Praise for *Shadows We Carry*

Most Anticipated Historical Fiction Novels of 2023

—Hasty Book List

"*Shadows We Carry* is an insightful novel that probes the complex, painful question of what it means to be Jewish in a post-Holocaust world."

—*Foreword Clarion Reviews*

"A different era, but oh so current: The late 1960s of *Shadows We Carry* was a time of turmoil — political and social turbulence, cultural upheaval, and fraying of the bonds of convention. Meryl Ain, the author, has delineated those years beautifully. We feel right there with the novel's main characters, Bronka and JoJo Lubinski, twins from Queens, New York. Yet their stories will have great resonance for contemporary readers. Each sister must fight for her own rights as women and as Jews. But each needs to look beyond herself toward a society free from the cruelty of discrimination and the brutality of hatred. *Shadows We Carry* is a memorable novel."

—Susan Isaacs, *New York Times* best-selling author

"When I finished *Shadows We Carry* by Meryl Ain, I cried. Reading this book was akin to going home . . . . To say it is moving is an understatement. For many readers, the tale of twin sisters Bronka and JoJo will be an eye-opener to Jewish life in a New York gone by. Bravo."

—Marilyn Simon Rothstein, author of *Crazy To Leave You, Husbands and Other Sharp Objects*, and *Lift and Separate*

"*Shadows We Carry* transports you into the multi-faceted lives of Jewish Holocaust survivors and their children during the 1960s and 70s in America. Her fully developed characters wrestle with guilt, love, marriage, Judaism, sexuality, politics, and the unraveling of family secrets. Ain, with impeccable research, has made a significant contribution to our understanding of the Holocaust and its dramatic impact on survivors and their descendants."

—Esther Amini, author of *CONCEALED: Memoir of a Jewish-Iranian Daughter Caught Between the Chador and America*

"Meryl Ain's sequel to *The Takeaway Men* is a novel that I couldn't put down . . . . the story brings to life the turmoil of the era—the Vietnam War and the demonstrations against it, the marches for women's equality and the fight for pro-choice . . . One of the most successful elements is how Ain has incorporated events of the day, as well as the history of earlier times, to the fabric of her story. This adds weight to her novel, grounds it in such a way that also lends authenticity and realism to each of her characters."

—Jacquie Herz, author of *Circumference of Silence*

"*Shadows We Carry* by Meryl Ain is an important new book. It is not necessary to read her debut novel, *The Takeaway Men*, to understand this sequel, whose merits stand on their own. Its themes include: immigration, assimilation, questions of identity, how we define ourselves, and whether Holocaust survivors' families have a responsibility to track down Nazi perpetrators. I was deeply affected by the novel's characters and events. The issues raised are as valid today as they were 50 years ago. Book clubs, congregations, and other groups must read and discuss this work. Bring plenty of tissues with you.

—Linda Ettinger Lieberman, Blogger, *The Times of Israel*

Past Praise for Author
For *The Takeaway Men*

2020 Best Book Awards Winner in Fiction: Historical
2020 American Fiction Awards: Winner in Historical Fiction
2020 Canadian Book Club Awards Winner in Fiction
"17 Books to Read Before the End of Summer"—Buzzfeed

"The author's tale is sensitively composed, a thoughtful exploration into the perennially thorny issues of religious identity, assimilation, and the legacy of suffering."

Kirkus Reviews

"Ain builds a layered world of many different characters to create a complex, difficult, and well-researched novel around the identity of the Jewish community following the Holocaust and the problems and debates it faced."

—*Booklist*

"A wise and sensitive work of historical fiction...ties in many themes: stories of Righteous Gentiles, a suspected Nazi living in the neighborhood under a new identity and working in a kosher deli, the stigma then of mental illness, questions of defining Jewish identity and reacting to evil, and the popular culture of the '50s."

—The Jewish Week

"All too often, books focus on what happens to people persecuted by the Nazis during the war, but I rarely find a novel that tells the story of what happens to a family after liberation . . . I would definitely recommend this book to anyone who loves historical fiction…"

—Readers' Favorite, 5 Star Review

"At a time when the darkness of the Holocaust is being whitewashed, Meryl Ain's remarkable debut novel illuminates the postwar Jewish American landscape like a truth-seeking torch. An emotionally rich and lovingly told saga of survivors, with great sensitivity to what was lost, buried, and resurrected."

—Thane Rosenbaum, author of *The Golems of Gotham*, *Second Hand Smoke*, and *Elijah Visible*

"In *The Takeaway Men*, Meryl Ain tells a gripping story of lives intertwined and shaped by the horrors of the Holocaust and its aftermath. With sensitivity and compassion she makes her characters come alive and remain in our heads and our hearts long after the novel ends. A powerful read!"

—Francine Klagsbrun, author of *Lioness: Golda Meir and the Nation of Israel*

"An exceptional and vibrant first novel . . . a portrait of the power of love and the ability of family to embrace and heal."

—TBR News Media

SHADOWS WE CARRY

SHADOWS WE CARRY

A NOVEL

MERYL AIN

Published by SparkPress, a BookSparks imprint,
A division of SparkPoint Studio, LLC
Phoenix, Arizona, USA, 85007
www.gosparkpress.com

Published 2023
Printed in the United States of America
Print ISBN: 978-1-68463-200-8
E-ISBN: 978-1-68463-201-5
Library of Congress Control Number: 2022919517

Formatting by Kiran Spees

For Stewart

Encourager, Empowerer, Helpmate

THE CHARACTERS IN *SHADOWS WE CARRY*

MANY OF THE CHARACTERS IN *Shadows We Carry* first appeared in my 2020 novel, *The Takeaway Men*. This sequel was written in response to the requests of numerous readers who wanted to know what happened to these fictional characters after the book ended.

There are also a few new characters.

Here is some brief information about some of them that will help refresh the memories of those who read the first book and will provide background to those who have not yet read it.

THE LUBINSKIS

Aron – A Holocaust survivor whose first wife and unborn child were murdered in the Kielce Pogrom in 1946.

Judy – Aron's second wife and the mother of his twin daughters. Although she was born and raised Catholic, she adopted the practices of Judaism for her husband but never converted.

Bronka and Johanna (JoJo) –Aron and Judy's fraternal twin daughters.

Faye and Izzy – The older cousins who welcomed the Lubinski family into their home when they first arrived in New York from a Displaced Persons Camp in Germany in 1951. They became the twins' surrogate grandparents. In addition, they also taught Aron the bakery business. and made him a partner in the bakeries they owned.

THE SMITHS

Brian – A news photographer, who becomes a friend and colleague of Bronka's.

Roy Smith/Rudolf Schmidt/Rory Dougherty – Brian's father, who came to the U.S. after WW II claiming he had no Nazi past. In *The Takeaway Men*, it is discovered that he was a guard at Auschwitz, but when confronted, he claimed he has repented.

Margaret –Roy's wife, mother of Brian and Doreen.

Doreen – Sister of Brian.

THE MORGENSTERNS

Mindy – Friend and neighbor of Bronka and JoJo, whom they first met days after coming to their new home in Queens. Since she was a little girl, Mindy has been trying to solve the mystery of who her biological father is.

Lenore – Mindy's mother, who was arrested in *The Takeaway Men* for suspected involvement in the Julius and Ethel Rosenberg Spy Case. She has led Mindy to believe that her father is dead.

Jennie – Lenore's mother and Mindy's grandmother, who helped Lenore raise Mindy.

Al Springer – A hugely successful entrepreneur in the burgeoning deodorant business, he served time in prison during the Red Scare in the early '50s. He is actually Mindy's father, but Lenore has forbidden him to reveal this secret to her.

THE STERNS

Bruce – JoJo's longtime boyfriend

Doris – Bruce's overbearing mother

Leon – Bruce's father

OTHERS

Irv Rosen – Irv is a neighbor of the Lubinskis. A very successful magazine photographer, he was born and raised Jewish but agreed to raise his three daughters as Catholic to please his Catholic wife, Connie. He had a confrontation with Roy Smith/Rudolf Schmidt about Roy's Nazi past in *The Takeaway Men*. Irv's daughter, Christina (Tina), is the same age as the twins and is a good friend of theirs.

Ned Jakes – A young man Bronka first met as a colleague on her high school newspaper and with whom she has remained friends. Bronka is intent on getting him to marry her.

Monsignor Stanislaw Kowalczyk ("Father Stan") – A Catholic priest who was born during the Holocaust in Poland. His family emigrates to New York after World War II.

Oren Lieberman – Nazi hunter and son of Holocaust survivors

PROLOGUE

NOVEMBER 22, 1963

WHEN BRONKA AND JOJO REMEMBERED this day for the rest of their lives, it was not for the unseasonal weather, although the anomaly of spring visiting a week before Thanksgiving certainly made it memorable. It was much too warm and bright for November in New York. It felt almost as if it were May with its luminous and dazzling sunshine and gentle breeze. People cheerfully threw off their coats and breathed in this gift of nature.

The fraternal twins bore little physical resemblance to one another. Bronka favored her father with dark hair and chocolate brown eyes, big-boned, but trim, who now towered over JoJo, who was five feet two inches with blonde hair and blue eyes. As they headed toward their lockers at the end of the school day, friends and classmates kept coming over to congratulate JoJo on her performance. The night before, she had starred in the premiere of her high school's production of *The Boy Friend*, where she played the lead role of Polly, the daughter of a millionaire in the 1920s. Her leading man was the strikingly good-looking, blonde and blue-eyed Bobby Bass, who played Tony.

JoJo was convinced that she was on a path toward the dramatic career she had craved since she was a little girl. She had even settled on her stage name—*JoJo Luby*. Whenever she daydreamed, she wrote the name *JoJo Luby* in her curling, expressive script, experimenting with hearts for the *O*s or filling in the *O*s with smiley faces.

"You really brought down the house last night with the song, 'I Could Be Happy with You,'" said Bronka. "You know all those cheers were for you. Bobby was clearly chosen for his looks rather than his singing voice."

"Thanks," JoJo said with a smug smile. "And thankfully, Papa finally relented and I can do it again tonight even though it's Shabbos. I'm sad Mama and Papa won't be there, but . . ."

"I've been meaning to speak with you about that," Bronka interrupted, somewhat sheepishly. "But I just want you to know that I can't come to the show tonight."

"You can't or you won't?"

"I guess, it's both," Bronka said, always straight with her sister.

"How will that look for the star reporter on the school newspaper—who happens to be my twin sister—to be missing, along with my parents?"

"I'm happy for you; I really am. I was there last night and I'll be there on Saturday night and Sunday afternoon, but tonight is Shabbos. I don't feel right about being out and especially leaving Mama and Papa. It's a big deal that they're letting you do this and if I go too, it's like a double whammy."

Before JoJo even had a chance to respond, they heard the booming voice of Mr. Mendelson, the principal, on the loudspeaker.

"Students, I have very sad news to report. President Kennedy has been assassinated. He was shot when he and Mrs. Kennedy were traveling in a motorcade in Dallas, Texas. All after-school and evening activities are cancelled tonight. All sports events and all performances of *The Boy Friend* will not take place this weekend. Please stay calm and safe. May the memory of President Kennedy always be for a blessing."

JoJo screamed, Bronka knelt down to the floor sobbing, and other crying and screaming boys and girls, who moments before had been anticipating a fun-filled weekend, responded to the shock.

JoJo extended her hand to help Bronka up.

"This is the end of the world," Bronka said. "Nothing will ever be the same again."

PART ONE

THE LATE SIXTIES

CHAPTER ONE

BRONKA REMEMBERED HOW SHE HAD been dumbfounded when JoJo revealed the shocking news to her just the night before in the bedroom they shared.

She blushed, remembering how clueless she had been when her twin sister began by giving her hints, telling her how she had actually fainted on the bus the previous day.

Bronka had jumped to the conclusion that JoJo had epilepsy, relying on a distant memory of a film she had seen about the condition when she was in junior high school. But the truth was that JoJo, even though she had managed to get herself into this terrible situation, was only about to enter her junior year at Queens College.

"No, I don't have epilepsy—I'm pregnant, Bronka! I missed two periods. I had a test and I'm pregnant; I'm due in April. Can't you see how bloated I am?

Bronka couldn't see it at all. Her sister always looked tiny and skinny to her.

All through dinner, JoJo gave Bronka signals to follow her upstairs and forgo the Huntley Brinkley Report. The twins could communicate without speaking a word and Bronka could sense her sister's concern, especially because JoJo was always thought to be the happy-go-lucky sister. Skipping dessert, the girls climbed the stairs to their attic bedroom with its slanted ceiling. It was still pink after all these years, the same color it was when they slept there the first night after getting off the boat from Europe. Plush stuffed animals and pillows with psychedelic colors and peace signs had replaced many of the dolls that used to sit on their flowered matching bedspreads.

Surviving were the worn pink teddy bears Tante Faye had given them on their first day in America when—at three-and-a-half—they arrived from a Displaced Persons Camp with their parents. Where the toy chest once stood was a stereo sitting on a cabinet that housed a stack of 45- and 33-rpm records ranging from Barbra Streisand to the Beatles' *Rubber Soul*. On their bulletin boards, The Beatles, Julie Andrews, the martyred President JFK, Martin Luther King, Jr., and the Mets were all represented with magazines, posters, or souvenirs.

They each plopped themselves on their matching beds placed side-by-side, both strewn with registration materials. They were 20 years old and about to register for their junior year classes at Queens College the next day.

Ever since her success on her high school newspaper, Bronka wanted to be a journalist, majoring in history and political science, and minoring in education. She had acquired a passion for current events during John F. Kennedy's presidential campaign in 1960. She read the news, watched the *Huntley Brinkley Report* each night and *Meet the Press* on Sundays. As a prolific and enthusiastic reporter, Bronka caught the attention of Ned Jakes, a senior who was editor-in-chief of the school newspaper and who was headed to Columbia University the following fall. Bronka's passion for journalism was exceeded only by her infatuation with the introspective and talented Ned. She thought that his editorials were probing and profound, and she saw in his enigmatic dark eyes a person who was perhaps as sensitive as she was—a soul mate. She daydreamed about seeing her name in print and making Ned happy.

JoJo was majoring in music and also in secondary education. The education classes were a concession to their parents because she did not want to be a music teacher at all. She wanted to be an actress and she was proud that her talents had begun to be recognized in high school.

In fact, she had not wanted to go to college, and asked her parents if she could try instead to become an actress. But Papa, with Mama acquiescing, nixed that plan and instead insisted that she go to college first and then they would allow her to pursue a career in acting. They argued that she needed the education classes in case her dreams of being a famous actress did not materialize.

In return for promising to go to college and getting a teaching certificate first, they became more tolerant of her dreams. Throughout high school and college, she spent summers as a drama counselor and had starring roles in school and community plays. Her parents now looked the other way when she violated the Sabbath to perform.

But now, JoJo's pregnancy would put a stop to all of it.

"How did that happen?" Bronka blurted out before she realized what a ridiculous question she was asking. She might not have been experienced, but she certainly knew how babies were made.

To her surprise, JoJo answered: "I don't know; it was a shock to me and Bruce. He told me he didn't think I could get pregnant that way."

"What way?"

"He pulled out."

Bronka looked down. "I don't know what to say."

JoJo's boyfriend Bruce had fixed Bronka up with a few of his friends, but each time the assessment was the same.

"It just didn't work out," Bruce would tell JoJo later.

Actually, Bronka found all of Bruce's friends—like Bruce—handsome on the outside but vacuous and shallow on the inside. They were simply not interested in the things she cared about: politics, philosophy, history, and changing the world. There was only one boy for her and that was Ned Jakes. Tall, dark and handsome, articulate, a social activist and a deep thinker. She had hung out with him in high school before he graduated and went on to Columbia University. While he was at college, he would take her to movies and concerts—and sometimes the ballet. They had even gone to a few peace demonstrations together. A couple of times, he asked her to accompany him to dances at Columbia as his date. He had even necked with her, but she was yet to make him her boyfriend. And now he was going to get his master's degree from Columbia University's Graduate School of Journalism. And she was hoping to follow in his footsteps there.

"I know the minute you tell Mama about the pregnancy, she will go and tell Papa," warned Bronka. "So, I think you have two choices—either tell them now or take a chance and discuss this with Tina and Mindy. They're our oldest friends and are much more experienced than we are and they might have some ideas. And we better do it right away. Especially because Tina is headed back to Georgetown next week."

The time and place were Bronka's idea: Brodsky's Kosher Delicatessen after lunchtime, before the early dinner rush.

When they arrived at Brodsky's there were only two diners who were about to leave their upfront table. As they waited to be seated, JoJo inhaled the smell of corned beef and pastrami and she told her sister that she felt a little queasy.

They took seats at a table in the back of the narrow restaurant and were soon joined by Mindy, who was a year and a half older than the twins and whose unkempt non-descript brown hair hung almost to her waist. She wore a flowing, sleeveless maxi dress with large red, blue, and yellow flowers. When she bent over to give them each a kiss, they could see that she had long ago dispensed with shaving under her arms.

Just as Mindy was seated, in came Christina Rosen. At 20, she didn't really look like a college girl. Even without the stark comparison with Mindy, she was incredibly put together. Her blonde hair was perfectly coiffed, her blue eyes were framed with brown eyeliner and curled eyelashes, she wore a cute little white mini dress and she smelled ever so slightly of Chanel No. Five.

"So, what's the story?" Tina asked.

"Let's order first," said Bronka. "And then we'll discuss."

The waiter, a young man of medium build with blond hair and sideburns, came to take their order. His round wire rimmed eyeglasses framed his green eyes.

"Hi Bronka," he said, looking straight at her. "I know you. You were in my political science class with Sol Bramson last semester. I understand he's a tough grader. Thankfully, I got a *B*. I heard he doesn't give *A*s."

"Yes, I remember you, Brian Smith. There's a reason they call him B.C. Bramson; he's got a reputation for not giving many *A*s. I only got a *B* also. But he's a very good teacher."

"So, introduce me to your friends, Bronka."

After introductions, he took their orders and placed them. Chicken soup and ginger ale for JoJo and turkey sandwiches and cherry sodas for the others.

"He's cute," said JoJo. What's his name?"

"Brian Smith," said Tina.

"You know him too, Tina?" Bronka asked.

Tina put her finger to her lips and in a tiny whisper, said, "My father knows him. He told me that when he came in here a couple of times, he commented on my father's camera equipment and asked him questions about photography. He wants to be a news photographer like my dad. Shush, don't say anything, but I think Brian is the son of the deli man, that stocky guy with the German accent."

"So what if he is?" Mindy said, always ready to contradict Tina. "What's the crime in having an accent?"

"Oh, Mindy, it's impossible to have a civil conversation with you," Tina said. "Never mind. Just never mind. I can't deal with you. Bronka asked me to come here for JoJo and that's why I'm here even though I'm really busy. And my mother and sisters and I have plans to shop for a wedding gown later this afternoon."

"But you're not getting married for a year," Mindy said.

"Look, Mindy, I understand that the kids you hang around with probably don't bother with the trappings—if they get married at all. But Frank and I want a big church wedding with all the trimmings. That's what we want and it's a free country." She said this with emphasis as she lifted her hand to her face, showing off her round diamond in a princess setting.

"It's not that free," Mindy retorted, twisting her lips. "You're just going to become a cog in the Military Industrial Complex. And what about your fiancé? Bad enough that some boys get drafted, but how do you feel about being engaged to a midshipman—someone who goes to school to learn how to fight? You may like his fancy uniform now, but he'll probably end up in Vietnam as soon as he graduates."

"Look girls," Bronka interrupted Mindy's tirade, "we didn't ask you to come here for a political or philosophical discussion, even though I would like that much better than what we have to talk about. We have a problem here and we're asking for your help."

"What's wrong?" Both Mindy and Tina said at once.

"First promise me you won't tell." Tina and Mindy both nodded.

"I'm pregnant," JoJo whispered.

Simultaneously, both Mindy and Tina's eyes opened wide.

"Doesn't Bruce know?" Tina asked.

"Yeah, of course he knows."

"Not your parents?"

"Not yet," said JoJo.

"A few girls at Barnard have gotten abortions," said Mindy, who was a year ahead of the three others in school.

"There was one girl, freshman year, who got pregnant and her older sister was a nurse. She got a fellow nurse to do it but she bled so much and ran such a high fever she had to be admitted to the hospital. She almost died. Then there was another girl, who told her parents and they agreed to pay for it. They sent her to Puerto Rico and she came back a week later and she was fine."

"Yeah," said Tina. "For that matter, you can go to Sweden where they're legal. Remember Sherri Finkbine, the *Romper Room* host in Arizona? It was all over the news about five years ago. She had taken Thalidomide, which causes serious birth defects and not one hospital in our whole country would help her. After she got the abortion in Sweden, they said the fetus had one leg and no arms."

"Papa hates Europe; he'll never send her there," Bronka said.

"Sweden was supposedly neutral in World War II," Tina added.

"He'd never spring even to send me to Puerto Rico, let alone Europe. He's much too tight," JoJo added.

"Isn't there a doctor down on Union Turnpike who does abortions?" Mindy asked. "Name starts with a *D*—Drake, Davis, Denning, something like that?"

"Oh no, you don't want that quack," Tina screwed up her face. "It's Dunninger. He's out of business anyway—for a few years already—thankfully. He went to prison, as well he should."

"What happened?" Bronka asked.

"Do you really want to know while we're eating?"

"I have to know," said JoJo.

"I can't believe you girls missed this story," said Tina. "It was all over. My father even took some photos of his house and also at his trial. It was the worst thing you ever saw. He botched an abortion, which killed the mother and then he cut her body into pieces and flushed them down the toilet. He was caught when he called for a plumber. Now, how stupid can you get?"

"Dis-gust," Bronka said, screwing up her face. JoJo held back tears.

"Have you considered marrying Bruce?" Tina asked.

"Well, we're planning to get married eventually; we're pinned. But I want to try out acting first—see if I can get anywhere professionally. I'm going back to the Berkshires this summer to do summer stock. A baby just doesn't fit in right now. And Bruce is starting law school—it's three years until he's finished."

"I'm really sorry I have to go now," said Tina, as she got up from the table. "There just aren't a lot of options. I wish I could have been more helpful."

As tears welled up in both of the twins' eyes, Bronka squeezed JoJo's hand. Their friends had not been helpful. After this meeting, they both understood that the only course of action was to discuss the situation with their parents.

"Are you walking back home?" Mindy asked. "I'm going to stop by and see my grandmother before I head back to the city."

"Sure," said Bronka. "Let's walk together."

"I just want to stop at the counter and get some comfort food to take home for her," Mindy said. "She misses me, and a corned beef sandwich and a cup of matzoh ball soup could cheer her up. And my mother is so busy these days. She's either at work or since they got engaged, she's hanging out with Al all the time."

"So you're going to see your grandmother and then head back to the apartment in the city and your other life in college?" Bronka asked.

"Yup, that's the plan. Can I walk with you?"

"Of course," said Bronka.

Holding the paper bag containing the cup of soup and sandwich, Mindy, Bronka and JoJo walked the three blocks to their respective homes—right across the street from one another—on 253 Street.

"I'm so sorry, JoJo. I wish I could have been more helpful. I feel so bad for you."

"That's OK, Mindy. I really don't want to talk about it anymore," JoJo said. "Let's change the subject."

"Remember the first time we met?" Mindy asked, trying to switch gears as the girls walked together on Union Turnpike towards their street.

"Sure," said Bronka. "I think I remember it or we've talked about it so many times that it's become a memory. JoJo and I were right off the boat from the Displaced Persons Camp in Germany and you showed us your television, your Tiny Tears doll, and all your Howdy Doody paraphernalia. We really couldn't understand English, but we were impressed."

"That was just a couple days before my mother was taken away by the FBI for questioning in the Julius and Ethel Rosenberg spy case. Remember how we talked about the takeaway men for years after?"

"Yeah," said Bronka. "We were really terrified that we would be taken away."

"On another topic," Bronka continued, "may I ask what's with the hostility towards Tina? She done anything to you lately?"

"No, of course not," Mindy said. "I don't have anything to do with her these days. She's just so establishment and so sure of herself. She appears to have it so together. So blonde and perfect—and conventional.

"My mom and her fiancé, Al, are totally establishment too. Lenore is thrilled with the designer clothes she wears, courtesy of Al, and the two-and-a-half carat, pear-shaped diamond she's sporting on her left hand. Do you think I'm a hypocrite?"

The twins also knew that Al was footing the bill for Mindy to go to Barnard, and even though they suspected Mindy thought he was a capitalist pig, she was willing, at least for the present, to look the other way.

"I didn't say a word," JoJo said. "My mind is on other things."

"How long have your mother and Al been engaged now?" Bronka

asked, attempting to change the subject. "It's probably only a matter of time until your family moves. Right?"

"Well, they've been 'engaged' for three years now," Mindy said making quotation signs with her fingers, "while he keeps his huge house in Great Neck and my mom keeps this house with Bubbie Jennie. Honestly, I'm glad that I haven't yet been uprooted and can come home from the city. As conventional as it is, the familiar childhood neighborhood is still comforting.

"I have to say, though, I do have a special place in my heart for Al. He's been nothing but kind and generous to me. He'll be my stepfather someday, but he's probably as close to a father as I will ever experience. Whatever I need, whatever I want, he gets it for me before I even have to ask. And he's also easier to have a conversation with than my mother. She's still so uptight. Of course, Bubbie Jennie is my special person. She's always been there for me while Lenore was off gallivanting."

"So you started to tell us about the Rosen sisters. What's the story there?"

"As far as Tina and her sisters go, that's another matter," Mindy responded. "They never included me in their circle. I always believed they thought they were better than me. But I have to respect the long-time friendship you guys have with them. It's just that everyone is so impressed with their father, the famous news photographer. Gosh, they never stop talking about how Irv Rosen photographed JFK, LBJ, Jackie Kennedy, the astronauts, and just about every famous person on the planet. They bragged about how Irv was even in the news himself, being mentioned in *Talk of the Town*, Ed Sullivan's society column in *The Daily News*."

"So, that's why you hate Tina—because she's proud of her father?" Bronka asked. "After all these years, I don't understand why that still bothers you?"

"You really want to know?" Mindy responded with an angry edge in her voice. "I'll tell you straight. Maybe it's because I don't have a father myself and despite my best efforts, I've been unable to unlock the secret of why I have absolutely no information whatsoever about him."

As they turned onto their street of identical brick bungalows, Mindy started humming Pete Seeger's song, "Little Boxes."

"Well, the houses on 253rd Street are certainly all the same," said Bronka. "Except, of course, for dormers and other extensions. But the people aren't all the same."

"Most of them are. Just like the houses, they're all made out of ticky-tacky, just like the song says," Mindy said.

"Look, my mother and Tina Rosen and her sisters will all end up in boxes. It's up to you whether you do or not. I think both of you could go either way. But I sure as hell will not. I'm going to find a different path. But first, I have to find out who I really am."

CHAPTER TWO

AS BRONKA STOOD AT THE mirror over the blue sink in the upstairs bathroom, she brushed her long, dark hair and reflected on the situation at hand. Thankfully, she thought to herself, Izzy and Faye were out of the house—on vacation. If JoJo was going to broach the traumatizing news of her pregnancy to their parents, it was much better not to have her cousins' well-meaning but loud and intrusive opinions in the picture.

The older Lubinskis had welcomed and embraced the survivors and their twin girls into their hearts and their home when they first came to America. And Judy and Aron and the girls had lived with them ever since. Now, sixteen years later, Aron was a full partner and running both of the bakeries Faye and Izzy had started, leaving the retired senior citizens free to spend most of the year in Florida. From September through June, they lived in a beautiful and spacious apartment at the Crystal House, a spanking new luxury building in Miami Beach. They had set up Faye's daughter Becky, who was afflicted with schizophrenia, in an efficiency apartment at the Whitelaw Hotel, where Faye checked in with her every day. The set-up worked—close enough to monitor, but far enough away not to be stifled. Faye made sure that Becky took her medication and also escorted her to the movies, shopping, and out to lunch. In the summer when Izzy and Faye were in Queens, Becky came to visit. They would break up the time with a week or so at Grossinger's with sumptuous meals, card games, entertainment, and swimming pool.

Each summer, Bronka enjoyed spending time with Aunt Becky, who had been so kind to her as a child, before she witnessed her hitting rock bottom. But now, with medication, she seemed like the original Aunt Becky she loved.

Judy had taken over both the home and business responsibilities where Faye left off. Not only had she become a good cook, but she also inherited the bakery bookkeeping from Faye. She found that she enjoyed the job and also liked chatting with the customers when she chose to work behind the bakery counter.

We better get this over with before Faye and Izzy return, Bronka said to herself, wondering how her parents would react.

When she was fifteen her parents finally revealed to her and JoJo what they had experienced during and after the Holocaust and how their mother had literally saved their father's life. The disclosure had cleared the air, but it raised more questions than answers. Answers that Bronka was determined to discover. True, the wall of secrecy had been breached, but there was still so much more Bronka had to work out about her family's legacy.

While both twins had a better understanding of their father's moodiness, he was still subject to fits of depression and anxiety. Bronka did not know if it was her imagination, but she thought that her mother had become somewhat less meek since the revelation, giving her opinion more frequently and seemingly less squelched by her husband.

What's more, both parents looked the other way when JoJo went out on Friday nights and at least verbally tolerated her desire to become an actress, and they seemed genuinely proud of Bronka's writing. But it was only in her diary, which she shared with no one, that she chronicled her innermost thoughts. She often wrote about her crush on Ned Jakes, the boy she hoped to marry, although as Faye said, much to Bronka's annoyance: "I don't think this dough is going to produce any bread."

Bronka remembered that she was mildly annoyed at Faye for making the comment, but she figured that although Faye believed she was an expert on all things, she really wasn't. As impressive as she was for someone her age, her thinking was rooted in another era. Her surrogate grandmother was loud and opinionated and she loved her, but didn't necessarily take everything she said to heart.

In addition, Bronka had written in her diary about her brief flirtation with an Orthodox boy when she entered Queens College. She had never reread it; it was much too embarrassing. But neither could she rip out the pages in her diary, which she had contemplated doing. She had kept the documentation as a reminder, a warning of a dream that had been quickly dashed.

Shmuely

Bronka had been put in her place by her dalliance with Shmuely Ehrenberg, but there was something in a more observant life that still attracted her. Maybe it was the certainty or the centrality of values in religious practice, which she longed for. Maybe religion was the antidote to a world gone amok. And then there was the matter of her own religious heritage.

Unquestionably in the eyes of his peer group—the men who donned tallis and tefillin and with whom he prayed every single day—Aron Lubinski was a super Jew, even a *tzadik*. He went to minyan every day and often led the service. On Shabbat he read Torah and assisted the rabbi in giving out honors. He put up a sukkah in the fall, and in the spring for Passover he insisted that his wife turn the house upside down removing every trace of leaven.

Yet, in this group of pious men, he kept his family secret. When they were teenagers, he and Judy had been forced to reveal to their daughters and JoJo that their mother had been born and raised Catholic and that she had embraced Aron's religion—to be fair, wholeheartedly—after she saved his life in Poland. But there was a catch—one that profoundly affected Bronka. Although she considered herself a Jew by choice, their mother had never officially converted. While Judy did not initially grasp the magnitude of the problem, her husband did. And this was something that Aron insisted on keeping secret, but refused to rectify. Bronka often thought that if her father had encouraged her mother to convert, she would certainly have done so. Judy was so anxious to please others, especially her husband, and she had fully embraced Judaism. But he never even suggested it. He had slipped her into the Displaced Persons Camp as a Jew and then continued the subterfuge.

If Judy had converted before the twins were born, they would have been born Jewish, but she had not. And once the die was cast, Aron did nothing to solve it; and Judy continued to function as an observant Jew. So it was a secret that bothered JoJo not at all, but tore at Bronka.

But the first time she had dipped her toe into the Orthodox pool, it had not gone well.

During freshman year she had attended a party in Shira Yudenfreund's basement. Shira was the daughter of their synagogue's cantor. Shira's Orthodox social group at Queens College sponsored the party. And there Bronka met the rakish Shmuely Ehrenberg. He was from Boro Park and was considered a bit of a rebel in the Brooklyn College Orthodox set.

"You know, all of these kids have been together forever," he told her. "We've all gone to the same yeshivas and to the same shuls.

There's absolutely no cross pollination of ideas, let alone people. They've labeled me a bad boy because I'm open to interacting with all kinds of people—even those from Queens," he said as he winked at her.

Much to her pleasure, Bronka found out that he was also a student of philosophy. And after an evening discussing Buber, Franz Rosenzweig, and Samson Rafael Hirsch, she was ready to perhaps forget about Ned Jakes, don a *sheitel* and commit to the security of an Orthodox lifestyle.

And Shmuely was clever; she had to admit, although Bronka was surprised when he told her how he and his friends had devised a way of avoiding serving in Vietnam.

"I'm learning with a rabbi, who will give me *smicha*."

"Wow," exclaimed Bronka. "So you're going to be ordained a rabbi, that's exciting."

"No, I have no intention of becoming a rabbi. I'm just studying part time with a rabbi, who will give me a piece of paper that says I'm an ordained rabbi and I'll get a draft exemption."

"Oh, sort of a like a draft dodging yeshiva?" Bronka asked. "Can you get into trouble?"

"No, not at all, my dear," he said as his hand brushed hers, seemingly unperturbed by her comment. "I have the paper that says I'm a rabbi."

After the evening, Shira warned Bronka that Shmuely was considered a rebel, especially by the "no-touchies," who would not even hold hands with girls. She added that it was even rumored that he dated non-Jewish girls.

None of this information bothered Bronka at all; in fact, it empowered her. Here was an Orthodox person who was a real intellectual, exciting, and open-minded. And his body language was actually more welcoming than Ned's. *Why couldn't she be Orthodox? It wouldn't be a big stretch.* After all, she still went to shul every Shabbos, kept kosher inside and outside the home, and apparently had a grandfather and great grandfather in Poland, who had been esteemed rabbis.

Even before he called her for a date, she ran to the library and took out *This is My God* by Herman Wouk. As she read it, she became increasingly certain that she would be able to embrace an Orthodox lifestyle.

When Shmuely came to the door to pick her up for their first date, she was surprised that he wore a black hat, although it didn't detract from his rugged good looks: he was handsome and well-groomed, unlike many of her peers. He smiled devilishly as he looked her up and down in her sleeveless pink mini-dress. Sitting in a kosher restaurant on Union Turnpike for three hours, they discussed philosophy and religion. At the door, he gave her a tender kiss.

"How did your date go with Shmuely?" Shira called the following day to ask.

"Great," said Bronka. "I want to learn more about becoming Orthodox. Tell me what I need to do."

After three dates and heavier kissing, Bronka decided that she would try to forget about Ned Jakes, become Mrs. Shmuely Ehrenberg and move to Brooklyn, have six children who would go to yeshiva, and make cholent for them every Shabbos. She could make herself fit into the Orthodox world. An Orthodox life would give her a foundation from which to convey important values to her children. She was three-quarters of the way there anyway; she could easily do more.

Shira had told Bronka that if you made it to six dates in the Orthodox world, you could expect a proposal. True, she was only eighteen, but that's how they did it in their community and engagements were short. She could expect to get married within six months, and then attend college until she had a child.

"Forget about becoming a journalist," Shira told her. "But as a writer, you can always do that in your spare time—if you have any. Maybe you'll write a book."

Bronka had dreams of not only being a journalist, but thought she might want to be on television, although you could count on one hand the number of women who did serious news. Bronka knew that was a pipe dream; she was much too shy and inhibited for that. And it was only too easy to convince herself that she could give up that unrealistic dream for a secure, predictable, and happy life.

On the sixth date, Shmuely took her to Lou G. Siegel's, a fancy kosher restaurant in Manhattan. By then, Shira had informed her that sleeveless mini-dresses were not appropriate for the Orthodox crowd, so she wore a very pretty red dress, which skimmed her knees and had three-quarter sleeves.

After a glass of kosher wine and a lovely dinner of coq au vin, they ordered a slice of the restaurant's signature babka to share for dessert.

"So, Bronka, you're really a treasure. I've never met a girl who is so knowledgeable and thoughtful about the things I care about. You're well-read and pretty too. Tell me about your family. I know you said your grandfather and great grandfather were rabbis in Poland and your father's family perished in the Holocaust. And you mentioned your father goes to minyan every day. Does he daven in an Orthodox synagogue?

"Well, the rabbi has Orthodox *smicha* and I would imagine it's the same service."

"Is there a *mechitza*?"

"You mean, is there a barrier between the men and the women?"

"Or perhaps the women sit in a balcony?"

"No, they sit together," Bronka said.

"Oh, I see," said Shmuely. "And what about your mother's family. Does she also come from a line of Polish rabbis?"

"No, not at all," Bronka giggled.

"So, what did her family do in Poland?"

"Her mother was a nurse, who died before the war, and her father was a policeman."

"A Jewish policeman in Poland?" Shmuely asked with a quizzical, almost smirking look on his face.

"No, of course not," Bronka said. "Neither of her parents were Jews. But my mother adopted the religion of my father after the war. She keeps a kosher home and has raised my sister and me in the faith."

"Do you know if an Orthodox rabbi converted her?"

The dessert came and the waiter put it in the middle of the table for both of them to share, but Bronka couldn't take a bite. She had a sinking feeling that there would be no engagement.

Bronka said nothing, but realized that her mother's choice based on her father's influence continued to plague her. Her heart sank as she observed that Shmuely stopped looking directly at her and instead focused on the huge piece of chocolate babka, polishing it off all by himself.

After Shmuely didn't call her for two weeks, she called Shira.

"He really liked you, Bronka. But as much as he poses as an open-minded guy, his family is obsessed with *yichus.* Even though you passed the test on your father's side, his parents would never accept the lack of family background on your mom's side. It has nothing to do with you; they liked you when they met you. His family would probably not accept ninety-eight percent of the Jews in Bellerose. The Conservative synagogue alone might have been a deal breaker, but a Polish policeman during World War II—that was a giant red flag. I'm so sorry; I know it's not fair, Bronka, but that's just the way they are. They're very insular. It's all about the gene pool."

Bronka hung up the pink princess phone, threw herself on her bed and, clutching her pink teddy bear, sobbed and sobbed for an hour and a half.

When JoJo came into the bedroom and saw her sister's contorted, red, bloated face, she raised her eyebrows.

"What happened, Bronka? Talk to me."

Bronka could barely speak. In between wrenching sobs, she told her sister about her rejection.

"And it's not my fault at all," Bronka moaned. "All of these decisions were made before we were even born."

"Well, look at the bright side," JoJo said. "If Papa hadn't survived because Mama saved him, we wouldn't even be here. Shmuely and his lot are tied to the old world. We're Americans, Bronka! We don't have to be concerned with our lineage. Why don't you just lighten up and find a nice American boy like Bruce."

Bronka was not in a position to insult Bruce so she went in another direction.

"I don't know about that. Shmuely's world is safe and meaningful."

"Don't kid yourself. Those people are just as dysfunctional as everyone else. It just looks good from the outside. Actually, I think what you're looking for is a safe, comforting cocoon, like Papa. His religion comforts him. When he wraps himself in his tallis, it is the only time he is at peace. Except, maybe when he distracts himself by being a workaholic. Then, he can block everything out. But in between, you know how miserable he can be. You're not like that; you don't need it. What you need is a boyfriend."

"No joke," said Bronka. "But, JoJo, I'm drawn to religion and the meaning of life. I want to share that with someone."

"Well, perhaps Ned will call you and you can have some philosophical conversations with him. He really is very slow, although I understand he's the one you want. Think of this Shmuely thing as a little blip. Honestly, I can't picture you wearing a sheitel and making cholent."

CHAPTER THREE

THE QUEENS COLLEGE BOOKSTORE WAS crowded with students in advance of the fall semester. They hugged and kissed each other and shook hands. As Bronka wandered through the store, well-stocked with the new term's required textbooks and neatly folded sweatshirts and tee shirts with the school's insignia, she daydreamed. What would her friends say once they found out her sister was pregnant? How would she tell Ned? Would it affect his opinion of her? Would he think less of JoJo and her family? Or maybe, it might encourage him to be more assertive in the lovemaking department. After all, it was not lost to her that Shmuely Ehrenberg, a boy who hung out with the "no-touchie" crowd, had gone farther—with more passion and enthusiasm—than Ned ever did. Despite Ned's line, 'We could make beautiful music together,' he was rather timid and never seemed to have any problem calling their necking sessions quits.

Bronka was pretty sure JoJo's condition would not reflect negatively on Ned's opinion of her. He was a political activist, having just enrolled in a master's degree program at Columbia Journalism School. He had lived in the dorms when he was an undergrad and was moving into an apartment now with another guy near the J

School. And although Faye and Judy were of the opinion that Bronka radiated innocence and purity, she was astute enough to know that someone of Ned's sophistication did not care about those things. Rather, she thought Ned might be afraid to be ensnared—and just wasn't ready to make a commitment to her.

"Bronka, did you find everything you need?" JoJo said as she approached her with an arm full of heavy textbooks.

"Mostly," said Bronka. "They're out of Cecil Roth's book, *History of The Jews* for my Jewish History course with him this semester. They'll have more on Thursday."

"So since when are you so interested in Jewish History? I thought you were letting go of the tradition a little bit."

"I never said that. I'm curious about Jewish History from the standpoint of our own family. But also ever since The Six Day War, I want to know more about Israel—the people, the culture, the history, the ethos. In fact, looks like Professor Roth will have to update the book in light of The Six Day War. I'm honored to be taking his class. He's a visiting professor—one of the world's leading experts on Jewish History. He's working on a Jewish Encyclopedia.

"But most of all, I want to learn more about our family history. About what life was like before the war, not only for Papa, but also for all our relatives who were murdered. I want to study more about Jews throughout history. I believe we have a rich heritage on Papa's side, but I must admit that I'm still troubled that we're not really technical Jews because Mama never converted and Papa didn't have us converted either."

"You're crazy, Bronka. Just drop it. Why is that even an issue for you? Who cares about technicalities? Why are you looking for trouble? Our father is a super-Jew!"

"But what about our mother and her mother? Not to mention our paternal grandfather. I will get to the bottom of this one way or the other."

"You are definitely my intellectual and introspective sister. And in my opinion, you are asking for trouble. Let's pay for these books and head home."

The girls, lugging bags with their heavy textbooks, walked toward the bus stop on Parsons Boulevard.

"So, what did you decide about telling Mama and Papa?" Bronka asked her sister as they waited for the bus.

"I've been thinking about it and the more I picture the conversation, I can't do it with the two of them. At first I imagined a talk with you and me and them, but just because he's not as angry as he used to be, I'm afraid this might trigger him, and I'm afraid."

"But you have to tell them—you're not going to go to a quack abortionist where you could die. Are you?"

"No way," said JoJo. "I think I want to speak to Mama first by myself and see what she has to say. She's more reasonable."

"You can't expect her to keep it from him, can you?"

"I'm not sure."

"So, you don't want me there?"

"You can come if you want, but it's not necessary."

"I don't need to be there," said Bronka, a little hurt and a little relieved.

CHAPTER FOUR

AFTER DINNER WHEN ALL THE dishes were washed and put away and the kitchen was clean, Aron went into the living room to watch television, as was his pattern each evening. JoJo knew that Judy, especially when she worked a full day in the bakery, had the habit of going into Faye and Izzy's bedroom and lying down on their queen-sized bed for about a half hour. Her mother had told her that Faye had offered to move her and Izzy's things to the upstairs bedroom since they weren't there for most of the year, but Judy just didn't think it was right.

She insisted on keeping the attic bedroom with Aron, but when Faye and Izzy were gone, she permitted herself this one luxury. Actually, Judy and Aron's bedroom upstairs was larger than the one downstairs. With Faye's mahogany dresser and Izzy's matching chest, there was barely room for a portable TV. Tonight, JoJo was thankful that she could approach her mother alone in the warm and cozy dusty-rose-colored room. Often, either JoJo or Bronka would join their mother on the bed after dinner and have a special time alone with her.

JoJo closed the door as she walked into the bedroom and lay down on the bed next to her mother.

"So, what's doing?" Judy asked her daughter.

JoJo began to cry.

"Tell me about it, sweetheart. It can't be that terrible. You know I always say that nothing's permanent. This too, shall pass."

"I'm afraid this may be permanent, Mama."

Judy bit her lip and her eyes began to water as she looked at her daughter and stroked her tear-stained face. JoJo was sure that at that moment, her mother must have noticed that her face was fuller than usual.

"Speak to me," Judy said in a shaky voice.

"I think I'm pregnant."

"You think?"

"No, I am pregnant. I had a test."

"How far along are you?"

"Two months. I'm not really ready to have a baby. And I know that Bruce isn't either."

JoJo was relieved that her mother had the habit of weighing her words. She was not like Faye, who what was on her mind ended up on her tongue. JoJo guessed that her mother probably wanted to shake her and say: *Why didn't you think of that before?* But she was a practical person, so what was the point? What was done was done. Anyway, she had not exactly been upfront in discussing sex with the girls, especially the matter of protection. Hadn't her mother been deluding herself? *I've had a steady boyfriend for several years now. It's possible Mama feels a bit guilty and is blaming herself.*

"So what are you thinking?" Judy asked.

"An abortion?" JoJo answered.

"Well, you know abortions aren't legal, JoJo."

"I know, but I heard if you pay, you can get one."

"Do Bruce's parents know?"

"No. He hasn't told them yet."

"Well, I will have to discuss this with Papa and see what he says. Is there anything else you want to tell me?"

"No, not really."

Judy squeezed her daughter's hand. "There is a solution for every problem."

JoJo knew that Judy spoke from her heart, repeating one of Aron's stock sayings. After all of the suffering and death and destruction her parents had encountered in their lifetime, she was somewhat comforted to think that her mother believed that this was a problem that could be solved.

It was nine o'clock at night and after Aron had finished watching TV, he took a book from the coffee table in the living room to the kitchen table to read while Judy put out a pot of tea and two cups. She poured Aron a cup and took one for herself as she watched him settle into reading his book. She sat down opposite him and sipped her tea.

"I have something important to tell you," she said. "It's not very pleasant."

Aron lifted up his head from the book and looked at his wife, and after pausing, she said: "Johanna is pregnant."

His eyes opened wide and his jaw dropped.

"*Oy gevalt*!" He gasped.

Aron stood up and slammed the book onto the table, rattling the teacups as the hot tea spilled onto the table.

He shouted: "It's a *shanda un a chorben*." A disgrace and a disaster.

The twins, upstairs on their beds, had been dreading what was going to happen when their mother broke the news to their father. But still, they were startled by the loud thud and Aron's outburst.

"Get her down here now," Aron ordered.

"Johanna," Judy opened the door to the attic steps and called, "Come down now. Your father wants to speak to you."

Sheepishly and slowly, JoJo got up from her bed and walked down the eight steps to her mother who was waiting at the bottom of the stairs.

He was still fuming. He glared at his daughter.

"How could you? Where's your *kop,* vat's the matter with your head?" He went on with his rant, reverting to Yiddish. *"Du farkirtst mir di yorn!* And if you haven't figured it out, it means: You'll be the death of me!"

"Why don't we all sit down and calm down?" said Judy. "Aron, you sit at the head of the table."

JoJo walked past her father and took a seat on the other side of her mother.

"Mama tells me you've brought shame and dishonor on this family. It's a *shanda*—a terrible shame. After all we've been through—all the *tzuris*—the pain, grief, death, torture, suffering—and this is what you do to ME! To your mother? And you speak to her of an abortion—after the Nazis tried to wipe us all out! You dare to speak of an abortion when my first wife was murdered in the Kielce Pogrom, along with our unborn child.

"*Vos iz mit dir?* What's wrong with you? We have given you everything—food, clothing, shelter, education; we allowed you to follow your foolish dreams of becoming an actress. And this is the thanks we get.

"Who is this boy anyway?"

"You know," JoJo said. When he looked at her with a blank stare, she added. "Bruce, Papa."

"He's from a good family," she went on. "He's graduating from Hofstra in June, he's studying accounting, and he's hoping to go to law school. His father is in the cosmetics business. They live in Rolling Hills. His father was one of the founders of Temple Tikvah."

"Temple Tikvah? A *knacker.* So he's a big shot in a large Reform shul in Rolling Hills."

"Yes," said JoJo.

"Zol Got mir helfen," Aron whispered under his breath, asking God to help him.

"So, I guess we'll have to speak with his parents?" Judy said. "What are the Sterns' first names, JoJo?

"Doris and Leon," JoJo said as her voice cracked. She could not bear to think of the meeting between her immigrant parents and the apparently rich and fancy parents of her boyfriend. Not only had they paid tuition for Bruce to attend Hofstra, but they had provided him with his own car—a very cool Ford Mustang in candy apple red. Mr. Stern looked like a regular father, always crisp and fresh compared to her father's disheveled appearance and outdated, mismatched clothes. But Doris was something else; she was beyond the normal definition of rich and fancy—even by Rolling Hills standards—and she let everyone know it too.

"The sooner, the better," said Aron. "We will set up a meeting with Leon and Doris Stern and resolve this."

JoJo didn't say a word. She realized she no longer had any say in this matter. She knew she had to call Bruce ASAP and give him a heads-up. As she slammed the door to the attic behind her, she felt overwhelmed with nausea. As she mounted the first step, she looked up.

Sitting on the top step, Bronka—in her pink, flannel pajamas—closed her eyes and hugged herself. She had taken it all in from her perch. JoJo knew that Bronka could read her mind and was feeling her pain. Her sister was fully aware that her dreams of becoming an actress would be put on hold for a very long time. *But at least I have Bruce and we love each other. Bronka, on the other hand, is still trying to make Ned her boyfriend.*

CHAPTER FIVE

JUDY HAD INSISTED THAT BRONKA come along to meet the Sterns, especially after JoJo told her that Bruce's two sisters would be present at the meeting.

"We have to present a united front and show them what a lovely family we are. Not for nothing, we have two beautiful daughters and we are partners in two bakeries."

Bronka was sure her mother wanted to show off both of her daughters. Judy had also nixed the mini-dresses they had planned to wear for the occasion, saying they did not need to go into this situation "looking risqué." The girls had nothing but mini dresses and slacks, so they settled for bell-bottom pants and button-down blouses.

But Bronka also knew full well that it was Aron who wanted her to tag along. Essentially, it wasn't so much tagging along, but driving them there. Neither Aron nor Judy had ever learned to drive. They walked, took public transportation, or if they left Queens, Izzy occasionally drove them in his 1961 cream-colored Chevrolet Impala which mostly sat in the driveway, save for rare occasions. Fortunately, both girls had learned to drive by then. Izzy and Faye were still a few days from returning from their vacation in the Catskills. They and Becky had taken the bus and the car sat in the driveway. Bronka was certain that there was no way Aron was going to allow JoJo, his disgraced daughter, to drive them to Rolling Hills. That would put her literally in the driver's seat, and according to his thinking, that was not where she deserved to be. So for this occasion, he directed that Bronka would be the driver, despite the fact that JoJo was the better driver.

Unlike her sister, Bronka only drove on local roads to avoid the Long Island Expressway. So for this occasion, she decided to take the service road, which afforded the family the opportunity to view the outskirts of some of the developments that had sprouted in Nassau County in the '50s and '60s. As she got farther from Queens, the houses got larger and the greenery and landscaping grew more verdant and sculptured.

Aron sat next to Bronka in the front seat, silent and fidgety except for each time Bronka stopped short at a traffic light or stop sign. With each jolt, he muttered "*Oy vey.*"

Bronka was glad that JoJo was in the back seat with their mother. She was relieved that in the back, her sister did not have to look at their father's angry and disapproving face, which had seemed frozen in that expression for the last three days. JoJo had told Bronka that she dreaded this meeting with Bruce's parents, especially because their Pollyanna mother thought everything would be fine. But she also warned Bronka that their own parents were no match for the Stern crew.

"This is going to be a disaster," she told Bronka the night before as they sat on their beds.

Trying to comfort her, Bronka asked, "Why do you say that? You and Bruce love each other. You're pinned so you would've gotten engaged and married at some point. They know that. You've been in their home. You're beautiful and personable and talented. Even if they're shocked now, they'll get over it."

"I'm not sure, Bronka. They're considered to be superior."

"By whom?"

"By themselves, of course."

Bronka laughed. "That's actually funny, JoJo."

"Mostly it's Bruce's mother, but you'll see . . . and his older sister is like an embryonic version of his mom. Maybe we should just elope."

JoJo told Bronka that she had considered eloping, but she had ruled it out. She said she pictured Bruce coming in the middle of a night with a ladder she would use to climb out from her attic bedroom. But she told her that she knew that was a preposterous fantasy for many reasons, the most practical being: How would her suitcase get down? She said she pictured tossing it and hitting Bruce by accident, screaming, and waking up the whole house. "No, I am not equipped to elope; although I confess I'm afraid of an actual wedding.

"I'm cringing picturing Mama and Papa standing next to me at the wedding, compared to Bruce's parents. I can't imagine that our humiliated parents will buy new clothes for the occasion, although I'm quite sure that Bruce's mother is feeling no shame whatsoever. I'm sure she's rationalized that it's all my fault and that won't cramp her style. And although Mama is a pretty woman, she's been wearing the same plain shirtwaist dresses for years. And she never wears makeup except for lipstick, and her blonde hair is showing strands of gray. She won't even consider coloring it."

Rolling Hills Estates consisted of colonials and ranch homes on considerably larger plots than their home in Bellerose. "These aren't mansions," Aron observed as they approached the Stern's development. "Nassau County doesn't have all the services we have in the city and the school taxes are high. And if you live outside of the five boroughs and you go to Queens College, you have to pay tuition and drive a car. "

Although JoJo remained silent, Bronka guessed that her twin was rolling her eyes in the back seat.

"It's always about the two free tuitions we're getting while living in Queens," JoJo often complained to Bronka. "It's Papa's idea of one of the greatest perks of all time."

It didn't really bother Bronka that her father frequently talked about the fact that Queens College was free. She reasoned that you had to have good grades to be accepted, so it was an honor. And she had to admit that free tuition was one of the few things that gave her father real pleasure.

As Bronka turned onto Leggup Court, she asked JoJo for the number of the house.

"It's about four houses down on the right. There will probably be a Cadillac in the driveway. They have three cars if you count Bruce's, but they only have a one-car garage."

"Oh, there's the house. The coffee-colored ranch," JoJo added.

"It's a reddish brown," said Judy.

"It looks like a barn," said Aron.

"They call that color umber," Bronka declared.

"Umber? I never heard of that," JoJo said. "Where did you get that one from, Bronka?"

"Oh, from an English novel."

"So this is the big deal?" Aron snarled. "The rich Sterns live in a house with brown shingles, the color of a barn. My family's stone house in Kielce was much bigger than this!"

The house was actually a neat ranch house with an attached garage. There was a white door on the left, a bay window in the front and an attached garage with a white door on the left. Maple trees framed the house. There was a late model lemon yellow Cadillac in the driveway and Bruce's Ford Mustang was parked in front of the house.

"This is very pretty," said Judy. "It's a normal house, not as big as I expected, but very lovely—out in the country like this."

"It is, Mama. You know we could have moved here too," said JoJo. "We didn't really have to stay with Izzy and Faye in that tiny house for all these years."

"Why would we move? We have everything we need where we are and we don't need a car," said Aron. "And our house is all-brick; this is all shingle. And this barn is in the middle of nowhere—in *Yenemsvelt!* These people have to drive miles and miles just to buy a container of milk. *Meshuga.*"

They got out of the car and JoJo led the way to the white front door and rang the bell. Bruce came to the door and opened it. Bronka thought that his smile was forced and he did not kiss her or JoJo, as he usually did, and he extended a stiff handshake to Judy and Aron.

"Come in," he said, as he led them through the white living room, and past the dark mahogany breakfront that held figures and crystal bowls and goblets. There was a lone silver menorah in the case and a pair of silver candlesticks on display. There was not a newspaper or a magazine anywhere in sight. It looked like a model home, except that model homes usually had some reading material for decoration, Bronka thought. She knew about this from all the years she had gone with her parents visiting model homes, but never moving.

"It must be 90 degrees outside, but it's freezing in here," Aron whispered to Judy.

Judy raised her eyebrows and put her finger to her lips to shush him, but it was too late; Bruce had heard him.

"Oh Mr. Lubinski, we have central air-conditioning; you have to get used to it. I can turn it down if you like."

Bruce led them to a smaller room in the back of the house, next to the dining room, in which the sun shone brightly through the row of windows on the back wall. There was a white sectional sofa with bright red flowers, and a portable TV facing the couch.

Two young attractive dark-haired women were sitting on the couch. One appeared to be pregnant and the other was holding a baby dressed in pink, who looked to be about six-months-old. There was a little boy about four-years-old sitting on the lap of an older man, whom Bronka presumed to be Bruce's father. The two were snuggling on a brown leather recliner and watching cartoons.

"Who are they?" the little boy asked in a loud voice.

"They are guests, Mason," said the pregnant woman. "They are Uncle Bruce's friends."

Bronka saw JoJo's face fall as she steeled herself so as not to burst into tears. Well, JoJo had always said that Bruce thought his older sister was a bitch, she recalled. She could have at least said JoJo's name or referred to her as Bruce's girlfriend. She could have said we were going to be their family soon. But maybe this was all going to go terribly wrong.

Just then, Leon, an average looking sixty-year-old, grayish brown hair slightly balding, of medium height and build, lifted Mason from his lap and put him on the floor. He got up and walked over to the stunned JoJo and pinched her cheek.

"So how are you, my pretty, little *Mamala,*" he said with a smile and a wink.

"Ok, thanks, Mr. Stern, I'm fine," JoJo said reflexively. But Bronka knew that JoJo's stomach must be tied up in in knots and she was dreading the reaction of Bruce's mother. She had told her that Bruce's father was decent, but JoJo had no idea how Doris Stern was going to react to this situation.

"Well, I have to say you look very well. Please introduce me to your parents," he said, ignoring Bruce.

He shook hands with Aron and Judy and also pinched Bronka's cheek.

"I'd never know you were twins, but you're beautiful too, in your own way," he said to Bronka. "Let me introduce you to *my* beautiful daughters."

"This is Carol," he pointed to the pregnant one, who did not move, but nodded her head with a weak smile. "And that is our middle child, Jackie."

With baby in hand, Jackie got up from the couch, handed the pink bundle to her father, and much to their shock, proceeded to hug each of the four Lubinskis.

"Welcome to the family," she said cheerfully.

While Bronka could see that JoJo was somewhat relieved, she began to wonder what had happened to Bruce's mother.

"Where's your mother?" Leon said in an exasperated tone as if reading her mind. He seemed to speak to no one in particular, perhaps to any of his three children who would answer.

"Her hairdresser was running late, so she was delayed at the beauty parlor," said Carol. "She's just changing now."

"Well, let's sit down," said Leon. "Jackie, maybe you can get the Lubinskis something to drink."

Aron sat in a bridge chair, as did Bronka. JoJo and Judy headed for the sectional.

"No, that's perfectly OK," said Judy. "We're fine."

"Did you catch the last episode of *What's My Line?*" Leon asked making small talk. "I'm sorry it's going off the air. I'll miss it. I've been watching it for seventeen years and I feel like I know everyone personally. I'm wondering if John Daly and Arlene Francis will show up on any other programs. At least, we know Bennett Cerf has a day job."

Before anyone could answer, Doris Stern entered the room. Bronka took one look and her mouth opened wide. All she could think of was, *Except for her hair color, she looks like a cross between Zsa Zsa Gabor and Jacqueline Susann.*

Having graduated from Tante Faye's homemade dresses as youngsters to shopping for their clothes at Mays Department Store in high school, the twins had now moved up to the more upscale shops at The Miracle Mile in Manhasset. There they had observed the fancy ladies from the North Shore communities with their bleached blonde hair, jewelry, and expensive clothes. But Doris Stern was in a category all of her own.

An average sized woman, her strawberry-blonde hair was coiffed in a bouffant style. But her presence was commanding. Bronka wanted to whisper to JoJo and ask if they should curtsy, but she didn't dare.

Doris's eyebrows were penciled and she wore thick black eyeliner and mascara. Her lips were clearly outlined and accentuated and filled in with ruby red lipstick. Her hair was so teased and frozen in place it looked like a helmet. She wore white slacks and a silk Pucci blouse with a bold geometric design of turquoise and lavender. Her look was topped off with filigreed gold hoop earrings, a diamond pendant on a thick gold chain, and a large diamond engagement ring on one hand and a big diamond wedding band on the other. She exuded the fragrance of the perfume brand Joy.

Bronka observed that her mother, normally fresh and lovely in her own right—seemed to almost disappear from the scene, practically fading into the beige wall of the den. She wondered about the outcome of this discussion. Her parents had told JoJo in no uncertain terms that she was to marry Bruce and have the baby. Bronka knew that one of her sister's real issues with her boyfriend was that he seemed to be intimidated by his mother, always afraid of her criticism and disapproval. True, when JoJo had told him that her parents insisted that they marry, he had agreed right away. But JoJo had also emphasized that he could easily change his mind unless he received his mother's seal of approval. Although Bruce had assured her that he had spoken to his mother and she was okay with the marriage, JoJo told her sister that she knew that just "okay" wasn't a ringing endorsement and she was nervous that it was not yet a done deal.

Bronka also knew that if the wedding went forward, her sister must be realizing that she would be tied for life to him and his family. *What was that expression Faye always said? "You don't just marry the man, you marry his grandfather's chair."* Did her twin really want this to be her family?

CHAPTER SIX

WHILE ARON'S WIFE AND DAUGHTERS might have been intimidated, he was not at all impressed with Doris Stern and her trappings. He had come on a mission and after all, he was, first and foremost, a survivor.

"So are *ve* going to sit down and discuss the situation?" he said.

"Oh, of course," said Leon. "Make yourself comfortable. Doris, don't you have some refreshments for our guests?"

"Jackie, there's a plate of cheese and crackers on the kitchen counter," Doris responded in a soft, throaty, yet commanding voice.

Jackie left and returned with the platter, which she placed on the empty coffee table, save for a Waterford bowl opposite the couch.

"Please, let me get you something to drink," said Leon. "Water, seltzer, soda, orange juice, schnapps?"

"I'll have some seltzer," said Aron.

"Anyone else?"

"OK, well then, I'm going to have some Scotch. If anyone else changes their mind, let me know."

Leon came back with the glass of seltzer for Aron and Scotch on the rocks for himself and sat down.

"So, we have a situation here." Doris sat down and began the discussion. Her throaty voice remained low, but authoritative.

"Now, we have to fix it," she said slowly and deliberately; an emphasis on "fix."

"Yes, that is *vat ve vant* too," said Aron. "A *vedding*—the sooner the better. I *vas* thinking they could get married by Rabbi Herbert in his study. I'm sure he'd do it this *veek*."

As if she hadn't heard a word Aron said, Doris went on. "Actually, I've already called my caterer, Larry Marx, and he's available in two weeks. I'll order a tent and we'll set it up in the backyard. We'll have to phone people because there's no time to print and send invitations. It'll just be a small wedding; maybe forty, fifty people—tops. We can tell them Bruce is concerned that he will be drafted so he's getting married to his girlfriend. They were going to get married when she graduated, but they're just pushing it up a bit. No one will dare say a word. When the baby is born, we'll say it's premature. And you needn't ask your rabbi, Aron. I've already contacted ours. He's more than happy to officiate."

Bronka and Judy looked at each other with shock and sorrow on their faces. But JoJo did not look at all surprised. This was going to be her life now. She had better get used to it. Doris was in control.

Having survived the unimaginable, Aron had the ability to overlook things that other people couldn't. Forty or fifty was a small wedding by Rolling Hills standards. But he and Judy had gotten married with six other couples in a joint ceremony in the Displaced Persons Camp. Did that make them any less married? He recalled that each couple had been given two tickets for new clothes. One of the brides covered her head with a bandage in place of a veil.

He rationalized that his daughter was marrying into a comfortable family. She would not be having a child out of wedlock. So let Doris have a wedding in her backyard and invite forty of her closest friends and family. As far as the Reform rabbi officiating, he could live with that too. Better than having a more observant rabbi snooping around in their family history. The Sterns' rabbi would likely know that Aron was a pillar of his synagogue. He would not start inquiring.

Most important, as far as he and everyone else were concerned—he would have an ostensibly Jewish grandchild—a sign and a symbol from God that even into the next generation, Hitler had been defeated. Jewish life would go on.

CHAPTER SEVEN

BRONKA FELT SORRY FOR JOJO not having a big blowout wedding in a synagogue with a white, flowing bridal gown, a veil, and a bunch of bridesmaids. Her sister was so theatrical and concerned about appearances that she knew the lack of a traditional wedding must have been eating her up. Bronka told herself that she really didn't care about the trappings the way her sister did. She just wanted someone who would love her, understand her, allow her to be herself, and of course, marry her—and that was specifically Ned Jakes. She would have liked to invite him to the wedding, but the only guests the Lubinskis had asked were their cousins. Judy and Faye also said they thought it would be nice to have their neighbors, Jennie, Lenore and Mindy.

But Aron nixed that too. "We'd have to also invite Al, Lenore's boyfriend. There will be too many tongues wagging. They'll understand that it's just for family." He added that since the Sterns had refused to take any money from them for the wedding and they had virtually no one else they felt close enough to invite, that was going to be it.

But, of course, everyone knew that wasn't the only reason—he didn't want a bunch of prying eyes to invade his space. JoJo confided in Bronka that she would have liked to have a couple of friends there too, but she realized she was not in a position to bargain. And Bronka told her twin that since she was not officially Ned's girlfriend, she was okay with not inviting him. But deep down, she knew that she would have felt so much better with him holding her hand—literally and figuratively through this challenging event.

A few days after the meeting at the Sterns, Bronka had gone shopping with JoJo at A & S in Manhasset and they had found a sleeveless maxi-dress for the bride-to-be. It had an empire waist, which fortunately was in style and would also camouflage her sister's growing belly. It was light beige lace with white ribbon below the bust. And although it reached to her ankles, it was not a wedding gown per se. JoJo insisted that Bronka also get something new, since she would be the maid of honor. They settled on a sleeveless pink lace jump suit with bell-bottoms. JoJo assured her that it was fine for an outdoor wedding. And Bronka really wanted it because she had seen something similar on another girl when she was at a party with Ned at Columbia. She had gone to such pains with her appearance that night and was nearly knocked off her feet when Ned said out of the blue: "You see that gorgeous outfit that girl is wearing; do you think it's expensive?" This was months ago and it was still bothering Bronka.

Why was he looking at the other girl, specifically her outfit? Perhaps she needed to spend more on her clothing? Would he ask the other girl out and drop her? What was he thinking? She figured the wedding was as good an excuse as any to buy the pink lace jumpsuit and then she would wear it the first chance she got when she was out with Ned.

Izzy drove the family to the wedding in his Impala. Judy and the two girls sat in the back seat. And Aron sat on the bench seat in the front with Faye in the middle. Bronka was a little sad that Faye had decreed that it was probably better to send Becky back to Florida and they would join her right after the wedding. She decided that it was best for her not to be exposed to a high-pressure situation, which no one would be able to control. But Bronka thought that Becky should have been given the choice of whether she wanted to attend.

As they drove into the development, Izzy commented in his booming, cheerful voice, "Well, at least the sun is shining; it could be raining. Where should I park?"

I guess on the street," JoJo said, "unless there's room in the driveway."

"Don't park in the driveway, Izzy," Aron said. "Someone could block you and you might have trouble getting out."

So like Papa, Bronka thought. *We haven't even arrived yet and he's thinking about leaving. And it's his daughter's wedding!* But as they approached the house, there was no room in the driveway at all. There was a large powder blue catering truck that said "Larry's Classic Catering" in navy blue script. There were a couple of cars behind the truck.

"I don't think I'm familiar with Larry's," said Izzy. "I thought I knew all of the kosher caterers in the area."

"Doris said that it will be all dairy and fish, no meat," offered Judy.

Bronka saw that Aron rolled his eyes and raised his palms upward into the air. She hoped that this was not a harbinger of how he was going to behave at the wedding.

"Not a problem, Aron," Izzy said. "Even if they're not kosher, but I would think for a wedding, they'd have a kosher caterer. But what do I know? These fancy people in Rolling Hills have their own ways of doing things. And I eat everything."

Bronka had been a bit surprised when Doris had made it very clear beforehand that people must walk around the house to the backyard. So even though the bride and her family should have been the guests of honor, that's what they did.

As her eyes scanned the backyard set-up, Bronka gasped. It was not what she had expected at all. Indeed, none of the Lubinskis had ever seen anything like this before.

"You didn't tell me your mother-in-law was 'the hostess with the mostest,'" quipped Faye as she looked at JoJo, who responded with a wan smile.

The chuppah sat on the brick patio. When Bronka took one look at it, she was embarrassed that Aron had offered to bring the portable chuppah that Rabbi Herbert used for small weddings in his study. But she knew that her father always scoffed at excess; he thought the faded blue velvet canopy would have been fine. White drapery hung from the poles holding up this chuppah. The canopy itself was a striking display of pink and white roses.

On the lawn, there was a white tent with six round tables, pink damask tablecloths and matching cloth napkins. The tables were set not with the paper plates and plastic utensils of Bronka's imagination, but ivory china and gold flatware. At the center of each table in a crystal vase were flower arrangements with a dozen pink and white roses, baby's breath, and ferns.

And then there was Doris Stern herself, who stopped giving instructions to the catering staff long enough to air kiss her almost-daughter-in-law and her family. Doris was wearing a knee length hot pink dress with a matching coat and pillbox hat. Faye eyed it and whispered to Judy that it was custom made.

"Oh Bronka, you look lovely—and we coordinated with each other; we're both in pink! I didn't tell a soul about my dress, so what a lovely coincidence!"

Not a word about the bride or the rest of her family Bronka noted with sadness.

"We'll be starting in a bit," Doris told the Lubinskis. "JoJo, come with me, so you and Bruce can speak to the rabbi. The rest of you—have a drink and some hors d'oeuvres."

As Doris spirited JoJo inside to meet with her son and the rabbi, a black-tied waiter suddenly appeared with a tray of white and red wine in crystal goblets.

"Let's have something to drink," Izzy said.

Ten minutes later, Doris re-emerged with the bride and groom together and told the Lubinskis the wedding was about to start.

"Come," she said. "We are going to start the ceremony. There'll be no procession, but all the parents and Bronka and Bruce's best friend, Tom, will stand under the chuppah and the guests will stand around them. Izzy and Faye, there are some folding chairs if you need to sit down."

Bronka observed that Faye's mouth was half open about to say something—likely snarky—she guessed. She knew that Faye hated it when people assumed she and Izzy needed special accommodations because they were getting older. And Doris had a condescending way about her, even if she was trying to be kind. But Izzy quickly said: "That's quite OK, Doris, we'll stand. I'm sure we'll have a better view that way."

The rabbi was a short man, with curly white hair and a black robe. He stood in front of a bridge table covered with a damask white tablecloth. He did not wear a *yarmulke*. On the table was a large, ornate sterling silver wine cup, encrusted with colored stones. There was a wine glass for Bruce to smash with his foot when the ceremony was over, as well as the *ketubah*, the marriage contract, and a white prayer book.

The rabbi made a big speech about what a wonderful family the Sterns were and how he had officiated at Bruce's bar mitzvah and confirmation and the sisters' weddings. He mentioned that Leon was not only a founder of the synagogue and had been on the rabbinical search committee when he was hired, but could always be counted on to support the temple's needs. And of course, beautiful Doris, who he said looked like strawberry ice cream, had been a president of sisterhood. He mentioned that the Lubinskis were members of their synagogue and that Aron went to services every day. He mistakenly called Johanna, Joanne. And soon the ceremony was over as Bruce smashed the glass with his foot, breaking it on the third try—and everyone called out *Mazal Tov.* Bruce kissed the bride tenderly. Now it was time for the party to begin.

Bronka felt her tears welling up and she noticed that JoJo and her mother also had tears in their eyes. But she was reasonably sure that she knew what her father was thinking. *He's relieved,* she thought. His daughter was married; his family had avoided shame. Despite all of the aggravation she'd given him, Johanna had married a Jewish boy—and one whose family appeared to have money. Bronka knew that her father was capable of looking past the waiters walking around with trays of shrimp and cocktail dipping sauce, crabmeat blintzes and eggrolls and just figured that Doris's concept of dairy was a bit different than his. She imagined him saying to himself while he looked the other way: *Let the Sterns enjoy their treif.* Bronka also surmised that while Aron thought this entire show was a huge waste of money, it wasn't his money that had paid for it. In fact, she conjectured that he was also glad he hadn't invited anyone but Izzy and Faye—no need to explain.

CHAPTER EIGHT

WHEN SHE GOT HOME AND went upstairs, Bronka got out of the pink lace jumpsuit, and saw that it was soaked with sweat; she would have to bring it to the cleaners before she wore it on a date with Ned. As she jumped into the shower, she noticed that the upstairs was eerily quiet without her sister. This would be the first time she had ever spent a night without her. *I'd better get used to it,* she thought. She couldn't even discuss the wedding with her now—the couple was off to Puerto Rico for a quick honeymoon. Neither could they gossip about Doris, or Bruce's obnoxious sister, or talk about the pompous rabbi who had snatched a piece of shrimp from the waiter's tray. Her father's eyes almost popped out of his head, but she had been thankful that he didn't say a word.

She had suspected that everyone at the wedding knew JoJo was pregnant, but no one dared mention it. By the time the ceremony was over, the glass broken, and hearty Mazel Tovs intoned, the guests were ready to eat and drink. Most were happy to gorge themselves on Larry's Classic Catering delicacies—the vast majority of those in attendance were obviously non-kosher. Still, Doris, the perfect hostess, had provided salmon and plain vegetables and baked potatoes for the Lubinskis. And they could eat the creamy vanilla wedding cake with chocolate pudding filling, chocolate covered strawberries and ice cream for dessert. Bronka knew that her sister didn't care about the dietary laws and had had no say in the menu. But still, you might think Doris would have had more respect for JoJo's family. And, of course, Bruce was a wimp. She knew that it was totally out of the question—even if he had cared—for Bruce to muster up the courage to confront his mother.

Bronka felt very confident that her own wedding would be kosher, especially if she married Ned Jakes. His mother, Clara, was a lovely woman whom Bronka had met a few times. She was a widow and lived in Glen Oaks, the garden apartment complex on the north side of Union Turnpike. Ned's father, an electrician, had died from a heart attack last year, and Bronka had gone to pay a shiva call. Clara kept thanking Bronka for visiting and although the house was full, she insisted Bronka join her on a chair next to the low mourning bench on which she sat.

Bronka learned that Clara was also an immigrant and had come to America when she was six years old, so they immediately hit it off. And Bronka was hopeful that Clara would put her seal of approval on her as a potential wife for her son, which both tickled and reassured Bronka.

Bronka was certain Clara Jakes would never put a piece of shellfish or pig in her mouth, nor mix meat with milk, let alone allow it to be served at a simcha. She was also certain that she would be a much more loving and considerate mother-in-law than Doris Stern.

CHAPTER NINE

TWO WEEKS AFTER THE WEDDING, Ned called and invited Bronka to spend the following Sunday with him in Central Park. He suggested bicycling in the park, weather permitting. The plan was for her to meet him in the city since he would be at his apartment for the weekend. They arranged to meet in front of Carnegie Hall because the bicycle rental area was a short walk from there.

Bronka didn't mind that she had to go to Manhattan alone to meet him, although her father suggested that he might have come home to visit his mother in Queens for the weekend. That way, he could have at least, accompanied her to the city. But she knew full well that girls who lived in the outer boroughs were classified as "GUD." They were considered geographically undesirable. So she was thrilled that he had chosen her—a girl from Queens—for this date. She believed he could have had his pick of many girls who lived right near him in the city, including those at Barnard or graduate students at Columbia.

As luck would have it, it was a gorgeous fall day. Bronka was excited to experience the iconic park in its autumn splendor. And since she had not seen Ned for more than two months, she yearned to see him again.

Yearning, that was the word that Bronka thought best described what she felt for Ned and how she desired him during his frequent disappearances. It was an ache, a deep longing that did not go away until she saw him again. Still, in her heart of hearts, she knew she was on tenuous grounds. That's probably why she listened again and again to the Ian and Sylvia ballad, "Four Strong Winds." She thought it captured her on again, off again relationship with Ned. Its melancholy refrain captured her deepest fears: "I'm bound for moving on . . . . I'll look for you if I'm ever back this way."

Ned was someone who came and went, and when he was in her life he could be charming and attentive. But she couldn't remember that he ever asked her out twice in the same month nor gave her an explanation for why. He could discuss politics or philosophy or history—Bronka thought with insight and wisdom. He was funny and clever. But he could also be brooding and inconsiderate. For example, he was habitually late, often making her stand alone on a street corner waiting for him for a half hour or more when she met him in the city.

Her intuition told her that he struggled with demons, perhaps she surmised, family relationships, his father's death, maybe even illness. She couldn't pinpoint it. And Bronka was too polite to inquire if he did not choose to share. All she knew was that she adored him and wanted to heal him from whatever it was that made him behave erratically.

And why did he keep coming back to her if there was no attraction there?

The bicycling was energizing and Bronka was relieved that she was able to not only manage the bike after so many years of not riding, but also to keep up with Ned. Actually, she was delighted that she didn't fall off the bicycle and make a fool of herself.

After they finished with the bikes, Ned found a somewhat secluded patch of grass and they sat down close together on the ground. He reached into his pocket and pulled out a small cloth gift bag with a drawstring.

Bronka's heart began pounding. Was he going to ask her opinion about a present he had bought for someone else? Or was he actually going to give her a gift?

Awkwardly, he handed it to her without saying a word.

"What's this?"

"It's something I picked up. I saw it and thought of you. Go ahead and open it."

Bronka was shaking inside; she could not believe her good fortune. Maybe Ned had finally made up his mind about her or had solved whatever his issue was.

"Oh, it's beautiful, Ned," she said as she took out a small silver necklace. A peace sign, adorned with turquoise and sparkly beads, hung from the silver chain.

"Thank you," she said. "What's this for?"

"I don't know, I saw it and thought of you. I thought it had your name on it," he said with a smile so big his eyes twinkled.

"That's so sweet of you," said Bronka, totally beside herself.

"Anyway, I didn't get you anything for your birthday."

"My birthday was in July."

"I know. Sorry, I missed it, but I was in Mexico. Put it on."

After she fastened the necklace, she leaned over to give him a kiss. And to her surprise, he kissed her back, not a peck, but a long, deep kiss, exploring her mouth with his tongue. Before she knew it, he was on top of her, kissing her neck, touching her breasts.

While she was elated, it did not escape her notice that they were in the middle of the city's largest public park in broad daylight.

"Ned, we're in a public place. I think we should stop. People can see us."

"OK, if you think so," he said, seemingly unperturbed. "But we can make beautiful music together. You really should get your own apartment."

After that, they both got up and strolled around the park, holding hands. Then he walked her to the subway station.

"Thanks for a wonderful day, Ned," Bronka said.

He cupped her chin in his hand and gave her a kiss on the lips.

"Ciao," he said.

During the one-and-a-half-hour trip home on the subway and bus, Bronka smiled and kept fondling the necklace.

Could this be a turning point in our relationship? She wondered. He had been so romantic and had even given her a gift.

The next morning, she saw that Ned had left her yet another token of his affection—a prominent hickey on her neck. Bronka had never had one before, but her sister and her friends had spoken about hickeys. She knew they were caused by biting or sucking, but she hadn't even been aware that Ned had gotten so carried away. She was embarrassed by the purple bruise, but saw it as a badge of honor. Nevertheless, she certainly didn't want her parents commenting on it. She set about trying to conceal it with foundation and powder—but they didn't completely cover it. Next, she tried a scarf around her neck.

Bronka was disheartened that it took almost two weeks for the hickey to disappear. It took far longer than that for Ned to call her again.

CHAPTER TEN

IN JANUARY DURING INTERSESSION, NED invited Bronka to accompany him to New Hampshire to campaign for Senator Gene McCarthy. McCarthy, who was opposed to the Vietnam War, was challenging President Johnson for the Democratic Presidential Nomination.

Most of what Bronka knew about the war was from TV, her professors, and Ned. She also knew of a high school classmate who had been drafted after he dropped out of college. And, of course, Tina Rosen's midshipman was likely headed to the war zone after graduation from the Naval Academy. Mindy told her about a boy who had fled to Canada and one who was a Conscientious Objector. Most of the other boys she knew sought medical or educational deferments. Lloyd Miller told her that he was 4F because he was a diabetic, but generous person that he was, he had shared the urine in his cup with several young men who had also reported to the draft board that day.

Every bone in Bronka's body was opposed to the war—even though she had no personal connection. It was simply an unjust war, not like World War II. The idea of joining McCarthy's Kids' Crusade appealed to her as much as traveling and working with Ned. She reasoned that he must care for her; why else would he invite her to come with him?

Still living under the same roof with her parents, going to New Hampshire would be an issue. She imagined that Papa was only at ease when she was sleeping in her bed. If he could, he would lock her in a closet until she was ready to be married. There was no way he would allow his remaining daughter to ring strange doorbells and travel with a young man.

"It's cold in New Hampshire this time of year," said Judy. "You're really going to be comfortable ringing doorbells in the freezing cold?"

Judy and Bronka were sitting at the kitchen table, drinking coffee and eating graham crackers.

"I'll be with Ned."

"Is the reason you want to go to campaign or to be with Ned?"

"Honestly, Mama, both," Bronka answered as she teared up.

"That's what I mean, honey. You're so sensitive," Judy said as she looked at her daughter, dark eyes blazing with passion, "You have such a thin skin. I don't want you to get hurt."

"Mama, you can't protect me from getting hurt. Don't you think it's time you stopped trying?

"And what did you do yourself, out of passion?" Bronka continued. "Renounced your family, your country, your religion, to follow the man you loved. I'm not leaving the country. I'm going to New England for a couple of weeks to be with the boy I love. In addition, I want to take action for a cause in which I believe. Isn't that what you did?"

"Look, if that's what you have your mind set on doing, I'm not going to stop you, but I just wish you would appreciate how special you are—you could get any boy you want. I'm not going to stop you, but I'm not so sure I can give it my blessing."

The word, "blessing," was a trigger for Bronka. Even after JoJo got pregnant out of wedlock, disgracing the family, both their parents—even their father—ended up giving her their blessing, she recalled. Now her mother was invoking the word, *blessing,* for a political trip to New Hampshire.

"Mama, cut it out," Bronka said angrily. "I love Ned and I hope he loves me. He cares about what I have to say. No one has ever listened to me the way he does. And we both share a love of politics.

"I have no confidence," Bronka went on, "because you have none either. I inherited my inferiority complex from you. You were a hero; you saved Papa—and countless children. And you still let Papa control you. You wanted to be a nurse. But you didn't because Papa wanted you under his thumb. And you allowed it. And what are you doing with your life now? Working in the bakery? Still catering to Papa's every whim? You could still do something else."

"Bronka, I'm not unhappy. I know my place. First and foremost, it's as a wife and mother. What's wrong with that?"

"What's wrong? JoJo is married and pregnant. And I have one year left of college. There are no babies at home to nurse."

"I'm volunteering at the hospital, so that fulfills my need to care for people. And I'm responsible for the bakery's books. Papa wouldn't give me that job if he didn't trust me."

"It shouldn't always be about what Papa thinks," said Bronka. "Don't you get to choose?"

"Papa means well. And I know my place."

"The place of women in society is changing," said Bronka.

"Maybe so, but I was under the impression you wanted nothing more than to have a boyfriend and get married."

"I do, Mama. But I also want to make a difference in the world. Maybe if I marry Ned, I can be his silent partner. He can run for office and I can help him. Maybe write his speeches, do research for him."

"Really, Bronka, that doesn't sound so liberating. You just said you wanted more. How is that so different from what I do?"

Bronka dunked her graham cracker in the coffee and savored the taste before she answered.

"I don't know Mama," Bronka said as she teared up. "I'm confused. I want to marry Ned. I want a family. I want to be a good mother, but I also want to be someone. I just don't know what that is yet. But I'm pretty sure it's more than being a teacher."

"There's nothing wrong with being a teacher. You get out at three o'clock every day and get holidays and summers off."

"All the girls at Queens College are becoming teachers," Bronka replied. "And many of them have engagement rings already. I want to be loved too, but I want to do something different."

Bronka was aware that her mother worried about her anxiety. It was no secret; she had been riddled with it ever since she was a child—just like Aron. With her sister married and her relationship with Ned not progressing, she was more anxious and depressed and desperate than ever.

She knew also that her mother had big doubts about Ned. She had made it clear to Bronka that she thought he was a big gamble, had sized him up and strongly suspected that her daughter was heading for a fall.

"I don't want you to get hurt," Judy said. "But it breaks my heart to see you so depressed and anxious. And there's always the possibility that I could be wrong about Ned. I know you're not the type of girl who would just defy me and go anyway if I said no.

"Fine, if you're determined to do it, then go ahead. But you know, McCarthy doesn't have a chance," Judy added. "I'll handle Papa."

CHAPTER ELEVEN

ON THE ROAD TO NEW Hampshire, Bronka found herself on a noisy crowded bus with a bunch of other young people. She overheard conversations about shorn beards, haircuts, and the purchase of new clothes for the McCarthy's Kids Crusade. Sweatshirts and jeans were not allowed. The young people had been told to "get clean for Gene," and they dutifully followed instructions so they could participate in the political process.

On the trip up, a few kids had brought guitars and led the group in the lively singing of the popular folk songs of the day. One talented young man even had a repertoire of his own original McCarthy campaign tunes, which he taught to the others.

Bronka, always the curious reporter, eavesdropped on a number of conversations that indicated how coming to New Hampshire to campaign for McCarthy was a cathartic event for many of the participants.

A young man sitting behind her told the girl next to him: "A lot of us have been protesting in the streets for a long time and nothing's changed. We're pretty desperate. It seems to me that McCarthy is the only guy who had the courage to take a stand and challenge LBJ's war policy."

When she wasn't talking, listening, or singing on the bus, Bronka wondered what the sleeping accommodations would be. Would she be with Ned? Would they have any alone time? Would this trip bring their relationship to the next level?

When they arrived at their destination, the young people were given their housing arrangements. New Hampshire's citizens stepped up to the plate, embracing and housing them in church and synagogue basements, spare bedrooms and on living room floors. Bronka soon discovered that she and Ned had been assigned to an old farmhouse in Nashua where they slept in an attic room in sleeping bags with three other college kids.

Each day Bronka and Ned, along with hundreds of other young people, went door to door in the freezing cold and even snow. They urged voters to come out on Primary Day on March 12 in support of McCarthy. Bronka was pleased that most of the people they canvassed were warm and welcoming. The students even got a big compliment from the chairman of the Nashua Democratic City Committee. "These college kids are fabulous," he commented to a reporter from a local TV station. "There are so many people who have kids of their own of the same age, and they can't talk to their own kids, it's another generation. These kids knock at the door, and come in politely, and actually want to talk to grown-ups, and people are delighted."

The work in New Hampshire was energizing, the discussions inspiring and the optimism boundless. Bronka basked in the heady experience of being involved and making a difference, but also being in Ned's presence for two whole weeks. She saw it as an intense meeting of minds and purpose—politically, intellectually, and spiritually. But aside from hand-holding and a few kisses, it was regrettably still a platonic one.

"I'm switching my support from McCarthy to Kennedy," Ned told Bronka on the phone one evening. She was in her bedroom, seated at her desk, listening intently to Ned's words on her pink princess phone. Kennedy had announced his candidacy just four days after McCarthy surprised everyone by coming in a close second to President Johnson.

"Really? Why? We worked so hard for McCarthy in New Hampshire and now he's got momentum," Bronka said.

"Gene is a moral and idealistic choice; Bobby is a realistic one," Ned opined. "Anyway, McCarthy was a bit of a stiff. You remember that guy who wrote all the great campaign songs? They refused to use any of them.

"I've already been down to the Kennedy headquarters in the city and it's huge. If you want to join me, we'll have a blast."

Bronka was torn—for about thirty seconds. She reasoned that Bobby Kennedy had the Kennedy looks, speech pattern, and machine behind him. If Ned said McCarthy didn't have a chance, she believed him.

"Sure, Ned," Bronka said.

"OK, great," he said. "Now we just have to find a place for you to stay in Manhattan for the weekend. I'd love to have you stay with me, but my roommate is a bit finicky so it might be uncomfortable for you.

"Actually," he continued, "my friend Eleanor is having a party in the city at the end of March. Maybe you can skip school for a couple of days and we can go."

"Sure, I'll see if I can find a place to stay," said Bronka, thinking Thursday and Friday were light days for her anyway. The only person she knew in Manhattan with her own apartment was Mindy, her friend at Barnard, who would let her stay there for free. Mindy actually paid no rent at all; the apartment was owned by her mother's fiancé, Al.

CHAPTER TWELVE

THE FOUR-DAY-ADVENTURE IN NEW YORK, rather than providing answers for Bronka about her relationship with Ned, just added layers and layers of more questions. On Sunday night, Bronka and Mindy sat on the gray couch in Mindy's living room, munching on potato chips and cheese and crackers that were laid out on a folding snack table. Ned had insisted on mixing apricot sours for the girls and he poured a Scotch on the rocks for himself.

Mindy had offered them pot, but Ned declined, saying the last time he had smoked it while in Europe, he had had a paranoid experience. Bronka was glad, not sure if she wanted to try it either. Although many of her peers were experimenting with drugs, she was afraid. First and foremost, she was queasy about putting a foreign substance in her body. She did not want to lose control over her words and actions or have a scary experience like the one Ned described. But most of all, she was concerned about the long-term effects on her body and the impact on the future children she wanted so much. She was not about to endanger them in any way.

Bronka sliced a piece of Brie with a special cheese knife on Mindy's teakwood cheese plate as she got ready to watch *The Smothers*

Brothers, a program which she looked forward to each Sunday night. Then, at 9:01, the surprise announcement came: "This program is being interrupted to bring you a message about Vietnam from the President of the United States, Lyndon Baines Johnson."

They listened as Johnson began by speaking about a pause in the massive bombing campaign that was destroying much of Communist North Vietnam. But it was the end of the speech that caught them by surprise.

"With America's sons in the fields far away, with America's future under challenge right here at home, with our hopes and the world's hopes for peace in the balance every day, I do not believe that I should devote an hour or a day of my time to any personal partisan causes or to any duties other than the awesome duties of this office—the presidency of this country," Johnson said in his southern drawl as he looked solemnly into the TV camera.

"Accordingly," he continued. "I shall not seek, and I will not accept, the nomination of my party for another term as your president."

At first, the three young people just looked at each other speechless—as if not completely comprehending what LBJ had just said.

It was Ned who broke the silence.

"That's it! We did it! We have a great chance now to elect Bobby and end the war!"

Bronka and Mindy got up at once and started jumping up and down in a delirious dance of excitement and joy. Ned joined them, putting his arms around both of them at once.

"I'll walk you to the subway," Ned offered when Johnson finished his message, signaling that the evening's festivities were over.

Bronka had been hoping that Ned would take her out again that night, perhaps she might have slept at Mindy's again and gone straight to Queens College the next morning. And now there was something to celebrate, and they were together. So why not?

The visit to the RFK headquarters on Thursday afternoon before President Johnson withdrew from the Presidential race had been both exhilarating and perplexing for Bronka. Ned took her around and introduced her to several handsome young men. It was clear that Ned had already ingratiated himself with the Kennedy staffers. Just as they were about to leave, one of the good- looking guys ran after them.

"Hey Ned," he called. "Stop right there. I need this lovely lady for a minute."

"What for?" Ned asked.

"We're filming a documentary about Bobby's supporters and we have some newspaper guys photographing it. Do you mind if I borrow her?"

"Sure thing," said Ned.

Why didn't he ask Bronka herself? She was standing right there. And he didn't even ask her for her name. On one hand, she felt like an object; the other, she was delighted he called her "lovely."

He led Bronka through the cavernous room of desks with envelopes and flyers piled high. The only decorative touch were the large RFK posters that dotted the white walls. Soon, they were outside where a film crew and some newspaper photographers were snapping pictures.

There was a line of four other girls who had already donned white brimmed hats with red and blue bands and matching sashes that said "Kennedy." At five foot six, Bronka was about the same height as the other girls and they blended well. The handsome guy put the sash and hat on Bronka and gave her a shopping bag to hold. Then another shorter, but also good-looking young man, told the girls to line up in front of the building's tall line of windows, each plastered with a face of Bobby. For the still newspaper photo, he asked them to all point to Bobby's face. Then for the movie camera, they were instructed to parade around the building.

"Okay, thanks girls," the tall handsome guy said. "You can go now."

"So you're gonna be in pictures, lady," said Ned, as he took Bronka's hand and walked her away from the building.

"Yeah, I guess so," said Bronka. "But I really want to contribute to the campaign. What can I do?"

"Well, you can come back and stuff envelopes," said Ned.

You must be kidding, Bronka thought to herself, but did not dare say. *I have a brain too, just like you.*

Bronka didn't have the courage to ask him if that was what he would be doing, but she knew it wasn't. Was that what the girls on the campaign did while the guys got more important work? Neither did she ask him why they had chosen her for the filming. Did they just need another girl? Or did they choose her because she was pretty? Why couldn't he just say complimentary things to her? Maybe he didn't think she was attractive at all.

As they walked away, Ned said, "Let's go back uptown. I'll show you my apartment and then we'll grab a quick bite near Columbia."

With that, Bronka perked up.

Ned's apartment was located on 110 Street. Was it in Harlem? Bronka thought so but didn't want to ask. She had heard all about the crime and the drugs there and she was frankly surprised that Ned would choose to live there—although if he were there to try to make things better for its residents, then she understood fully. He was putting his money where his mouth was. Ned had spent a summer in Mississippi petitioning against white supremacists while trying to register Black people to vote.

The apartment was twice the size of Mindy's and it had high ceilings and crown molding. The furniture was sparse and old. The living room consisted of a fake black leather couch, some folding chairs, a coffee table, a TV, and bookshelves on the wall.

"Here, I'll show you my room," Ned offered. There was a typewriter atop a small desk with a chair, a wooden chest of drawers painted bright green and a full-size bed, perfectly made up with purple sheets and a purple comforter. There was a scratched-up wood veneer night table on the left side of the bed. On it was a yellow telephone and a lamp. On the green chest, there was a blue box of Cheer Detergent and the neatest pile of men's underwear that Bronka had ever seen.

There was a large bulletin board on the wall with news clippings and two photos. One was a black and white picture of Ned with Andrew Goodman that was taken in Mississippi in 1964 shortly before the 20-year-old Queens College student was murdered by the Ku Klux Klan, along with Michael Schwerner and James Chaney. Along with Ned and many other young people, they had come to Mississippi for Freedom Summer to register black voters.

The other was a large color photograph of Judy Garland.

"You like Judy Garland?" Bronka asked, thinking Ned was more of a Bob Dylan kind of a guy.

"Yes, I love Judy. She's a survivor, and she understands suffering."

Suffering and surviving were her father's motif; saving was her mother's specialty. It entered Bronka's mind that Ned also was suffering. That was the only explanation for his erratic behavior and disappearances. She wanted to heal Ned from whatever it was that was haunting him.

Bronka was curious to see the other bedroom too, but Ned did not offer to show it to her. She heard the strains of the Beatles' recording of *Norwegian Wood* coming from it and concluded that the roommate was in there.

"OK," Ned said with a sly smile and a wink. "Now you've had the grand tour. Sometime when Preston isn't here, we can make beautiful music together."

Just as they were headed for the door, Preston emerged from the other room, exuding the spicy, earthy tones of Brut, and looking like he had stepped off the cover of Ebony Magazine. He was elegant and debonair in his pink shirt and brown and pink plaid sports jacket. He was tall with broad shoulders and a small waist—and a huge wide smile.

"Bronka, meet my roommate Preston; Preston meet Bronka."

"Hi pretty lady," said Preston with a wide grin that exposed a mouthful of gleaming white teeth. "And where is my friend taking you?"

"Oh, we're going to get a bite to eat at the chicken place on Amsterdam," Ned answered for her.

"That's the best you can do? This beauty deserves fine dining."

Ned rolled his eyes: "Maybe you can afford it on your assistant professor's salary, but hey, I'm still a student."

"Well, gotta run to class," said Preston. "Don't want to keep the students waiting."

It seemed strange to Bronka that Preston could not get out of the apartment fast enough and neither he nor Ned suggested that the three of them walk uptown together. After all, they were all headed in the same direction—the chicken place was only a few blocks from Columbia. She was intrigued that Ned had a black roommate, and one who was an assistant professor at Columbia. *This is all good,* Bronka thought to herself. *Ned will change the world—not only with words and public actions, but also with his personal behavior.* Meeting Preston only convinced her even more that she just had to spend the rest of her life with Ned.

CHAPTER THIRTEEN

THE FOLLOWING NIGHT WAS FRIDAY and the party at Eleanor's. Bronka was glad she was not at home where her father would remind her that she was desecrating the Sabbath by going out. Mindy happened to know Eleanor also and was going to the party too. Bronka was happy to have her as a crutch.

"Which should I wear?" she asked Mindy as she took out the jumpsuit from JoJo's wedding and a little orange mini-dress she had packed in her overnight bag.

"Both are a bit dressy," Mindy said, rolling her eyes. "You can wear either of those outfits or one of mine."

Bronka didn't want to be rude, but she was not going to wear the flowing dresses with the psychedelic colors Mindy favored. She wanted something that would show off her figure, which she had been working hard to get in shape for this weekend; she had lost seven pounds in the last few weeks.

"Well, which outfit makes you feel the most beautiful? Or are you going to tell me you still think you're ugly."

"You don't think I'm ugly?"

"Bronka, cut it out. A flea has more self-esteem than you do.

You're a beautiful, intelligent young woman, but I'm not going to keep saying it over and over. Grow up—now which is it going to be?"

"I want your opinion, please Mindy."

"OK, I vote for the lace jumpsuit. It might be a little much for this event. But I know you had Ned in mind when you bought it. And you look great in it."

As Bronka donned the lace jumpsuit, she was still debating with herself. Was it worth it? Would Ned think she was overdressed? What if she had to go to the bathroom? It was a pain to pull on and off.

She looked in the mirror again and again. She had decided to wear her dark hair long and loose, although she thought she looked more sophisticated with it pulled back. Well, this was a college crowd, long was probably better. She dared not ask Mindy another question; she would yell at her. She surveyed her face—foundation, eyebrow pencil, eye shadow, mascara and lipstick. Mindy wore no cosmetics.

She was beginning to sweat, so she sprayed some more deodorant under her arms. The sleeveless jumpsuit felt a bit scratchy, so she pulled it off and put on the orange minidress with the short sleeves.

Mindy walked in. "You're a nut job, my pretty friend."

Bronka felt the tears welling up; she felt completely overwhelmed. "I guess so, but I want to make a good impression on Ned's friends."

"Are you ready?"

"I guess so," said Bronka as she took one more look in the mirror.

"Honestly, I don't know why he can't come here first. Eleanor lives near Washington Square. He's got to hop a subway down to the Village too. I know you have a thing for him, but he dragged you here for the weekend."

Bronka felt herself choking back tears. But she was not going to ruin her makeup. She took a deep breath and said nothing.

At Eleanor's apartment in Washington Square, she came to the door wearing a white lace pants suit, very similar to the one Bronka had nixed. Her blonde, silky hair reached below her shoulders, and she greeted the girls with a wide smile. Bronka was instantly taken aback, wondering whether Ned had a thing for her.

The living room was crowded with about fifteen young people chatting, drinking beer in plastic cups, and munching on pretzels and potato chips. Most of the young men had sideburns, some had facial hair and they were all dressed casually. The female students ran the gamut from hippie to fancy.

Most of the kids were standing, but there were a few who sat on the couch or one of the two upholstered chairs or the folding chairs.

"Hi Mindy." Two girls who were dressed in brightly colored long dresses with matching bandanas came over to say hello, along with a boy with auburn hair who wore an olive-green tee shirt and jeans. He didn't look like a hippie, just a regular guy with black horn-rimmed glasses and long sideburns.

"This is my old friend and neighbor, Bronka," Mindy said as she introduced her to the three young people. "We've lived directly across the street from each other since we were little kids. Bronka was actually born in a DP Camp. And when I first met her, she hardly spoke any English. These are friends from my philosophy class—Autumn, Annabelle, and Oren. Have you seen a guy named Ned? He's who invited Bronka here."

"No, but I'm sure he'll surface soon enough," said Oren with a friendly laugh.

"Are you a student at Barnard, Bronka?" he asked.

"No, I go to Queens College," Bronka said apologetically, rolling her eyes.

"Queens is a good school," said Oren. "I thought for sure I'd end up at Brooklyn College, but then I got a scholarship to Columbia. So here I am. I'm a political science major. You?"

"Me too," said Bronka. "Do you know what you're going to do with it?"

"Probably go to law school. You know, I was born in a DP Camp too. And I think that because my parents had their own dreams squashed, they insist on me becoming a professional. And since I'm not a science person I can't be a doctor, which would be their number one choice. So it looks like I'm headed to law school—whether that's what I want or not."

Hmmm, Bronka thought to herself. Part of her really wanted to continue talking to this boy; he seemed nice and kind too. But when she looked around, she saw Ned heading toward her with a big grin and his distinctive swagger.

She was annoyed at him; he should have come to pick her up or at least designated a meeting spot. Mindy was right. If Mindy hadn't come with her, she would be standing alone in this group of strange people, looking like a lost lamb. Grateful that another boy was talking to her, she turned toward Oren smiling and with a look of great interest, said, "Where do you think you'll go to law school?"

"It all depends on the scholarship money," he said. "My first choice is, of course, Harvard, but unlikely that's gonna happen. We'll see."

Just as Bronka was about to ask whether he had a better chance of getting into Columbia since he was an undergrad there, Ned interrupted the conversation. He had a big smile on his face.

"So, this is where you've been hiding out. Introduce me to your friends."

Hiding out? Was he kidding? Bronka was disappointed and a bit disgusted that Ned was showing his bossy side. She not only wanted to continue the conversation with Oren, but she also wanted to show Ned she could be attractive to another guy. But he had other plans and after the introductions, he grasped her hand.

"Let's get some beer," Ned said after pulling her away from the group and leading her to the couch, which had been vacated. "Let's sit for a while," he said. "Come, sit on my lap."

Although Bronka thought this was a peculiar request, she

complied. *Why would you ask a girl to sit on your lap in the middle of a party like this? Was Ned showing off for someone? Was he using her to make Eleanor jealous?*

Bronka actually felt embarrassed. This party of Eleanor's was basically a mixer; everyone had come stag. And the swift way Ned had asked her to sit on his lap seemed unnatural and forced. It was as if he was trying to make a statement—and she was the prop. She wondered what Mindy and her friends thought of this scene. And she was so sorry she had selected the orange mini-dress, which rode up on her and revealed her thighs. The lace jumpsuit would have been better.

Later, when they returned to Mindy's apartment, they sat at the kitchen table analyzing the evening. Mindy had a few choice words about the situation.

"You know, Oren liked you, but if you're going to sit on another guy's lap in the middle of a party, that's kind of a turn-off. Don't you think?"

"But I didn't go to meet anyone else. I thought Ned was asking me on a date."

"Some date! Free beer, free pretzels. You go there without him and you leave without him. Everyone else is there to meet someone and he puts you on his lap. What do I know? But it seems strange to me. Should I give Oren your phone number?"

Bronka was so confused that she began to cry. "You mean you don't think I have a chance with Ned?"

"I'm not sure anyone has a chance with Ned."

"What does that mean?"

"I don't want to say; I could be wrong. But I'm pretty sure that you have a pattern going for guys who are unavailable."

"I'm not sure what you mean, Mindy. Why do you think Ned is unavailable?"

"All of his actions and all of his gestures indicate that he is. Think about it. How does he treat you? When you're ready to face it, I'm here for you."

Bronka began to cry.

"It's been a long day; we'll talk about it another time," Mindy said.

CHAPTER FOURTEEN

THE THURSDAY NIGHT FOLLOWING THE party, Bronka lay in bed reading after trying to convince herself that she would never land Ned as a boyfriend, let alone a husband. She still hadn't heard from him. And she was still thinking about what Mindy said. She told herself that she really needed to move on with her life. But of course, when her pink princess phone rang, she immediately jumped, then remembered to let it ring three times before she picked it up.

"Bronka," Ned said breathlessly. "Did you hear the news? I'm just devastated and Preston is hysterical. Bobby Kennedy had to calm down a crowd in Indianapolis by talking about losing JFK."

"Ned, you're not making sense, what are you talking about?"

"Reverend Martin Luther King, Jr. was assassinated in Memphis! He was there for a sanitation workers strike and he was shot and killed in cold blood. This is going to unleash a lot of really bad things, I'm afraid.

"And Preston wants to get on a bus and go to Memphis—like right away. But I'm telling him that doesn't make any sense. We should wait until they announce the funeral plans and maybe go and pay our respects wherever it is. It's surely not going to be in Memphis. Will you come with us if we go?"

"Sure," said Bronka, having immediately forgotten her consternation with him, soaking in the sound of his voice.

"OK, well that's all for now. Turn on the TV and I'll speak to you soon."

Bronka went downstairs and turned on the television and the full horror of it hit her. Only her candidate, Bobby Kennedy, had stopped a riot in Indiana.

Two minutes of exulting in the conversation with Ned after she hung up with him, the phone rang again. Somehow, Bronka could always sense when it was her twin sister calling.

"Bruce still isn't home. I just cleaned out the refrigerator and ate two Carvel sundaes I found in the freezer. I'm so tired and I feel like I'm going to burst. They say that when you get the nesting instinct, you're close to delivering. I wish you would come over and keep me company."

"I'm already in bed, JoJo. When is Bruce coming home?"

"He's going to come home and just crash after his night class and I need company. Please, pretty please with sugar on top."

The last thing Bronka wanted to do was get out of bed, get dressed, and head over to her sister's apartment. Seeing her there in all of her pregnant splendor secretly bothered her.

Maybe Mindy was right about Ned being unavailable; other than a few deep kisses, she couldn't even get Ned to make love to her although he constantly implied that he wanted to. But now she thought she was making progress. She was thrilled that he had invited her to go to Dr. King's funeral with him and Preston, although she was acutely aware that this would likely be another platonic adventure since Preston would be along. But still, she would be in his company, partake in the historical experience, and have deep and meaningful conversations with the two intellectual young men.

On the other hand, JoJo was already married and about to become a mother. True, she hadn't planned it that way and she would have to put her dreams and plans on hold. But knowing her twin sister, she also was convinced that she would figure out a way to get what she wanted. She always did.

Now, JoJo was already a week late, and could go into labor at any moment. Bronka would never live it down if she abandoned her sister now.

JoJo and Bruce lived in a large apartment in Great Neck. Most of the Bellerose brides, if they stayed in the area, lived in Glen Oaks, a garden apartment complex off Union Turnpike. From there, they usually moved on to buy their first homes. But Doris wouldn't hear of the young couple staying in Northeast Queens. It just wasn't fancy enough for her. So they moved to a two-bedroom apartment in a three-story building on Wooleys Lane with a 23-foot-long living room and mirrored walls in the dining area, which made the space look even bigger.

Inside, JoJo was curled up on the couple's new red paisley couch in the living room. On the wall opposite the couch were shelves with a TV, surrounded by a few books and knickknacks. Bronka couldn't help notice how bloated JoJo was—from her face to her feet. For the first time in her entire life, she felt slim in comparison to her twin. Yet, JoJo was still beautiful—blonde hair and blue eyes with the glow of impending motherhood.

"There are two more Carvel sundaes left," said JoJo. "Should we finish them?"

"What about Bruce? He might want one when he comes home."

"Nah, it's tax season. He usually gets a bite to eat while he's there and then he just comes home and keels over into bed."

There is nothing more soothing than Carvel, Bronka thought to herself. She got up to take the two remaining sundaes from the freezer just as Bruce walked in the door.

"Hi Bronka—and how are you doing, Jo, my lovely little mother to be?" Bruce asked cheerfully although he looked exhausted. His tie was undone, his eyes were bloodshot and he was pale.

"I feel like an elephant," JoJo said, "although eating Carvel all night didn't help. I think it's going to be soon. Why don't you try and sleep for a couple of hours in case I go into labor? I have Bronka here."

"Sure, honey sounds good. I'll just take a shower first. Bronka, thanks for being here. Just wake me up if anything happens."

Just when JoJo was about to take her first spoonful of ice cream, she winced.

"I feel like I'm having a contraction," she exclaimed as she pushed the dish aside. Bronka promptly finished both sundaes.

Ninety minutes later, JoJo called out, "I just felt a gush of water. I'm soaked. I'm going to call the doctor and then change."

When JoJo returned to the living room, she told Bronka that the doctor had confirmed that her water had broken.

"He told me not to eat anything and when the contractions are five minutes apart to head to the hospital. I'm going to wake up Bruce now."

"Do you want me to stay or do you want to be alone with Bruce?"

"Please stay, Bronka."

"OK, I will.

Three hours later, JoJo, Bruce, and Bronka headed for the hospital. At six o'clock in the morning, JoJo delivered a seven-pound, two-ounce baby boy.

CHAPTER FIFTEEN

DORIS HAD LOBBIED FOR A huge catered affair at either her home or their club, but since it was still tax season and the young couple had a very large living room, she capitulated and they had the bris in their Great Neck apartment.

The aroma of lox, sable, whitefish, pickled herring and onions, permeated every corner of the apartment. While Leon had sprung for the food, Aron insisted on choosing and paying for the mohel; he was going to make sure that the most kosher of kosher mohels would circumcise his first grandson. Rabbi Pinchas Kupietsky, gray haired, with a full beard and a black hat, was about sixty years of age, but looked fifteen years older.

Aron was the *sandek*, holding the eight-day-old infant triumphantly on a white satin pillow on his lap, beaming and confident. The women scurried into the kitchen with JoJo, so as not to watch the actual cutting. Bruce and Leon had no choice but to watch squeamishly, commenting that they were hopeful that the gauze soaked in Manischewitz that the baby had been given prior to the ceremony, would numb his pain a bit. The actual circumcision was short and the baby cried lustily for a few seconds and then it was over.

Rabbi Kupietsky intoned prayers and then gave the baby his Hebrew name. Bronka could see that Aron was a trifle disappointed that his own father had gotten second billing on the English name, Ian David, Doris's father having gotten the top slot. But he grinned from ear to ear when the Hebrew name was announced—David Yehudah. David was his father's name and Judah was Doris's father. And even the name Yehudah meant Jewish, so how great was that? David, the Jew, thought Bronka. She knew what her father was thinking: How could a child with that name be thought of as anything but Jewish?

Bronka was amazed that once again, her father proved to be more flexible than she gave him credit for. Gone was the anger at JoJo for getting pregnant out of wedlock. Gone was the disdain for Bruce and his family. JoJo had delivered what was most important to him—a Jewish grandson.

CHAPTER SIXTEEN

BRONKA SAT AT THE ROUND kitchen table in Mindy's apartment, drinking coffee. It was the end of April. Soon it would be May and spring would be in full bloom. The day before had been a tease—beautiful and sunny and in the mid-seventies, but today it was cold and raining. The young women had hoped to spend the day in Central Park, bicycling and hanging out. But the dreary weather had forced them inside. And they wanted to catch up.

"How's JoJo handling things?" Mindy asked.

"She's OK, hanging in. She's busy with Ian and she gets together with other mommies and their kids during the day and goes to school at night. She has a built-in babysitter in me. And Ian is delicious and I love him to death."

Bronka still maintained the twin code of her childhood. She would not complain about nor betray JoJo to anyone. She was not about to tell Mindy that she actually resented that she spent so much time in JoJo's apartment, babysitting and changing diapers, and that JoJo always assumed that her own plans came first, forgetting most of the time that Bronka had the right to live her life as well. And yet, on some level she felt sorry for her sister, despite her outward trappings.

Bruce was a workaholic, who couldn't make a move without consulting his mother.

And JoJo sometimes wondered aloud to her sister whether she would have ended up marrying him if it were not for the baby. Doris freely criticized JoJo's housekeeping, cooking, and parenting, and Bruce had the unfortunate habit of repeating whatever his mother said. When JoJo asked him to defend her, he was incapable of doing it. Still, Bronka was confident that JoJo could take care of herself.

"So, she's given up her dreams of acting?"

"For the time being, but you never know with her. She'll probably teach first, but I wouldn't rule it out. She knows how to make lemons out of lemonade."

"You should take a page from her book. Think about yourself for once. Don't take this the wrong way, but you're way too tied to her. You probably don't want to hear this—but I think the best thing for you would be to get out of that house and our neighborhood."

"But don't you remember when we were little, I was so shy and fearful and she was always there for me."

"But you're not a little girl anymore, Bronka."

"I'm trying, Mindy. I'm trying," Bronka said. "I'm going to apply to Columbia University Graduate School of Journalism.

"Good for you. But I will absolutely kill you if you teach."

"But you're going to teach, Mindy, and so is JoJo—what's wrong with it? Mama says it's the perfect profession for mothers. You get out at three o'clock, and get school vacations and holidays and the entire summer off," Bronka said, trying to convince herself.

"Well, I can't say anything," Mindy said. "I took the teaching route too. But you don't have to do that. And who knows, with me? It's an easy fix for now.

"It's tough to get a job in secondary education now anyway," she continued. "And I sure as hell don't see you teaching elementary kids. You're much too serious and intellectual for that. And getting a job in the humanities is even more difficult than science. All of these draft-dodgers, not that I blame them, are going into teaching to avoid serving in Vietnam. There's a lot of competition. But you know my mother's boyfriend, Al, has some connections on Long Island, so I might get a job there. It will be a pain commuting from this apartment, but I have a couple of interviews lined up.

"And speaking of this apartment, that's what I really think you should do—unless you want to leave New York for graduate school."

"I just want Columbia," said Bronka.

"Then you should definitely consider moving to Manhattan. Why, you could even live here with me. I have this whole apartment to myself and it gets lonely."

"Well, I'm going to try," said Bronka. "And hopefully, things are changing. Not sure about moving out, but thanks for the offer, and I'll definitely consider it."

"There's always a choice. Anyway, I'm meeting my mother and Al for dinner tonight. They said they want to speak with me about something important."

"What do you think it's about?" Bronka asked. "Your job search?"

"I have no idea, but it must be a big deal. Ostentatious Al is taking us to The 21 Club."

"Wow," said Bronka, "I wonder if you'll see any celebrities there?"

"Al is a celebrity in his own mind."

"Still, Mindy, he's not so bad. And he's extremely successful—why he practically invented the deodorant business. And he's been very generous to you."

"Yeah, I know, but he's such a capitalist pig. But Lenore is just nuts about him."

"Do you think they'll ever actually get married?"

"Who knows? They've been engaged for years."

"Well be sure to tell me what happens. And by the way, what do you wear to The 21 Club?"

"I'm going to wear my interview suit, the gray one—no point in biting the hand that feeds you."

That evening, Mindy pulled her hair back in a ponytail, and even put on some pink shimmer lipstick and the gold hoop earrings Al had given her for her birthday. Bronka knew that she was a clever enough girl to understand that she wouldn't get a job if she went looking like an unkempt hippie, and she was not about to embarrass Al—not to mention her mother—in one of his favorite haunts. And there was also something about Al that Mindy actually liked. She had told Bronka that she couldn't pinpoint it, but she felt a connection to him in an intuitive way—something that endeared him to her. At times, she confessed, she actually thought she liked him better than her mother.

Bronka knew that Bubbie Jennie always interceded when Mindy criticized and fought with Lenore, pointing out her mother's virtues. Mindy didn't want to fight with her grandmother, so she usually backed down. Still, Mindy was well aware that it was Jennie and her late grandfather, Harry, who had raised her while Lenore was off working, traveling, socializing, and who knows what?

The 21 Club on West 52nd Street was the very definition of an exclusive restaurant. Operating more as a private club, it was constantly being written about in the gossip columns as the place to be. Everyone knew that the corner tables were reserved for celebrities. The limousines were always lined up in front of the building, which was extravagantly decorated with wrought iron and the figures of lawn jockeys named for famous patrons.

Mindy had decided to take a taxi to the restaurant—why not? She told Bronka that no one ever took a subway to The 21 Club.

CHAPTER SEVENTEEN

DESPITE HER SCORN FOR TRADITION and opulence, when Mindy walked into the posh legendary restaurant, she gasped. The grandeur of it all was overwhelming. There were original works from Frederick Remington and cartoon dedications from Walt Disney, among other collections decorating the walls. After she gave Al's name to the maître d', his face lit up. Al's customary generous tip likely ensured a warm welcome for her.

"Mademoiselle, I will escort you," he said, as he led her into the grand main dining room. She did a double take as she saw Al chatting at a corner table with Dean Martin, who was accompanied by his wife, Jeannie, and another couple.

She caught Al's eye and he motioned to her to come over.

Despite her desire to be hip and cool, Mindy's heart started racing at the thought of meeting this handsome, charismatic star—although he was old enough to be her father. And always lurking in the forefront of her mind, was the indisputable fact that she did not have a father herself. As she approached, Dino's smile got wider and he extended his hand to take hers.

For once, Mindy was glad that she had decided to dress in

appropriate establishment attire for the evening, but if she had known Dean was going to be there, she would have gone a little less professional.

"Hi, I'm Dino." Mindy was speechless as he kissed her hand and said to Al, "Now who is this lovely young doll, Al? And she's a knockout and dressed so professionally, not like a lot of other young people these days."

"Mindy is my youngest daughter."

"Let's get a photo," Dean said as he motioned to a photographer who was snapping pictures. "Al, you get in the picture too."

As Mindy got swept away in the excitement of meeting Dean, Al's words did not register with her. The photographer told Mindy to stand in the middle and both Al and Dean put their arms around her. After he took the pictures, he gave the men his business cards, saying he was with *The New York Post*. Then he took out a small notebook, asking for the correct spelling of Mindy's and Al's names. "Look at Page Six in tomorrow's *Post*."

"You mean we're going to be in the newspaper? Mindy asked.

"Of course," said Dean. "When you're with Dino, you make the news."

"You know everyone loves Dean," Al said.

Mindy nodded.

"We better get back to your mom, Mindy" he added. "She's sitting over there in the corner by herself. Great seeing you Dean, Jeannie."

Al put his arm around Mindy's shoulder and led her to a table for three in a corner on the other side of the restaurant, where Lenore sat nursing a glass of wine.

She appeared happy to see her daughter smiling because with Mindy's volatility, one never knew what to expect from her. Mindy gave her mother a peck on the cheek before she sat down next to her.

"You look very happy, Mindy."

"Yeah, Dean Martin is very nice."

Mindy perused the menu.

"I'm lining up a few interviews for you, Mindy," Al said after they ordered. "My friend, Carl Meiselman, is President of the Board of Education in New Rochelle, and Sheila Wasserstein, my next-door neighbor, is on the board in Great Neck. They'll both speak to their respective superintendents and make sure you are interviewed."

"Thanks, Al," said Mindy with a smile.

"There are openings in secondary science in both places," Al said, "so submit an application and they'll call you for an interview. Hopefully, you'll be offered a job before the summer and then as your graduation gift, I'd like to treat you to a vacation of your choosing."

"Wow, that's so generous of you, Al," Mindy exclaimed with a big smile. "I'm not sure where I want to go, but I'll certainly think about it."

For the next half hour or so, Al recalled his myriad vacations, suggesting this and that travel spot for Mindy to consider.

During the evening, Al's largesse was on display. When the three finished their appetizers and main courses, out came the flaming Baked Alaska, which the waiter set down on the table with a flourish. Once the flame flickered and died, he cut the dessert in three.

Lenore, who had barely said a word during the dinner, spoke first. "Mindy, we wanted to have this special dinner to tell you our news. Al and I are getting married next spring."

Mindy glanced at her mother's flashy engagement ring.

"Well, it's about time. Honestly, what were you waiting for all these years?"

"We didn't want to disrupt you, but now that you're out of school and going to be working, we think it's time. Al's going to build a bigger house for us in Kings Point and there'll be a separate wing for Bubbie and she won't be that far from her friends and the old neighborhood.

There are also lots of activities for senior citizens in Great Neck. And, I assume you'll still want to live in the city—unless, of course, you end up working in Nassau County. Don't get me wrong, you'll have your own space in the new house too."

"No, that's okay, I'll stay in the apartment."

"Well, we just wanted to have your blessing," said Al.

"Sure," said Mindy. "No problem."

"Great," said Al. "And you'll meet my other children soon—my son and older daughter. I want you to meet them before we get married."

"Will you have a big wedding?"

"No, we're too much like an old married couple already—just the immediate family."

"Hmm," said Mindy, her face turning red and her heart rate escalating, as the truth that had been hidden in plain sight, suddenly hit her smack between the eyes.

"Al, you've made two comments tonight that are making me wonder. First, you introduced me to Dean Martin as your youngest daughter. Second, you just said you wanted me to meet your other children. What, exactly, did you mean?"

"Mindy, Al is your father. I was embarrassed because Al and I weren't married. You were born out of wedlock," Lenore interceded. "Al was a married man with a family. He had a wife and two children. Things were a lot different then. I didn't want to walk around with a scarlet letter."

Mindy's face turned beet red and she pounded the table in exasperation.

"Mom, you mean my father is *not* dead? You mean you have been lying to me my entire life? Don't you remember how sad and lost I was as the only child on the block without a father? I felt deprived when I saw the other kids with their fathers—playing with them, driving them places, buying them ice cream and comforting them when they cried. And not only did you hide my father from me, but you were also an absent mother. You were too busy gallivanting about town to take care of me. You left me with Bubbie and Grandpa every day, and now you're telling me that my father was simply hiding in the shadows."

"Who do you think sent you a bicycle, a Tiny Tears doll, all your fancy clothing and the other expensive gifts, Mindy?" Lenore raised her voice and narrowed her eyes. "Why were you the first one on the block to have the latest toys? Who do you think made sure we were the first home on the street to have a TV? I remember the day you first met the twins and told them about Howdy Doody. You showed them all your Howdy Doody dolls and paraphernalia. Poor little girls off the boat, they were mesmerized by your toys and the TV."

"Al, all that came from you?"

Al nodded sheepishly.

"And you know," Lenore added, "he paid for you to go to Barnard and Columbia Teachers College and you're living in his apartment rent free."

"So that makes your lying to me all right? That excuses you? What world do you live in anyway?"

Lenore looked crestfallen.

"Whose idea was this, anyway, to tell me my father was dead? It's clear it was yours, Mom. And why?"

Scowling, Mindy turned to Al. "And you went along with this? You condoned this? You thought this was just fine?"

"Things were much more complicated then. I wasn't around when you were little."

"Where were you?"

Al turned to Lenore and she nodded her assent.

"It's a long story, Mindy," Al explained. "It's really a history lesson about a shameful period in our nation's history called The Red Scare. I was one of many who were caught up in it. I was falsely accused of spying, tried, convicted, fined and imprisoned for six months. After I got out and my wife finally divorced me, your mother was so enraged at me that she didn't let me see you. Believe me, I wanted to, Mindy. I really did."

"But when you showed up at Grandpa's shiva so many years later, why didn't you identify yourself to me then?"

"I just didn't think it was the appropriate occasion," Al said. "Your mother didn't know I was coming; I surprised her."

Mindy curled her lips. "What a surprise, Al! And, if you hadn't slipped tonight and called me your daughter, would you guys have ever told me the truth?"

"It wasn't a slip. That's why we asked you to come here tonight," said Lenore.

"So, it was *you*, Mom, you deliberately kept me from knowing my father all these years? And worse still, you deprived me of my father because all you care about is yourself and what people might think of you.

"This is too much; I can't take this! I am done with both of you. I will never speak to either of you again. I might as well be an orphan." Mindy yelled as she pushed her chair back and stormed out of the restaurant, leaving her stunned parents aghast.

CHAPTER EIGHTEEN

WHAT A CRAPPY SUMMER *this has turned out to be,* Bronka thought as she waited on Union Turnpike for the Q44A Bus to come, the first of the two buses that would take her to Queens College for summer school. *It's my own fault. What was I thinking?* This was the second summer in a row that Bronka was attending summer school—with the express purpose of graduating early.

Her other friends, like Esther Zilberman, made plans to spend the summer of '68 in a ten-week study program at Hebrew University. She knew a bunch of people who had started enrolling in *ulpans* and some even began talking about making *Aliyah.*

Not so, Bronka. The thought of being enclosed on an airplane for ten or more hours made her break out in hives. Still, she yearned to follow in the footsteps of her fearless friends. She simply did not know how to shake her anxiety, and she kept it to herself.

Even Aron expressed delight at the miraculous outcome of the war: Jerusalem was now unified. Bronka rarely saw her father in such a state of unadulterated joy.

"It's about time!" he kept exclaiming.

But that was last summer. This summer was a different matter.

With a segment of her classmates scruffy and unwashed and extolling the virtues of dropping out and taking drugs, it was increasingly difficult to find her place with them. She found herself wishing that she had gone to Israel with Esther. She should have known that as the Vietnam War dragged on, with more and more students disaffected and disheartened, it would only get worse on the Queens College campus.

Anyway, this was not her scene and not her group. The truth is that she had never really found her niche in the school. Before her pregnancy, JoJo was in the drama crowd—and even joined a sorority—but Bronka, while she took everything in, could not find her place.

Now—a year later—with many of her classmates sporting multicarat round and pear engagement rings as a badge of honor, it seemed to Bronka that there was no place for her at all.

While she would have loved to have a boyfriend, she was not about to settle. Those who weren't marrying embryonic doctors, lawyers, or dentists for the most part were engaged to accountants or engineers or what Bronka considered other careers that attracted people with whom you could not have philosophical discussions. That was paramount for her, finding someone—like Ned—with whom she could ponder the meaning of life.

Bronka felt strongly that she did not belong with either group. So with no boyfriend or prospects, she decided to expedite her exit from college the following January. Then she would work, save some money and hopefully, start Columbia Graduate School of Journalism in the fall.

Summer session was almost over and then, she thought, JoJo would want not only her company, but also her newly acquired babysitting skills on a full-time basis. Since summer school was finished by noon three days a week, almost every day she would head over to JoJo's apartment and either keep her company, stroll down Middle Neck

Road with her and Ian, or let her twin take a few hours for herself—to go shopping, have lunch with a friend, or go to the beauty parlor.

What a mess my life is! What a mess I am! Bronka was miserable and depressed.

CHAPTER NINETEEN

THE FOLLOWING FALL, BRONKA THOUGHT her heart would break. She could not stop crying. How was it possible for Nixon to win the election? How did she go from the rush of being one of McCarthy's kids to the exhilaration of a possible RFK victory to Nixon in a few short months? What would happen to the country? She didn't think for one minute that he was really going to end the war. The dream had died. She was done with politics.

To be exact, it was the assassination of Bobby Kennedy, which ushered in the summer and fall of discontent. Bronka was inconsolable after he was shot in cold blood shortly after he won the California primary in June. She was dismayed that the assassination resulted in the nomination of Hubert Humphrey, LBJ's vice president in August. Bronka and her parents sat glued to the television as the drama unfolded at the Democratic National Convention in the convention hall and on the streets of Chicago. They all gasped as police billy clubbed and tear-gassed young protestors on the street. And Aron sobbed as he watched Sen. Abraham Ribicoff accuse Chicago's Mayor Daley of using *Gestapo* tactics on the streets of Chicago.

"It never ends," he cried.

Ned called Bronka after the election and invited her to have dinner with him at a little Italian restaurant, where he ordered a bottle of Chianti. They drank the wine and shared eggplant parmesan and baked ziti, eating off each other's plates. And later, in recalling the evening, Bronka was totally positive that he was looking deep into her eyes and smiling at her. She mistakenly interpreted it as the look of love.

Once they had finished, Ned wiped his mouth and a serious expression came over his face.

"Bronka, I wanted to tell you this in person and I didn't want you to hear it from anyone else. Preston and I simply can't stay in this country any longer. We must get out. Nixon is evil and the politics are toxic."

Bronka could hardly process what was happening, yet she was suddenly holding back her tears.

"But I thought you wanted to get into politics to change things for the better. You're just giving up—just like that?"

"For now, yes."

"What will you do; where will you go?" she asked, an errant tear running down her cheek.

"Preston is going to teach at McGill and I'm going to join him in Canada. I'll just write—see if I can get a job for a newspaper there, writing about America from the perspective of someone who's left."

"How long will you be there?"

"Could be the semester or if it works out, could be indefinitely."

Bronka's heart began racing and she tried to stifle it, but it was as if a wave came over her and she could not stop it. *If I don't say it now,* she thought, *I may never have another chance.*

"But Ned, I love you."

The minute the words were out of her mouth, she almost regretted them. *But no, I need to know,* she told herself.

He looked at her quizzically and with what she later remembered as a cruel little sardonic laugh, said: "You love *me*?"

"What's so funny about that?"

He shrugged his shoulders.

Later, everyone would tell her that you never tell a guy that you love him before he tells you.

"Don't you love me?" She couldn't help but ask.

Again, with the cruel giggle and the shocked look. Faye was correct: no bread was coming from this dough! Mindy was right: there was something weird about Ned. Still, Bronka had never felt like this about anyone in her life and she was convinced she would never again.

"No, I like you very much—as a friend. You're smart and interesting."

"Do you have a girlfriend I don't know about?"

Again with that stupid laugh. "No, I don't have a girlfriend. I've never been in love with a girl. Don't worry, you'll find someone else."

"How do you know?"

"You will. You're attractive and someone will marry you; I think you better forget about me. Let's get out of here."

And with that, she grabbed her coat, he put on his, and they walked out together.

"Shall I walk you to the subway?" Ned asked.

"No, that's OK, no need, Ned."

He cupped her chin in his hand and looked at her with what she would have thought on any other day was affection and kissed her on the forehead.

"Ciao," he said.

"Have a nice life," Bronka said as she walked as fast as she could away from him and her tattered dreams.

CHAPTER TWENTY

AFTER FOURTEEN HOURS OF NON-STOP sobbing, Judy went upstairs to see Bronka in her bedroom. Her face was red, her eyes were puffy and she was still in the clothes she had worn on her date with Ned.

"Come downstairs. We'll have some ice cream. That always cheers you up."

"I don't want ice cream. I want to die. "

"Maybe it will all work out."

"No, that's not gonna happen. I'll die an old maid."

"Bronka, come downstairs with me and I'll make some tea. Let's talk this out. This is over the top. Tell me what happened."

Bronka began sobbing again, deep wrenching sobs, which came from a place she did not understand. They overtook not only her body, but her entire being.

"I can't. I can't ever tell anyone."

"OK, then, but wash your face and come downstairs."

Bronka got up, went to the bathroom and obeyed her mother. She looked at herself in the mirror—red, bloated, swollen eyes. She was not only unlovable, but ugly too. After all, Ned could have said she was beautiful, but he didn't. *But why,* Bronka asked herself, *do I need him to say it?*

The two women sat at the kitchen table. Without JoJo in her own house, Bronka felt alone, but her mother also had a soothing way about her.

"So you broke up with Ned?"

"You could say he broke up with me, but in his eyes there was nothing to break up. I think I was just a friend to him." Although during fierce necking sessions she did not mention to her mother, he had given her a different opinion.

"What about the necklace he got you?"

"He broke up with me," Bronka cried again.

"Bronka, I've lived long enough to know that things are never as simple as they seem. Maybe he's just not ready. I always say if a boy isn't ready you can stand on your head and do cartwheels and he won't marry you. But if he's ready, walk into his line of vision and he'll marry you."

"No, I'm done. I will never see his face again in my entire life, I'm sure," said Bronka, breaking out into sobs again. "I'll never find anyone else."

"Of course, you will, Bronka. I'll give you a million-dollar guarantee. I promise you that you will find someone else to love and he will love you back."

"How do you know?"

"I just know. If that's what you want, you'll get it. And it won't be this difficult. But in the meantime, Bronka, I think you need to find your own path. Mine was a zigzag and that's okay."

"But you've always put Papa first," Bronka said. "If not for Papa, you could have been a nurse."

"I chose to follow the man I loved. That's what most women did back then."

"You could still do it, Mama."

"Not anymore. I should have done it when Faye and Izzy were still here full time. Now, Papa needs me too much in the business and I'm too old to go back to school. But I do enjoy volunteering in the children's ward at the hospital.

"Listen, Bronka, if you want to get married, then find a husband. If you want a career, pursue the career. You want to be a journalist, try it. In the meantime, it's good that you listened to Papa and minored in education. You can always fall back on teaching. It's a good career for a mother—summers off, out at three o'clock, lots of holidays."

"Mama, I don't want to be a teacher."

Bronka thought about the end of JoJo's acting dreams, and the beginning of her path to being a teacher. It would just take her longer now that she had to go at night.

Bronka also thought about the cuteness of little Ian. She wanted to get married and have three children; she wanted to be a journalist. Despite her sister's problems, she was still envious, and at that moment she could not envision anyone marrying her.

"Mama, sorry, I'm going to apply to Columbia Journalism School for a master's degree and then I'll be able to get a good job."

"Good, I'm glad you stopped crying," said Judy with a relieved sigh. "Anyone who wants to get married, can get married. That much I know. I'm positive you will find the right person. And your husband will be a very lucky man—whether you are a journalist or not."

"I'm going to become a journalist; I've made up my mind."

"Do whatever you want, dear. I just want you to be happy."

"I'm doing it," Bronka said.

CHAPTER TWENTY-ONE

BRONKA GOT OFF THE UPTOWN subway at 116th Street and found that it was only a short walk until she reached the large, imposing gates of the Columbia University campus. She walked along the path, admiring the snow-covered grass and shrubbery framing the august brick buildings that surrounded the commons. At the Journalism School, she took the elevator up to the administrative offices to see the dean.

A tall, slender, man with brown hair and black horn-rimmed glasses in his 50s came out to greet her. He smiled and extended his hand to her.

"Nice to meet you, Miss Lubinski. Let's go into my office and we'll chat."

"So, Miss Lubinski, you want to be a journalist?" he asked after they sat down.

"Yes, very much, Dean Atkins."

"Well, I have to say you would make a very attractive journalist. Do you have any clips?"

While always pleased with a compliment, Bronka wondered what her physical appearance had to do with her skills as a journalist.

She took out the red faux-leather scrapbook where she had lovingly scotch-taped all her articles—beginning with her piece on President Kennedy's assassination in the high school newspaper and the one on the space program that landed in the *Long Island Press*. The dean looked through pages of her work, including all her contributions to the Queens College newspaper and literary magazine.

"Well, you certainly are a prolific writer. But do you think you have what it takes to be a journalist? Do you think you're assertive enough—actually aggressive enough—to do what it takes to chase down a story?"

"Yes, I do," Bronka answered, mustering every bit of confidence she had. "I've done it numerous times on my assignments for the school newspaper. And I'm also very competitive; I want to be the first one with the breaking news."

She knew—deep in her heart—that she absolutely would be able to get over her shyness when pursuing a lead. Even in school, when she was on an assignment for the paper, it enabled her to do and ask things she couldn't do in real life. Sitting in the dean's office at the Journalism School made her forget Ned and all her troubles. When she was running after a story and writing it, nothing else mattered.

"Well, you are a very impressive young woman, Miss Lubinski. And your credentials are top notch—stellar grades and a track record of performance in the field. And I did mention earlier that you're easy on the eyes. I do have to tell you, though, we only admit one hundred graduate students a year—that's from the whole country—actually the entire world; you know, we have foreign students too. Out of the one hundred, we have a quota for women—it's about 20 percent. So, we will only be admitting 20 women this year. So, here's my last question, I ask every woman this question—and I must ask it of you too.

"Do you plan on getting married and having a family? You see, because our enrollment is so limited, we want the women we admit to stay in the field. It's been our experience that women don't have the same staying power as men in the profession once they have a family. It's a fact."

"But things are changing," Bronka retorted.

"Maybe so, dear, but change is always slow. And right now, that's what the statistics tell us. We make a serious investment in all of our students and we want to see the results. So, please answer the question. "Do you plan on getting married and having a family?"

Bronka's face turned red and she scowled. *This is patently unfair,* she thought to herself.

"I certainly have no immediate plans to get married or have a child."

"So, you don't have a boyfriend? No steady fellow? Surprising for a girl as pretty as you."

"No, I don't. And what I want—more than anything—is to come to the Journalism School and learn from the best. I want to make my mark as a journalist and bring honor to this institution."

"Good answer," said the dean as he winked at her.

Afterwards, she thought she should have smiled more during the interview, but her mouth naturally turned down, making her look at best contemplative, at worst sad. But that wasn't the real reason for the sinking feeling she had. She knew that there was a different standard for men and women.

"I got rejected from Columbia Journalism School." Bronka called JoJo as soon as the letter in the thin envelope arrived.

"At the interview, the dean went out of his way to compliment me on my outstanding credentials."

"But you told me after you went for the interview that they only admitted twenty women. Why are you taking it so personally?"

"I just am."

"Oh right, you take everything personally," JoJo responded. "This is really not personal, Bronka. Either go somewhere else or try to get a job for a newspaper and prove yourself that way."

"I don't want to get a master's from any other place right now. I think I'll just try to get a job for a newspaper."

"Like Lois Lane—the token woman on *The Daily Planet*?" JoJo joked.

"Well, I was thinking more like Nancy Dickerson or Barbara Walters. I heard that some of the papers are hiring women to do features, so if that's how I have to get in the door, that's what I'll do."

"I'm sure you can do whatever you set your mind to. And you're totally free to follow your dreams."

PART TWO

1973–1977

CHAPTER TWENTY-TWO

IN 1973, BRONKA, WHO WOULD turn 26 that year, was still living at home with her parents. Her parents—mostly her father—made it very difficult every time the subject of her moving out was broached. He constantly reminded her that he was living in a bunker in the forest at her age! Why did she need to spend her hard-earned salary on rent when she had room and board for free? He also pointed out that he gave her extra cash for helping out in the bakery, which was only a few blocks away from their home.

When both Bronka and Aron had said their piece, they would often separate to calm down. One day, Aron came into her room and said, "If you're not married by the time you're thirty, you can move out and I will help you move. Here's some money so you can start saving now."

But her father's concerns notwithstanding, the most salient reason for not moving to Manhattan was her job at *The Jewish Dispatch* in Queens.

It was the first job that came along and Bronka grabbed it, relieved that someone wanted to hire her. She immediately accepted the salary offered, although she later found out that the male reporters were paid more. The *Dispatch* catered to the many Jews who lived not only in Queens but to the Conservative, Orthodox, Reform, Reconstructionist and unaffiliated Jews who resided in 100,000 homes in the metropolitan area and beyond. The award-winning publication covered breaking news, not only in New York, but also throughout the United States and even had an Israeli correspondent. It was the paper of record for rabbis as they composed their weekly sermons. Heads of major Jewish organizations barraged the office staff with press releases to get their organizations featured in the publication. Leaders in the Jewish community vied for coverage, making themselves household names.

The offices of the newspaper were in a storefront right on Union Turnpike near Utopia Parkway, and the commute from Bellerose could not have been easier. Bronka just needed to hop on the bus to get there. The space on the main floor housed a grandmotherly receptionist named Lillian, as well as desks for Bronka and the three male staff writers. Twenty-seven-year-old Steve Arlin, who Max, the publisher, had brought with him from *The Journal-American*, moved fast, talked fast, and somehow could sense when a story was about to break. With his black horn-rimmed glasses and short hair, he almost resembled Clark Kent. He was a newlywed who was constantly trying to fix up Bronka with his friends.

Manny Gottlieb, a middle-aged balding guy, who lived on Long Island with his wife and two kids, had been with *The Daily Mirror* before it folded. And then there was the pensive and cerebral Jeremiah Krinsky, who wrote thoughtful opinion pieces, book reviews, and probing interviews with Jewish intellectuals and newsmakers. Bronka judged him to be about thirty. He had longish brown hair, and a trimmed beard and mustache, giving him the air of a professor. He said he was modern Orthodox, wore a knitted *kipah* and was first out the door on Friday afternoons in the winter so as to get home to his pregnant wife before Shabbos.

The other staff member was Brian Smith, the blond, bespectacled, green-eyed, and eager staff photographer. Bronka knew him from college and from Brodsky's deli, where he worked part time; he was about two years younger than she was.

Upstairs was Max Wernick's office space and conference room. Max, the tough short and stout cigar-smoking editor/publisher, had explained Bronka's responsibilities to her on her first day of work, as well as his credentials. He had been in Europe during World War II as a war correspondent and later as a reporter and news editor at *The New York Journal-American*. When the paper folded in 1966, Wernick brought his experience, expertise, and nose for news to *The Jewish Dispatch*.

"So I'm carving out a specific beat for you, Bronka," Max said after giving her the office tour. "We need to cater more to our female readers. I want you to discover and cover the stories that women like. I need you to profile the leaders in the big women's groups like Hadassah and Women's American ORT, also the women's division of UJA. Also, I have a stack of cookbooks here in the office; anyone comes out with a cookbook, they send them. They're my welcome gift to you. I'd like you to do a weekly cooking column featuring these and any other food ideas you might have. And then, of course, you will go out into the field.

"If you have any other ideas, I'm open to them, so please let me know. That should keep you pretty busy to start. Oh, and we'll need a name for your cooking column. I'm thinking about *The Kosher Gourmet*. Of course, if you have a better suggestion, please let me know. So, welcome aboard, Bronka, I think you're going to love it here."

Bronka didn't have a better idea for the name of the column. She did, however, have some other ideas for the best use of her talents. The truth is that she was not a cook. When Faye lived with the family, she did all the cooking, and she had taught Judy well. Although Bronka often hung out in the kitchen with her mother, she could not remember executing a single dish or a meal by herself.

Bronka thought of her father, the survivor, the aspiring doctor who had to settle on becoming a baker. She thought of all those survivors who had avoided being murdered by claiming to have skills they didn't have. This was just a momentary blip. She would be the best Kosher Gourmet and women's reporter *The Dispatch* ever had. But she was also determined to move on to real news—one way or the other. Maybe if she could become a crusading reporter—exposing suffering and injustice—she could save the world in that way. But first, she would have to write about food.

During the first year of Bronka's employment at *The Dispatch*, she bonded with the other members of the staff. Lillian took her under her wing and became her confidante. The men enjoyed having an attractive young woman around and teased her, always noting that Bronka didn't have a sense of humor. But the set-up was easy and comfortable. So, Bronka, Lillian, and the guys became a platonic work family, going out for lunch, dinner, and drinks and discussing what reporters and friends talk about.

After four years at *The Dispatch*, she loved the camaraderie, but wanted to expand her professional repertoire—branching out into hard news and thoughtful opinion pieces. But that was easier said than done, since she had become something of a phenomenon. She was shocked to learn that her *Kosher Gourmet* column was a huge hit, read by housewives religiously each week. She received more mail than any of the other staff members, asking her food-related questions and offering their own recipes. While she was happy with her colleagues and flattered with the attention she received, she still wanted more.

Bronka still had dreams of moving out, and—selfishly—she often thought about how different it might have been had her sister not rushed into marriage with Bruce. Perhaps the two sisters would have shared an apartment in Manhattan or gone to graduate school out of town. Maybe they would have toured Europe. While she knew they had always been different people, her sister completed her in a way that she liked. Now older and still in the same place she had been four long years before, Bronka again felt alone.

JoJo, however, appeared to be well taken care of. Ensconced in Syosset in a late-1950s split-level with three bedrooms, a family room, and a finished basement, she now had two children—Ian and six-month-old Tracy. She got her degree from Queens College two months before her daughter was born and was now thinking about starting a master's degree program at Hofstra University. Bruce had gotten his CPA, but abandoned the idea of law school and was now in the cosmetics business with his father, drawing a very comfortable salary with plans to take over when his father was ready to retire.

JoJo shopped and also had lunch with friends, especially Charlene Grossman, her neighbor who lived across the street. Better known as Charlie, she was married to an orthodontist and had a son, Todd, about Ian's age and a one-year-old daughter named Bethany. Charlie was an expert on everything—from where to go clothes shopping, to where to have your hair done, to what restaurants to go to, to the best nursery schools. She taught JoJo how to play mahjongg and invited her to join her weekly game. The two women and their kids—both with absent husbands—spent a great deal of time in each other's home. Bronka was jealous.

Though it was rarely mentioned, Bronka felt the pressure mounting on her. Soon she would be twenty-six and then twenty-seven, and before she turned around she would be thirty. But she still thought about Ned and compared every young man she dated to him. None was smart enough, deep enough, or clever enough to measure up. In his five-year absence, Bronka had idealized him, and his sudden disappearance and the fact that he never tried to contact her again haunted her.

Additionally, Bronka feared that while she had once been viewed as the compliant, caring—even favorite twin—now she had been replaced as her parents' pet by her sister and her two adorable children. Aron and Judy doted on their grandchildren, so relaxed and effusive and different than they had been with JoJo and Bronka.

JoJo had already fulfilled her mission as far as their father was concerned. Bronka was still floundering.

CHAPTER TWENTY-THREE

ON SUNDAY MORNING, JULY 22, sleeping soundly in her bedroom in Bellerose, Bronka was awakened by a seven o'clock phone call. She reached for the pink princess phone and was surprised to hear Max Wernick's voice.

"Good morning, Bronka," he said cheerfully. "Hope I didn't wake you, but I have a story that you might want to cover if you're free today."

Bronka groaned to herself. Not only did Max wake her up at the crack of dawn on a Sunday morning, but now he was probably going to ask her to cover some kosher food festival. She had grown tired of being *The Kosher Gourmet.*

"So are you free?"

"Tell me why," she said skeptically.

"I'm gonna be honest with you, hon. This isn't your beat, but it's the middle of the summer and it's a Sunday morning. Steve is trying to track down some Jewish connection to Watergate, which is easier said than done. Manny's on vacation at the Jersey shore, and Jeremiah is not answering the phone. The event is scheduled for 10:30 and who knows if he gets up before noon on Sunday. Look, it may turn out to be a nothing burger, but I know you've been wanting to do some straight news.

"Here's your chance and here's the story."

Max went on to tell her about a community out on Long Island—in Suffolk County—called Yaphank. In the '30s, there was a housing development there created strictly for German-Americans. In fact, you still needed German blood to live there. Before the war, they had a youth camp inculcating kids with Nazi propaganda. The streets in the development all were given Nazi names, like Hitler Street, Bund Boulevard, Eichmann Avenue, and Himmler Drive. Those names were gone now, but they were having a ceremony to rename the last street.

"It's probably about an hour or so drive from where you are," Max said. "I'm sending Brian to take some photos, so he'll pick you up about nine-thirty if you're game."

Bronka was both excited and revolted at the same time, like the feeling she had when she was the last to be chosen on a sports team in elementary school gym. Still, this was her big opportunity. It was beyond intriguing—a German enclave on Long Island with Nazi street names. *Holy crap!*

Brian Smith picked her up at 9:45 in his brown Plymouth Fury. The only non-Jew on the staff, Brian was handsome and very pleasant and friendly. In the two years he had been with *The Dispatch*, the staff joked that he had become an honorary Jew, throwing around Yiddish expressions like *schmooze*, reminding the others about forthcoming Jewish holidays, and demonstrating a knowledge of Jewish food from working at Brodsky's Kosher Delicatessen as a student.

As they headed east on the Long Island Expressway, Brian said, "I can't believe there was a Bundist Youth Camp so close to us."

"Well, you know my parents were Hitler refugees," said Bronka. She had not told them where she was going, and simply said she was covering a story. "My father still gets upset every time he remembers what he went through and whenever it comes up. You know, he lost his entire family—all murdered by the Nazis."

"Yes, it's mind boggling," said Brian. "My mom is 100 percent Irish and she was born here, but my dad is German. He came here after the war because he couldn't tolerate living in a country that had treated people in such a vile and evil way."

"But what did he do during the war?"

"Oh, he was a soldier in the German Army," Brian explained. "He had no choice but to serve. He didn't even know concentration camps existed at the time or that they were starving, torturing, and murdering Jews. He was suffering himself on the Eastern Front, fighting the Russians. He only found out after the war. Then he left Germany as fast as he could."

"Wow," she said.

Brian Smith was sweet and earnest, Bronka thought, and she had no doubt he believed his father. But it occurred to her that she was yet to ever hear of a single German who admitted knowing about what was going on during the war. For that matter, some of their American neighbors—even Jewish ones—claimed that they had no idea of the scope or magnitude of the evil at the time. *And perhaps they didn't know,* thought Bronka to herself. *Or maybe, they didn't want to know.*

CHAPTER TWENTY-FOUR

ON A SUNDAY MORNING, BRIAN and Bronka pretty much had the Long Island Expressway to themselves. The only glitch in the trip was that Brian kept complaining that he was afraid that he was losing air in one of the tires. So, he stopped twice at gas stations to fill the tire with air.

When they reached Yaphank, a sleepy little hamlet with a rural suburban feel, they headed to Fatherland Gardens, the small housing development, which was hosting the name-changing ceremony.

As they entered the community, Bronka was shocked to see swastikas hanging in many of the windows. The tidy little community was filled with winding paths, and modest-size homes on large plots of land. The steps in front of each house were adorned with flowering plants and there were wind chimes hanging from the front doors.

According to Max, Goebbels Drive was the last street name to be officially changed in the housing development. Hitler Street had been the first to be renamed when the U.S. entered the Second World War. Max had also told her he had it on good authority that you still had to prove German ancestry to buy a home in the community.

Bronka and Brian were among the last to arrive due to the tire problem. From a distance, off to her right, Bronka was appalled to see a small band of about a dozen men, standing around and chatting. They were all wearing red armbands with a black swastika on a round background of white, as well as brown shirts, boots and helmets. She heard one of them yell "*Achtung*" and they came to attention.

Brian parked the car in a small lot and said to Bronka, "Just stay put for a minute, I'm going to see if I can change the tire. I don't want to get stuck on the Long Island Expressway on the way back."

"But we're already late. We don't want to miss anything. Don't you want me to help you?" She asked.

"Why, do you know anything about changing tires?"

"No, not a thing."

"That's what I thought. Just stand by the side of the car, please. My camera equipment is valuable and I don't want any of these thugs getting their hands on it.

While Brian was bending down at the back of the car changing the tire, his glasses slipped off his face and the lenses shattered. "Damn it," he said.

Meanwhile, Bronka began to squirm as she saw one of the men in Nazi regalia break from the group and come a bit closer as if to check out Brian's car.

While his attire was anathema to her, there was something vaguely familiar about him, but she could not place it. *That's ridiculous, I don't know any Nazi-sympathizers,* she told herself.

After Brian repaired the tire and closed the trunk, he opened the back door to get his camera equipment, but Bronka could see that he was totally flustered. "My glasses broke," he said. "And I don't have another pair with me. Can you drive home?"

"Sure," she said. Bronka had been trying to conquer her fear of highways anyway, and she realized she had no choice, but to comply with his request. She was aware that Brian was uncharacteristically rattled, and she knew he couldn't see well enough to drive without his glasses.

Since she could see that Brian was so agitated, Bronka hesitated for a minute or two, before saying, "One of the Nazi thugs was snooping around your car; it looked to me like he was checking out your license plate. And I know it sounds ridiculous, but he looked familiar to me."

"How could that be?" Brian asked. "Impossible. But let's go take a look and see what's going on. This is a disaster. What kind of photographer am I if can't see clearly?"

"Damn, he disappeared," she responded, her face flushed with the feeling of foolishness. "I'm telling you he was checking out your car and then he ran away. I wonder where he went."

In the fifteen minutes that Brian had taken to change the tire, a large group of demonstrators in favor of the name change had parked their cars and buses and assembled in front of the microphones. As per Bronka's instructions, he began shooting right away so as to capture the broad representation of those assembled—from the Anti-Defamation League, the NAACP, the Jewish Defense League, the Long Island Board of Rabbis, The Diocese of Long Island, to a multitude of synagogue, church groups, and elected officials. The supporters of the name change carried signs that read: *Smash the Nazis, Never Again, Remember the Six Million,* and *No More Nazi Streets.* This enthusiastic group far outnumbered the neo-Nazis. Bronka estimated that there were close to two hundred of them. The Long Island dailies, *Newsday* and *The Long Island Press* were there, and so were *The Daily News* and *The New York Times.*

Bronka headed over to the podium and microphones to survey the set-up as she was satisfied that Brian was shooting furiously—even without his glasses. From the way Max had indicated that covering this event was the booby prize, she was shocked at the turnout of both the public and the press. The wheels started to turn in her head: *This is my big chance; I can't just cover it the same as everyone else. Well, of course, there's the Jewish angle. But maybe I can think of something else too.*

As she watched Brian capture the unfolding events on film, Bronka saw New York City television stations videotaping the event. The twelve neo-Nazis goose stepped in a circle behind the podium, screaming "Heil Hitler," "Jews will not replace us," and "Fatherland forever." Bronka was a bit concerned that without his glasses, it was all a blur to Brian, but she convinced herself that all they needed were a few good pictures to accompany her story.

As Brian snapped away, Father Stan, his former teacher and youth group leader at Bishop Malone High School in Fresh Meadows, approached him.

"Hey Father Stan," Brian smiled at the priest, who was accompanied by Rabbi Arthur Bernstein from the Long Island Board of Rabbis and Reverend Basil Freeman, a civil rights activist. The two other clergy were dressed in sports jackets and ties, but Father Stan was wearing his clerical garb—all in black with his white collar.

"Move in a little closer, please," Brian called to the three clergymen. He began snapping as Father Stan, who was in the middle put his arms around the other two.

Bronka stepped forward from behind the podium just as Brian finished taking the pictures,

"They wouldn't stop their goose stepping to talk to me," she said in disgust.

"Hey Bronka," Brian said. "Look who I found here, my favorite high school teacher, Father Stan. He was a superstar social studies teacher at the school and also coached the debate team."

"Yes, Brian was one of my best debaters," the priest said.

"And if that weren't enough, he also made himself available to counsel kids who needed it," Brian said.

"I'm flattered that you remember that, Brian," Father Stan said.

"Of course, Brian was probably one of our most well-adjusted students—a much loved son in a model Catholic family. And I remember, Brian, how your mother had insisted on a religious education through high school for both you and your sister."

The priest put out his hand and shook hers and then formally introduced her and Brian to the Rev. Freeman and Rabbi Bernstein.

Bronka began to get some quotes from the clergy and then decided she'd speak to the representatives of some of the other groups and the elected officials. She was starting to resign herself to the fact that there would be no scoop here. *But at least it's a real news story, not a cooking column.* Perhaps her life could still change.

"So, what newspaper are you two working for?" Father Stan asked.

"*The Jewish Dispatch*," said Bronka.

"These thugs are chanting, 'Jews will not replace us,' but they fail to remember that Christianity came from Judaism," the priest pointed out. "Jesus was a Jew. We are all one family."

Bronka began scribbling furiously in her reporter's notebook as Brian snapped photos of her interviewing Father Stan.

"Brian, I'm not supposed to be in the story; I'm the reporter. And besides, did you get pix of the neo-Nazis? Even though they're refusing to talk to the Jewish reporters, their horrific comments and signs need to be chronicled. I think you should go back there and snap a few photos. All the other news outlets have been shooting pictures of them like crazy. You're a pro even without your glasses."

"OK," Brian said, walking away.

Bronka stood with Father Stan.

"Is that your full name?" she asked him.

"No," he said with a smile that made his eyes crinkle and his nose look even more prominent. He was tanned from the sun and she noticed he had a rugged look to him.

"Actually, now I'm Monsignor Stanislaw Kowalcyzk; I recently started working for the Diocese of Long Island. I get to concentrate on important issues like this, but, of course, I miss the kids. Brian's such a wonderful young man."

"So as a Catholic clerical leader, why are you here today?"

"How is it even possible that in 1973," he answered, "there is a street named after Goebbels, Hitler's diabolical henchman? This ceremony should have been a simple, no-brainer event, with little fanfare. The fact that it is now going to garner all this media attention is insane. You're going to see it on the news tonight. But what will be newsworthy are not the two hundred people in support of the change, or the officials who belatedly demanded it, or the people of good will of different creeds and races and backgrounds who are here to take a stand, but the dozen middle aged losers trapped in the past who should know better. Who are they? Where did they come from? Why are they spewing hate? And, tomorrow, you will read all about *them* and their sick beliefs in *The New York Times* and *The Daily News* and *Newsday* and every local outlet that's here. The story will be about them. That's sad."

"I don't agree with you," said Bronka. "Both sides will be covered."

"Perhaps," he said. "But the emphasis will be on the bad guys. We shouldn't be giving Neo-Nazis print space or air time."

"But there's freedom of the press in this country," Bronka responded. "We have to cover all aspects of the story. You think I like seeing these Nazis?"

"Maybe when people wake up to the fact that there are still Nazis in America and a community like this," she continued as she raised her voice and talked with her hands, "it will spur them to take action. Perhaps reading about this will make them think twice when they generalize about a race or a religion or a nationality. Maybe they will open their mouths or take action the next time they see evil in the world. Maybe they will join a civil rights demonstration, or help the homeless or the sick."

Bronka went on to explain more about her reasons for being so passionate, including her father's history. She suddenly felt herself talking for too long.

"Oops, I'm sorry, I shouldn't have said any of that," said Bronka. "And certainly not so vociferously." It occurred to her that she had messed up her first time out on a real news story. She imagined the Diocese of Long Island complaining to Max about how unprofessional she was, raising her voice and giving her own opinion. She hoped the priest didn't think she was yelling at him.

"I'm the reporter," she said. "I'm supposed to be interviewing you and I have to speak to a bunch of other people as well, so I must apologize I have to get moving."

The priest gave a kindly smile, and Bronka was shocked, but flattered when he touched her cheek. She noticed that his dark brown eyes gleamed with the spark of intelligence and religious fervor. She began to understand why Brian was so fond of him.

"Of course, Bronka," he said. "I didn't mean to monopolize you that way when you have work to do. I just so enjoyed hearing how your mind works.

"This is all my fault; please forgive me. You know, I was born in Poland. I emigrated to America with my parents when I was a little boy."

Bronka turned pale and stood silent, dumbfounded. Both she and the priest were born to Polish parents. She had only the bare facts about her family; there was much she didn't know about both sides. Did she really want to pursue this—with this priest?

"Bronka, did I offend you so much that you won't even respond? Perhaps we can continue this conversation over a cup of coffee some time. And we didn't even get a chance to talk about what my favorite rabbi and thinker, Abraham Joshua Heschel, would have said about this event today?"

"Monsignor," she said with incredulity. "You're familiar with Rabbi Heschel?"

"Of course, so sorry that I never got to meet him personally before he died last year. I've read all of his books and he was such an inspiration—a clergyman who had the courage to put his faith into action by speaking out and marching for civil rights and against the War in Vietnam. He was born in Poland too."

"That's a coincidence," said Bronka. "He's my hero too. I just finished *Man Is Not Alone.*"

"Splendid," said the priest. "Now you must read *God In Search of Man.*"

Bronka was speechless. Her perfect man, she thought ironically—tall, dark, and almost handsome. And so intense and intellectual and interested in every word she had to say. And he had touched her cheek in what seemed like an act of affection. It was her luck that he was a Catholic priest. And, what a bizarre coincidence, he was from Poland, the scene of her family's secrets.

CHAPTER TWENTY-FIVE

THE NEXT MORNING, BRONKA ALLOWED herself the luxury of getting to work a few minutes late. She was usually a punctual person, but this Monday morning her daydreaming had slowed her down. *The Jewish Dispatch* was a weekly, so what would be the Jewish angle after all the dailies had reported on the event? If the priest was correct, and the focus was on the dozen Nazi losers, how could she write something different? Mostly, though, she could not stop thinking about Father Stan, even when she thought of what Mindy had said about how she had a pattern of being attracted to men who were unavailable.

As Bronka headed to her desk, she was surprised to see Max sitting in her chair with a smile on his face. The daily newspapers were on her desk, along with Max's buttered bagel and cup of coffee.

"Good morning, our own Lois Lane," he quipped. "Looks like your first hard news assignment is getting a lot of buzz."

On the covers of the tabloids were large photos of the neo-Nazis decked out in their odious regalia with hateful expressions on their faces. The accompanying headlines ranged from *Nazis in our Midst* and *Beware the Return of the Reich* to *A Sleepy LI Town With A Dark Nazi Past.* An editorial read: *Is a Name Change Enough to Stop the Hate?*

"Brian is in the darkroom developing the photos," said Max. "Hopefully, he'll have something a bit different. And I hope you can come up with a unique angle. Clearly, we have to mention the Nazi thugs, but I don't want the whole story to be about them."

"I hear you, Max, and I totally agree."

Brian emerged from the darkroom with photos in hand.

"Let's see what you've got, Brian."

Other than a couple of shots of a few of the Nazis, Brian had concentrated on the officials at the ceremony and the large group of supporters of the name change. Of course, he had many with Father Stan and the other clergy.

"Who's the guy in the collar," Max asked gruffly.

"Oh, that's Monsignor Stanislaw Kowalcyzk, from the Diocese of Long Island. I know him, he was my teacher at Bishop Malone High School and now he has a big job working with Archbishop McDonnell."

"Great," said Max. "And I see Rabbi Bernstein. And Reverend Freeman. That's what we'll use for your piece, Bronka: 'An Ecumenical Approach to Anti-Semitism.' I love it! Did you speak with them at the event?"

"Briefly," said Bronka. "I also spoke with heads of some of the other organizations and elected representatives.

"OK, great that's the story. But you need to flesh it out with the three of them—how they are working together against this scourge. So get in touch and interview each of them in depth. Maybe if they're interesting enough, we'll include profiles of each as sidebars. So Brian, you'll go with Bronka when she does the interviews."

So that settles it, thought Bronka. The decision of whether to contact the priest had been made for her.

CHAPTER TWENTY- SIX

BRIAN STOOD OVER BRONKA'S SHOULDER as they surveyed the coverage in the dailies. *Newsday,* the Long Island paper, gave the event a two-page spread, with several photos, including some historical ones of the former Nazi youth camp. There were long shots of the large group of sign-holding supporters of the name change in comparison to the paltry group of the dozen neo-Nazis. There was also a picture of the president of Fatherland Gardens, along with the backstory of the community.

"Leave it to *The Daily News,*" quipped Bronka, as she showed Brian the cover photo that accompanied the screaming headline, 'Nazis In Our Midst.'

"That's the guy who looked familiar to me, but you didn't see him. That's the guy."

She pointed to a stocky man with short blond hair and light brown eyes, who appeared to be about sixty. He wore a helmet, an armband with the swastika and a brown shirt. He had the look of a madman with his eyes angry and blazing, his arm extended in the Nazi salute and his mouth wide open, doubtless yelling "Heil Hitler," Bronka was convinced.

All of the color drained from Brian's face as he opened his mouth wide, but could not say a word.

"What's the matter, Brian?"

He did not speak.

"I'll be back in a minute," he said.

In the bathroom, Brian held onto the pedestal sink as if to prevent himself from falling and looked into the mirror. He observed that he resembled his mother more than his father—more Irish than German. But half of his genes belonged to his father, that ranting, raving lunatic in Nazi regalia on the cover of *The Daily News*. How had he missed him there? Was he really so nearsighted that he needed prescription lenses to recognize his father? But why would he even recognize his father in a group of Nazis? Now, he put two and two together. Of course, Bronka recognized him from Brodsky's delicatessen. But still, there must be some mistake. He wondered if his father had been lying. What had he really done in the war?

His mother would never have married a Nazi, he reasoned. She was a mass-going, charity giving, devout Catholic who had chosen nursing so she could help people of all races and religions. He had never heard a prejudiced word slip from her tongue. She worked with many Jews at the Jewish Hospital. Why, her friend and colleague, Grace Weingarten, was Jewish. Many of the doctors she worked with and respected were Jewish. Their family physician was Dr. Goldstein, and he didn't even mind when they called him at home. His mother was no antisemite.

And his father, for crying out loud, worked in a kosher deli. Why would a Nazi take a job working with Jews, serving Jews, and smelling corned beef and pastrami and pickles all day long? Impossible, there was some mistake here, unless he was some kind of undercover agent. That would be the only way, Brian thought as he tried to convince himself.

Brian was in the bathroom so long, Bronka asked Manny to knock on the door.

When Brian walked out, he had a sheepish look on his face. "Must've been something I ate."

He saw that Bronka was still studying the photo, so Brian asked her if she'd go with him to get some fresh air.

Outside, Brian led them two doors down to the candy store. Behind the magazines and mints there was a soda fountain with a counter and four high seats. A policeman sat at the counter eating bacon and eggs, a cup of coffee by his right hand.

At the rear of the store, there were two small booths. Brian guided Bronka by the elbow to the last one.

"What's up with you?" Bronka asked. "Is something wrong?"

"I don't know," he answered, putting his head in his hands.

"You can tell me, Brian."

Brian looked up into Bronka's eyes. "This is a thousand percent off the record."

He inhaled deeply and said again.

"Brian, you can trust me. I'm a repository of secrets. You have no idea how many secrets I have floating around in my brain."

"Would you keep a secret that could win you a Pulitzer Prize?"

"Hmm," she said smiling, pretending to think.

"This is no joke, Bronka. I'm deadly serious."

"Of course, Brian, I will give up my Pulitzer Prize for you. What the hell is going on?"

Brian took a gulp of his coke and leaned in closer.

"You've recognized the man on the cover of *The Daily News* because you have seen him before. If it's not his long-lost twin, I know him too—intimately, as a matter of fact."

"Who do you think he is?"

"You know the counterman from the deli?"

"Your father?!" Bronka said loudly as she screwed up her face.

"Shhh," Brian put his finger to his mouth. "Whisper!"

"I wish I had brought the paper with me. I'm going to buy another one right now and we can look at it," she said.

"Please don't," Brian said. "It makes me nauseous to look at it. You can study it when we get back to the office."

"So, what are you thinking, Brian?"

Brian thought Bronka was weighing her words, attempting to avoid the word, *Nazi*.

He frowned and tears began to form in his eyes.

"The only plausible rationale I can think of—besides his having a doppelganger—is that he's a secret agent, hired by the government to infiltrate the group," he said. "With his German accent and heritage, I can see why they'd want to tap him. Other than that, I'm stymied."

He shrugged his shoulders.

"Let's go back to the office and call Father Stan and see how quickly he can see us," Bronka suggested. "In the meantime, I'll try to set up phone interviews with the other two clergymen. You can take their pictures before Wednesday deadline. But I need to get started on this right away. It's my first real news story."

"And you're not going to mention the man on the cover of *The Daily News*?"

"Why would I? There'd be no reason to. He will not be in the story."

"And you will never write about him, ever?"

"I will never write about him, I promise. But keep in mind that I want you to remember that I'm forfeiting my Pulitzer Prize for you, my friend," she said, half-smiling.

CHAPTER TWENTY-SEVEN

BRONKA COULDN'T DECIDE IF SHE was lucky or unlucky. It was all falling into place so easily: in just a day, she was on her first real hard news story and Max was finally treating her like a real reporter.

She also had the new burden of Brian's secret.

She wasn't entirely comfortable with the prospect of Brian telling Father Stan with her in the room, but clearly he wanted and needed her to be there. Father Stan said he was looking forward to seeing them both at two o'clock that day.

That left her the entire morning to put in calls to Reverend Freeman and Rabbi Bernstein and interview them on the phone since she didn't have time to meet them in person. Despite everything, maybe if Max liked her piece he would give her more hard news.

"Have you ever been in a church?" Brian asked from the driver's seat of his brown Plymouth Fury. He was wearing his backup pair of glasses that he had at home. They were on the road to Nassau County and Father Stan.

"Of course," said Bronka. "Why, I attended a friend's wedding at Our Lady of Perpetual Help in Bellerose a couple of years ago."

She decided not to share with him that her mother had been born Catholic and that her mother's sister, the aunt she had never met, was a nun. This made her feel vaguely guilty, especially since he had shared his secret with her. But she was not ready to bare her soul to him. Yet.

The priest was waiting for them inside the cathedral, which was quite grand, with oak ceilings and wainscoting and a carved oak Bishop's Chair with a coat of arms. The elaborate stained-glass windows, and the marble pulpit, altar and floors Bronka found almost breathtaking. Brian shot a few photos of Father Stan standing in front of the pulpit and sitting in the pews. Once they were finished with the photo session, the priest asked if they wanted to sit in the pews while they spoke.

"We have the sanctuary all to ourselves" he said.

"Really, Fath . . . I mean Monsignor," Brian corrected himself. "The sanctuary has a calming effect on me."

"Yes it does, and it's OK, Brian, I actually prefer 'Father Stan.' But first before we get to your matter, let's do the interview with Bronka."

Sitting in the front row of pews, Bronka interviewed the priest for about a half hour. She was taken not only by his intelligence, but also by his charisma. Brian continued to snap photos, and then sat down in the pew behind them, leaning close to hear every one of Father Stan's words. The priest was clearly someone special. To put it simply, the way he responded, his thoughtful answers, and the way he looked at her made her feel listened to. Heard.

"Ok, I think that's good for now," she said.

As soon as she turned, Brian was already whipping out *The Daily News* from his camera bag. He held up the front page for the priest to see. "Do you recognize this guy?"

Father Stan creased his brow, looked closely, then took a big gulp of air.

"Your father?"

"Right on," said Brian sarcastically, but his teary eyes betrayed him.

Brian explained to him what his father had told him about being in the war, but how none of what he told him now made sense. How he couldn't get his head around it. How could his father be the leader—not even just a member—of this faction of the Nazi party?

"Hmm." The priest narrowed his eyes as he weighed the situation. "It seems to me that there are a few things going on here that are making you upset. First, why was he at the rally if he's not a Neo-Nazi?"

"I was thinking he could be a government infiltrator."

"Could be, I suppose that's a possibility."

"He could have a twin we don't know about."

"Also possible, but unlikely," said the priest.

"He lied to us and he's a Nazi," Brian said bitterly.

"Look, Brian, the first thing I advise you to do is speak with your mother. She may have a simple explanation for this. But I think you have to tell her. It's possible she's already seen the paper. You have to tell her you saw it too."

"OK, but what did he do during the war? My mind is going crazy. I am his flesh and blood. I have his genes. What if he's a monster?"

"My son, whatever your father did or did not do, does not make you responsible. I know that you have been diligent in confessing your own sins. Your father's sins are his, not yours."

He reached out his hands to Brian, who grasped them tightly. Bronka watched as they both prayed, heads down. The priest intoned: "Oh God of our Salvation, we thank you for making us new creations in Christ. We choose to walk in our newfound freedom in Christ. We refuse to be chained to generational curses from our parents' house.

We stand firm in our new identity and declare that we are of a different bloodline, and that is the bloodline of Jesus Christ, our Lord and Savior . . ."

By the time they finished it was almost five o'clock, but it was still an exceptionally hot and muggy day.

Brian drove Bronka home, turning on the radio, Bronka suspected, so they didn't have to speak any further in the car. She could see he was exhausted and believed that although he had much to say, he could not talk about it anymore.

CHAPTER TWENTY-EIGHT

WHEN BRIAN DROPPED BRONKA OFF in front of her brick bungalow, she almost tripped, so focused was she on Father Stan and Brian who were still on her mind (for very different reasons). But her focus was soon redirected as she suddenly became aware of a car honking. She looked up and saw Irv Rosen's blue Buick with the New York Press plates. He pulled up in front of her house and got out of the car.

"Hello Irv," Bronka said.

Graying and heavy, Irv had gotten older since he used to drive her and his daughter Christina and her sisters to school. But he still seemed just as friendly.

"You know, I thought I saw you yesterday at Fatherland Gardens, but there were so many people there and so much going on, I didn't get a chance to say hi. Also, Christina told me that you were doing cooking and lifestyle features for *The Dispatch*, so I wasn't expecting to see you at such a hot event."

"It was a hot event." Bronka smiled with pride. "My boss couldn't find anyone else so he finally gave me some real news to cover."

"Well, good for you. I'm proud of you. I'll tell Christina when I call her later. That's just wonderful. You know, if you're working on the story, I may have an angle for you. I happen to know one of the neo-Nazis lives in this neighborhood. And believe it or not, he works in Brodsky's Deli. I had a confrontation with him about sixteen years ago—in fact he was at your tenth birthday party."

"Oh, come on, Irv, that's nothing to joke about," she said.

"No, Bronka, it's the absolute truth."

How could this be? Bronka thought to herself. She had never heard this story before. And it had happened at her birthday party.

"No, really. He delivered the cold cuts to the party for you and JoJo. And Jakob Zilberman, remember Esther's father, recognized him from Auschwitz. The deli guy was an SS guard when Jakob was a prisoner there. Anyway, it's a long story. I said hi to Brian yesterday but I don't know if he spotted his dad; he kind of disappeared after I saw him. But I'd like to speak with Brian if he's interested in the back-story. Poor kid, he's such a nice boy. I've advised him numerous times when I've been in the shop, giving him advice about photography and camera equipment. Tell him to contact me if he wants to chat."

Bronka's face fell and her heart started racing, but all she said was, "So it's true."

The Nazi had delivered the cold cuts. Well, it made sense, he worked in the deli. But why was it never mentioned? Certainly, Irv was such a yenta that the whole block must have known, especially her parents since they hosted the party. You would think in all these years at least Faye would have said something. So, everyone who patronized Brodsky's had come in contact with a Nazi. She wondered why Irv and Mr. Zilberman had just let it go.

"Look, we all carry shadows, but we have free will. And we defeated the Nazis. Brian's a great kid. So, just mention to him that I'm here for him if he wants to talk."

"Sure, thanks Irv," Bronka said.

Irv was a busybody, although he meant well. And his own lineage was a bit screwed up too, Bronka remembered. A Jew who married a

Catholic, raised his children in the Catholic faith, but still attended Yizkor Services faithfully each Yom Kippur. *Can you ever escape your family history?* Bronka wondered.

CHAPTER TWENTY-NINE

AFTER BRIAN DROPPED BRONKA OFF, he drove home to his family's 1950s Cape Cod, which was only fifteen or so blocks from the Lubinski home. No one else was there and the house was steaming hot on this torrid afternoon. He exhaled a deep and long breath as he entered. Brian turned on the air conditioner in the small kitchen and then headed upstairs to his blue bedroom with its slanted ceiling. He was breathing heavily from the excitement and the heat and cracked the window a bit so he wouldn't suffocate before the window air conditioner cooled the room. He went back downstairs and turned on all the room air conditioners on the first floor and then headed for the finished basement, the coolest spot in the house. He would start his hunt there.

Its walls were knotty pine and there was a pool table that took over much of the space, save for an old sofa and some chairs and a stereo. The other half of the basement was unfinished—only a furnace, a washer and dryer, and a second refrigerator. A long walk-in closet that housed the family's set of blue Samsonite suitcases and his late grandmother's cedar chest ran along the length of the wall.

He walked into the closet and scouted it out. Behind the neatly arranged family luggage, the cedar chest, an ironing board, and several cardboard boxes, he spotted an old, beaten-up looking valise. It was light brown, with darker brown straps on each side. Brian began to shake. Might the suitcase hold the answers he was looking for? Dare he open it?

Brian stood in the storage closet sobbing and arguing with himself for a good five minutes. Did he really want to know what was in the suitcase? It could be nothing and then he would be relieved. But he felt in his heart of hearts that this would not be the case. He was now perspiring and breathing heavily, and his hands were shaking. The suitcase could hold the secret to his father's past. All right, he convinced himself, he would open it; he had to know one way or the other. He lifted the valise from the closet and took it into the unfinished portion of the basement where it was cooler. He opened a brown folding chair and sat down with the luggage on his lap.

"Damn it," he said to himself. The suitcase was locked. "Where the hell did he hide the key?"

He went back into the closet, moving the blue luggage and the ironing board. He wondered whether he should start emptying the boxes, but decided to look first in the mahogany cedar chest where he found a white linen tablecloth with twelve matching napkins and rolls of fabric—pink and white gingham, blue shantung, and some cotton sheets and pillowcases. His mother, Margaret, was not a seamstress. This must have belonged to her mother, his late grandmother, Bernadette, Brian reasoned. Underneath the materials, there was a christening gown with a matching bonnet and booties. The gown was made from a white cotton fabric, trimmed with lace and embroidery. There were also a few knitted and crocheted baby sweaters and hats.

At the bottom of the chest was a white satin pillowcase. Brian opened it and found a Catholic Bible and a zippered rosary case with an image of the Virgin Mary and the Christ Child. On the reverse side of the pouch was a Byzantine-Russian style cross with a dove on the top. Brian unzipped the rosary case and gently stroked the fifty-nine green beads his grandmother used to hold. She had told him that they were Connemara Marble Rosary beads made from a very rare rock that is unique to Ireland. He felt comforted and close to his grandmother, reminding him of the deep and devout Catholic roots on his mother's side of the family. But then a small key fell out of the case. Brian wondered if this could possibly be the key to the valise. Had his father hidden it in the cedar chest, thinking that no one would ever find it there? Or maybe it was just his grandmother's key.

Before he could think further, he took the key, and slipped it into the lock of the valise. Even though it seemed obvious, Brian was still surprised when the lock turned. *Dumb luck or was I meant to find it?* he wondered.

The top layer within the suitcase was filled with pages and pages of documents in German. Some had swastikas on them.

Brian began to sweat and felt his heart palpitating. He believed he was too young to have a heart attack, but his hands were shaking and he was short of breath. Swastikas? Why would he have hidden them away? His father had a stash of documents with the heinous, odious Nazi symbol. He thought that if a creature from another planet suddenly appeared and asked him to describe its meaning, he would have difficulty putting it into words. It was the sum of everything evil and wrong in human nature—the symbol of mass murder, cruelty, torture, depravity intolerance, prejudice, hate, mindless obedience, there were not enough words in any language to fully express the meaning of the swastika.

Brian also recognized several copies of a newspaper named *Der Sturmer* that depicted Jews as horrific characters with grotesque facial features, huge noses, and distorted bodies. As he dug beneath the papers he felt more cloth, which he took out. Unfolding the grey-green material, he saw it was a uniform with SS shoulder board and insignia as well as a number of Nazi medals.

He ran the two flights upstairs and grabbed his backpack from his bedroom. So excited and nervous and nauseous, he tripped on the last few stops on his way back down to the basement and landed on his knee on the tiled floor.

"Damn it," he yelled, afraid to move for a few moments. His knee pulsated with pain, but he was able to move his leg so he decided it wasn't broken. He crawled to the couch, dragging his backpack and held on lifting himself up, and then sat down for a few minutes.

Good, he said to himself, as he pulled out a handful of eleven by fourteen cardboard envelopes that he used for his photos. He stood up and limped over to the suitcase and sat down on the folding chair. He placed the documents in the envelopes and put them in his bag.

He put on the backpack and slowly, gingerly ascended the steps, his knee throbbing. The house was still empty. He headed for the kitchen, opening the freezer for a package of frozen peas. *At least I know what to do,* he thought as he elevated his foot on a kitchen chair, lightly pressing the cold peas against his knee. Having a mother who was a nurse served him well, but *Oh no, my poor mother,* he suddenly thought, no longer distracted by his knee. *What will happen to our family*? He could hardly imagine telling his mother the news.

But first, Brian had to find someone who read and understood German.

CHAPTER THIRTY

THE NEXT MORNING, BRIAN HOBBLED into the office a few minutes late with his black and blue knee.

"What happened to you?" Bronka called from her desk the minute she spotted him limping.

"It's a long story," he said. As he approached her desk, he leaned over to whisper in her ear.

"I need to talk to you ASAP. When can you take a break?"

As they walked to the candy store shortly after, Bronka thought about the conversation she had had with her father when she told him she had covered the street name–changing event in Yaphank.

"*Vat* is Max doing, sending you to a neo-Nazi event? Doesn't he know our background? You should stick to cooking and ladies' issues. I don't *vant* you in danger, Bronka."

"I'm not in any danger, Papa, please," she had said. "There were hundreds of people there. Irv Rosen was there."

"Irv Rosen is everywhere; he has his nose in everything."

"That's his job, but I want to go beyond women's features. I want to do what the men do."

"I don't like it, Bronka. You're twenty-six. You should get married already and start a family. I *vant* someone to take care of *you*. And I need more Jewish grandchildren."

"All in due time, Papa. Please don't worry, I'm not in danger."

Brian and Bronka sat down in a booth. "So do you want to go first or should I?"

"You can go first," Brian said.

"This is hard, very hard," she began, as she narrowed her dark brown eyes, which shone with compassion.

Not only did she have to counsel Brian, but now she had her father's feelings to manage too. But she had been more than a dutiful daughter, and the opportunity Max had given her meant there was no turning back.

"So, you know Irv Rosen, the photographer?" Bronka asked.

"Of course, I know him from Brodsky's. He was very helpful to me when I first wanted to try photography. I owe a great deal to him. In fact, he shook hands with me at Fatherland Gardens the other day."

"Well, he lives on my block and he stopped me yesterday. He said he saw us at the event and he'd like to talk with you if you're interested."

"About what?"

"This is hard for me, Brian. I'm really uncomfortable that he put me in this position—he should have contacted you himself. He says he knows stuff about your father's background if you want to speak with him. Here's his number if you want to call."

Bronka could see that Brian looked stunned as he took the piece of paper that she handed him.

"Do you think you're gonna call him?" she asked.

"We'll see. But first, I have to get some papers translated that I found in my father's old valise. I think that Father Stan speaks several languages. I know for sure—Italian and French—and I'm hoping German too. Will you come with me if I set up an appointment with him?"

"Of course," Bronka said. She knew she was the kind of person who had difficulty saying no to others. JoJo called her a people pleaser. But her twin also often commented that Bronka was strategic.

"Thanks, Bronka; this means a lot to me," Brian said. "I'm so glad you don't mind going with me again to see Father Stan."

"Not at all. It's my pleasure."

CHAPTER THIRTY-ONE

WHEN BRIAN PULLED UP TO her house at seven o'clock the next evening, Bronka was waiting outside on the porch. As she walked to the car, she was astonished to see an attractive young woman with long blonde hair and hazel eyes sitting in the front seat next to Brian. As she peeked into the car, she saw the woman was slim with long legs, wearing red-and-blue hot pants.

Well, I guess Brian has been holding out on me. He has a girlfriend after all. But this is awkward.

"Hey, Brian, you didn't tell me you were bringing a date. I'll just drive myself. Izzy's car isn't being used."

"Nah, no way, Bronka. This is my sister, Doreen. Father Stan invited us to dinner so he could take a look at the documents and suggested that I include her as well as you in our meeting."

"Well, I still feel funny intruding on your family time."

"Are you kidding, Bronka?" Doreen said. "I'm glad to finally meet you and I'm so thankful for your support."

"Does your mother know about this?"

"No, not yet," said Brian. "We wanted to see what Father Stan said first, and I'm also going to meet with Irv Rosen. Then we'll take it from there."

"Are you sure you want me to come with you in the car? I can drive myself."

"Knock it off, Bronka. Hop in."

Bronka climbed into the back seat of the car.

"So, where are we meeting the Monsignor?"

"He asked us to meet him at The Alpine Inn. Ever been there?"

"No, but I've heard of it," said Bronka.

"You'll like it. It's a beautiful restaurant and there are some little shops in the same complex. And Father Stan emphasized that we are all his guests. It's his treat."

"Wow," said Bronka. "But I feel like I shouldn't be coming. I feel like I'm intruding."

"I told you to knock it off. We both want you to come. And what's more, Father Stan made a point of asking me to include you."

That was music to Bronka's ears. Father Stan had made a point of specifically asking for her to join them. She was correct in thinking that he liked her. They were on the same wave-length. He was so deep and intelligent—just the kind of guy she was seeking. She wondered why there were so few young men who met her standards. Too bad, he was a priest.

The Alpine Inn was a far cry from the eating establishments Bronka usually frequented. The building itself resembled a European villa, set back on several acres of manicured lawn with neatly shaped shrubbery. A path led to the old-fashioned shops, including an ice cream parlor, bakery, Swiss chocolate shop and a souvenir store. Once inside the actual restaurant, Bronka inhaled a strong scent of sauerbraten.

Everything about The Alpine Inn suggested old world elegance. The chandeliers were dark and subdued, and on each table there were two little bud vases with a single rose in each and two lit votive candles. Bronka knew what her father would have said about this place—*goyish*—a perfect hangout for the priest.

Father Stan was already seated at a table in the corner and he stood when the maître d' escorted them to him. The priest wore a black jacket and shirt with his white collar. He smiled with his whole face, his eyes crinkling. He wasn't really handsome, Bronka thought; it was something else. For a fleeting minute, Bronka had the sensation that had he not been wearing his collar, this swarthy man with dark eyes and dark hair might have looked equally at home at the kosher deli eating a corned beef sandwich.

As they sat down at the table, the priest welcomed them and ordered a bottle of red wine for the table. The waiter, dressed in a tuxedo, poured a bit for the priest to try and when he signaled his approval, he poured wine into each of the four wine glasses.

"Here's to understanding and serenity," Father Stan said, lifting his glass.

As they studied the menu, the waiter noted that should anyone wish to order the sauerbraten, there were two types—one with beef and one with pork.

Just as Bronka was about to panic, she spotted a broiled filet of sole on the menu and breathed a sigh of relief.

Father Stan crossed himself and recited grace: "Bless us, O Lord, and these Thy gifts, which we are about to receive from Thy bounty. Through Christ, our Lord. Amen."

When he was finished, he made the sign of the cross, then continued.

"*Baruch Atah Adonai Eloheynu Melech Ha'olam. Ha motzei lechem min ha'aretz.* Blessed Art Thou, King of the Universe, who brings forth bread from the earth. Amen."

When he looked up, Bronka couldn't control the expression on her face. Was he trying to impress her? She felt uncomfortable. Why was she even there? But tonight was not the appropriate time to ask, she knew, so she stopped herself from asking where he learned a Jewish prayer.

After they ordered dessert, Father Stan turned to Brian and said, "I believe you have something you'd like me to take a look at?"

Brian handed him two large cardboard envelopes with some of the contents of his father's suitcase.

The first thing the priest took from the envelope was the copy of Julius Streicher's, *Der Stürmer.*

"These vile anti-Semitic caricatures speak for themselves," said the Monsignor. "I'm sure you figured them out without having to read German, Brian. The whole idea of these was to demonize Jews; the Nazis wanted to show they were sub-human, so whatever they did to them would be accepted. And tragically, most people went along with it."

"Yes," Brian responded. "I really don't need a translation of the newspaper, but look at some of these other papers. There's one in particular that's handwritten. I think it's a letter to my father. I'm dying to know what that one says."

"Brian, I'm thinking the best course would be for me to take these documents with me, translate them for you, and have my secretary type them up so you can take your time reading them in English. I imagine there's a lot to digest here."

"But, but—" Brian's face began to turn red, "—but I thought we would have some answers tonight. I can't go through another night with at least something. Can you please just read the handwritten letter out loud?"

"Brian, you can wait. It's really nice of Father Stan to offer to do this for us and to invite us to this lovely dinner," Doreen piped in. "This is really above and beyond to continue to impose on him. We waited this long, Brian, what's another day or two?"

"Look kiddo." His lip curled as he sneered at his sister. "I've been dealing with this for several days already. But that's always the way it is. I'm the adult and you're the baby girl. You either just want to smooth things over or you're afraid to face the facts. I need answers now!"

Doreen looked shocked by her brother's abrupt change in tone, and it was evident to Bronka that she was trying to hold back tears. "I don't think we should be having a sibling argument in this lovely restaurant with the Monsignor," she said.

Bronka was also surprised by Brian's tone. The seemingly even-tempered puppy dog photographer had a bit of a temper. Well, she thought, she really shouldn't be shocked. People always take out their anger and frustration out on those they feel the closest to. *Why?* Bronka thought. *I guess because they can.*

"OK, kids, let's not argue," Father Stan urged the siblings. "You will need each other more than ever once you get answers. And you both need to be strong for your mother. Let me suggest a compromise. I'll translate the handwritten letter for you now, and then I'll take the other documents with me to transcribe. It shouldn't take more than a day or two.

"Sure," said Brian.

As their plates were taken away, Father Stan looked at the paper. Skimming the thin and crinkled paper in the neat, European handwriting, Bronka could see from his pained expression that he knew this was the smoking gun, and that the lives of Brian and Doreen would never be the same.

But she also wondered whether he had ever had to handle anything like this before—not even close. She expected that he had heard all manner of confessions as a former parish priest, and had observed and counseled kids and families in crisis at the school, but this was an extraordinary case. Former Nazis, neo-Nazis, swastikas, surely he had not been trained for this in the seminary. Now he could only do what he promised. He began to read aloud.

My Dear Son Rudolf

I want you to know, Rudy, your mother and I are proud of you. We cannot say how much because it is difficult to measure how our hearts overflow with pride. We know that you cannot tell us what you are doing, but we trust that it is furthering the work of our Fuhrer. We only want you to do it with courage and strength and belief in this important work. Do not question and do not falter, we are always here for you. And look forward to when you can return to us a proud German, fighting for our country.

As far as the Jews are concerned, I want to tell you that they must be done away with in one way or another. Already, due to the work of our Fuhrer, the five million German people unemployed are back at work and the war is not yet over. I know that many of the measures, carried out in the Reich at present are being criticized, but we should only have pity for the German people. The others had no pity on us.

So, whatever work you are doing in the furtherance of our sacred cause, take heart. Because of you and your comrades, we will be reunited in a clean and better world where we can live and love in peace. Your mother and I are glad that you are eating well and have made friends whose company you enjoy. Our mouths water when you tell us about the vodka, sausage, herring, and sardines you are treated to.

Stay safe and well.

Heil Hitler,

Your loving father

Bronka sat wide-eyed and uncomfortable, squirming in her chair, chastising herself for having come along. This was so intensely personal for Brian and Doreen; she felt she had no business being there.

What's more, it was hard not to think of what an amazing story this would be to write about.

She noticed that Brian's face grew redder and redder; he appeared to be steaming. Doreen began to shake and sob, first clearing her throat and then choking. She put her hands over her mouth and ran to the restroom.

Bronka got up to follow Doreen, and Brian followed close behind and waited outside the bathroom. When Bronka entered, she took one look at the traumatized girl at the sink and said, "Doreen, let's get you some fresh air. Do you want a Coke or something?"

"No thanks, I just wanna go home," she said, opening the door to the bathroom where Brian was waiting.

"I'll take you right now," Brian said as he put his arm around her.

"Bronka, please tell Father Stan I'm taking Doreen home. I'm sure you can hitch a ride with him."

CHAPTER THIRTY-TWO

JOJO'S TRYOUT FOR THE LOCAL production of *The Boy Friend* at the YMHA was scheduled for seven o'clock and she had asked Bruce to be home by six to help her make sure the kids would be ready before the babysitter showed up.

She believed that this could be her big opportunity—her second chance so to speak—especially because she had been the star of the same play when she was in high school.

Ever since she was a little girl, she had dreamed of becoming a famous actress. Even with two children and a house in the suburbs, she still harbored the dream of becoming JoJo Luby, her chosen stage name.

Recalling the terrible day JFK was killed, she remembered Bronka's words and thought how prescient they had been. *Nothing has ever been the same again. It was such a happy, innocent time.* But JoJo could not let go of her dream of performing again, even if it was just at the Y. Bruce had promised he'd be home early. She was counting on him to go with her for the audition.

When the phone rang at six thirty and JoJo heard Bruce's voice, she was frantic.

"Where the hell are you, Bruce?" she yelled. "Are you deliberately screwing up the best opportunity I've had in years?

"I do everything for you and you can't do one little thing for me," she went on. "Are you on your way home now? I'll be cutting it close, but I still can make it."

"Look, JoJo, something urgent has come up. I just can't leave right now. Can't you ask Bronka?"

"Screw you!" she said, slamming down the phone, holding back her tears so she would not ruin her professionally applied makeup.

She dialed her parents' number and her mother picked up.

"I need to speak to Bronka. Is she there?" she asked. She quickly explained the situation.

"I'm so sorry, honey, but Bronka's not here. I wish I could drive; I'd come to you and go with you."

"That's OK, Mama, I'm a big girl."

JoJo didn't need her mother to come. She needed her husband. She had especially wanted Bruce to come with her for moral support. And she wanted him to see her shining, all *farputzed* with her hair and makeup, acing the audition.

When Kim, the teenage babysitter who lived next door, rang the bell a few minutes later, JoJo considered telling her that she wasn't going. But when JoJo answered the door and Kim told her how beautiful she looked, she decided to rally.

She would go through the motions because they were expecting her and she wasn't about to send the babysitter home. But her courage and confidence had been washed away by doubt and despair. And the memory of JFK's assassination reminded her that nothing in this world was guaranteed.

CHAPTER THIRTY-THREE

WHEN BRUCE PULLED INTO THE garage at ten o'clock that evening, all the lights were off in the house. He peeked into the master bedroom and saw JoJo sprawled out on top of the covers with her street clothes on, her face buried in a make-up-stained pillow, her professionally coiffed blonde curls beginning to unravel. Instinctively, he rushed to the children's rooms to check on them, but each was fast asleep—Ian snuggled under his Sesame Street blanket and little Tracy a sweet bundle of pink, sleeping soundly in her white crib with the pink and purple flowers.

Alone in the bathroom, he noticed Charlie's pink lipstick on his white shirt as he undressed for bed. He rubbed the shirt to his nose, inhaling the sporty floral fragrance of her new signature perfume that bore her name. He was aware that the scent of Charlie was still with him.

Once they moved to the suburbs, JoJo filled her days with the children and her new-found mahjongg friends including her best friend and neighbor, Charlie, whose children were about the same age as theirs. Whereas in high school and college, JoJo had been one of the popular girls, now she was always in Charlie's shadow. Charlie was the style setter of the neighborhood. She organized card games, and kept the other women informed. She was the expert on the best hair salons, restaurants, and nursery schools. JoJo put great stock in Charlie's recommendations.

Charlie even insisted they go out for dinner with her and her husband, Steve, although the two men had little in common. And when they went out, Charlie dominated the conversation anyway, holding court with all of them. But after several dinner dates, Charlie began to turn her attention to Bruce.

She hung on to his every word, flattered him, asked him about his work, and even knew the latest scores for the Yankees, the Knicks, and the Jets. Everything Charlie did was the opposite of the way his wife approached the world.

Ever since the birth of Tracy, JoJo was not herself. She had shed her cheery exterior, and sometimes Bruce heard her crying in her sleep—sometimes screaming out loud.

"You're not exactly a quiet sleeper," she snapped when he asked her about it. "Maybe it's your snoring that bothers me."

He mentioned the situation to his mother and to his sister, Jackie. They said the same thing: "You have to talk to her about it."

But Bruce, not an adept conversationalist himself nor someone who could adequately express his own emotions, didn't have the skills to know how to discuss this with his wife.

It wasn't long before he reached out to Charlie. He told himself that he was phoning her to try to get a handle on what his wife was thinking and feeling. Soon, he was calling her several times a week to chat. It was easy; he felt comfortable talking with her.

Unlike JoJo, what was on her mind was on her tongue and Charlie freely expressed her feelings. She had an opinion about everything. Especially about his wife. And because JoJo had freely confided in her, she knew the couple's whole history.

She told him that JoJo, while she presented a smiling, happy exterior, kept it all bottled up. She just ploughed through, something that Charlie said on one hand was impressive, but on the other was also a liability. She explained that JoJo had made the best of the unplanned pregnancy and immediately went to work fitting in to her new role.

Charlie told Bruce that, in her opinion, she still resented that he had to give up going to law school and was now working long hours for his father. She also said that JoJo had become preoccupied with her home, her children, and her friends, to his detriment.

He countered by saying his wife always had dinner for him at whatever hour he returned from work despite his not wanting to chat after a long day. He said he knew this frustrated her at the beginning because she told him so—a rare departure from her usual behavior. She said that she waited the whole day for him to come home and tell her about his day, but he only wanted to eat, plop in front of the TV, and vegetate. While she didn't dwell on her feelings the way her twin did, Bruce never really asked her about them either.

One day, Charlie stopped by his office around lunchtime—ostensibly to proffer some helpful advice and to drop off a bag with two corned beef sandwiches, a knish, and two cans of Dr. Brown's soda: a Cel-ray and a cherry. He had forgotten how he had mentioned his favorites in passing.

"Let's get out of here," he said, shining with the glow her flattery had cast on him. And he led her to his car in the parking lot.

"Where are we going?" Charlie asked.

"There's a little pond about a mile away. We'll sit in the car and have lunch."

That was the first time, and not the last. But tonight, they had taken it to a new level.

And when JoJo went to gather the laundry the following morning, she smelled the evidence first. She pulled Bruce's shirt out of the hamper and sniffed the telltale scent of Charlie's perfume. As the expert she considered herself to be, Charlie had told the other women that if they wanted to be cool, they should switch their fragrance to Charlie. But then she saw Charlie's signature frosted pink lipstick on his collar and she broke down and sobbed.

CHAPTER THIRTY-FOUR

WHEN BRONKA RETURNED TO THE table without Doreen or Brian, the Monsignor's face flooded with concern.

"What happened?"

Bronka explained the situation, making sure to stress that Brian had told her to go back to the table.

"I understand how incredibly difficult this must be for both of them," he said, the frown lines on his forehead visible and his deep brown eyes reflecting his agony. "I'll translate the rest of the papers, but you can see that the letter from their grandfather says it all."

"Absolutely," Bronka said.

"And don't worry, I'll drive you home. But let's sit here for a while and debrief. You look like you've seen a ghost, Bronka. How about an after-dinner liqueur?"

"I don't think I've ever had one."

"Well, this seems as good a time as any to start," Father Stan said as he called the waiter back.

When the waiter brought the two Grand Marniers to the table, Father Stan looked at her playfully and said, "Now be sure to sip it slowly."

The orange-flavored drink gave her a warm feeling she was not familiar with. The liquor had a calming effect and she began to relax.

"You know, those kids just experienced a double whammy," the priest said. "It's bad enough to discover your father was a Nazi during the war, but to find out that your grandfather enthusiastically embraced and acted on that odious ideology is quite another."

Bronka nodded. "What's going to happen?"

The priest looked into her eyes and put his hand on hers.

"I really don't know, my dear. It's a conundrum. Of course, I will pray on it. And I will consult with my superiors. And I will go back to the sources. But this is hard. I confess: I've never dealt with a situation like this before."

Reflexively, Bronka squeezed his hand, but then she felt her eyes well up, and she removed her hand to use a tissue.

"It's beyond sad," said Father Stan. "They're such nice young people. And their mother, Margaret, is a pious woman. It's a tragic situation."

"Are you actually going to translate the rest of the documents? It could make it worse," Bronka said. "But, of course, I've already done that. I added my two cents to the fire. I told him Irv Rosen, the *Life Magazine* photographer, wants to speak with him. He has more information about what Brian's father did in the war. I know the truth is supposed to set us free, but I'm not sure in this case."

"I must translate the documents, Bronka. I promised Brian and he has to see this through. Proverbs tell us that there are six things that the Lord hates and the seventh is an abomination to him. 'A proud look, a lying tongue, hands that shed innocent blood, a heart that devises wicked imaginations, feet that are swift in running to mischief, a false witness that speaks lies, and he that sows discord among brethren.'"

"And Brian's father has committed all seven?" she asked.

"Correct."

“Let me ask you another question,” Bronka inquired, feeling more relaxed and chatty. “Do you think the children and grandchildren of Nazis and their sympathizers bear any responsibility for what their relatives did during the war?”

“If you’re asking me if evil is carried through bloodlines, I don’t believe it. But that’s a great question, Bronka, and two things come to mind. One, what is the significance, if any, of our genes? For example, I was adopted so am I the product of the family that raised me or do I have a responsibility to the heritage of my birth parents? Do I need to choose one or the other or can I live with both?”

“You were adopted? I’d love to hear your story.”

“Another time, I promise; it’s getting late and we both have to go to work bright and early tomorrow. But I just want to share my thoughts on the second point that you raised about bearing responsibility. Yes, I think children and grandchildren bear responsibility for the Nazi horror, but only in the same sense that every member of the human race does. How could a civilized, cultured country like Germany enable Hitler to take over and spread his venom? And they allowed it in increments; it happened over years, bit by horrible bit.

“Brian’s grandfather gives a clue in the letter. People were out of work so Hitler made Jews the scapegoat. Jews were forbidden to work and then five million Germans got their jobs back, so they loved Hitler and gave their allegiance to him.”

“You’ve given me a lot of food for thought,” Bronka said, thinking that she could go on talking to the priest forever. These were exactly the kind of discussions she loved, but rarely had with her peers.

“Yes, we will definitely continue the conversation. And thank you for being here tonight; it was good to share the events of this evening with such a sensitive and intelligent person. Let’s get the car.”

After the secretary typed up the translations a few days later, the priest took the papers and looked them over. While the letter from Roy's father was the linchpin and the grotesque cartoons of Jews in *Der Sturmer* were nauseating, these other documents seamlessly supported Roy Smith's pro-Nazi proclivity. The fact that he was demonstrating with neo-Nazis at Fatherland Gardens only corroborated that he had been a Nazi collaborator and continued to be one.

The monsignor sought counsel from the Bishop about how to proceed. He explained to him that he had done a lot of soul-searching and was tormented by the questions he continued to ask himself about this very difficult situation: Why had he been so quick to agree to translate these documents? Once he had shared the sickening letter from Nazi father to son, was there a point of pursuing this further?

"It's clear from the letter that Roy Smith was involved in something nefarious during World War II," he told his superior. "His proclivities were absolutely corroborated in the papers. But what is the point in sharing them with the Smith children at this point?"

"But wasn't it young Brian who asked you to look into it?" The Bishop asked. "Isn't he the one who is interested in truth—and perhaps justice?

"Yes, that's what he told me. But do I need to add more fuel to the fire?"

The bishop told him that this was a very complicated matter and to continue to reflect and pray on it. The answer would eventually come to him.

After the meeting, Father Stan went back to his office and reached into the top drawer of his desk, taking out a key chain with a St. Christopher's medal that held three keys. He walked over to the antique mahogany file cabinet that matched his desk and unlocked the cabinet. He placed the pernicious papers in the top drawer, and then he wept as he prayed for guidance.

CHAPTER THIRTY-FIVE

BRONKA WAS IN OVER HER head, and she knew it. But she had no idea how to extricate herself, nor did she want to. Her heart broke for Brian, but as a journalist, the whole story was fascinating.

And then there was the priest who she was drawn to in a way that she hadn't been since Ned. And like Ned, there was a mystery to him, as if he were harboring a secret.

They had spent hours together talking on the phone during the week. And while the conversations always began and ended with the Roy Smith situation, the discussions went far afield. They discussed the philosophy of Martin Buber, and the need for I–Thou relationships in today's world instead of the transactional I–It, which was so prevalent where one party uses the other for their own needs. They had even discussed dietary restrictions, Bronka explaining why she was trying to keep kosher in her own way.

"It's the same feeling I get by not eating meat on Friday," Father Stan offered.

She yearned to talk to him face to face again.

Bronka and Brian were getting out of his car when they saw Irv standing on the sidewalk waiting for them along with a short little man with a beaked nose.

"Hi guys," said Irv. "This is Jakob Zilberman and this is Bronka's friend and colleague Brian Smith, a wonderful young man in his own right." Jakob smiled and extended his hand; although Brian looked alarmed, he shook his hand with a firm shake.

Assessing Brian's reaction, Bronka excused herself, saying that she forgot something in the car. She could not think of another way to save Brian and get him alone.

Irv clearly sensed what was going on. "OK, Jakob and I will meet you in the backyard. The two older gentlemen turned to walk to the back. Brian looked panic stricken.

"Did you know that other guy would be here?" he asked.

"If you want the truth, you must listen to Jakob. He knew your father in the war."

Brian sighed, then looked at the sky. Bronka could see in his expression he was thinking deeply.

"Might as well hear the guy out," he finally said. "I started down this path and I have to see it through."

Irv led them down the six concrete steps and opened the outside door that led to the finished basement. They walked through a full green kitchen into another room with knotty pine walls, covered with Irv's photographs, and a dark room where he developed his pictures.

"Let's sit at the table," he said, pointing to a light green kitchen table, and they all sat. Irv brought four glasses of water for them to drink.

"I'm sorry Brian," Irv began. "I could have told you his story myself, but what happened during the war would have been second-hand. I was with Jakob sixteen years ago when we met your father in the deli. This will be an incredibly difficult account for you to hear, so please stop us at any time if it's too much."

"No, go ahead, please," Brian said, clasping his hands together.

"So vat happened," Jakob said, "is that your father delivered the deli platters for Bronka and JoJo's birthday party and I recognized him from the camp. I told Irv then that he was a guard who stood outside the gas chamber with a whip, herding naked Jews into the chamber, telling them they were taking showers. Now I'm sure your next question is how did I live to tell about it? So I'll answer.

"I'm ashamed to say that I was a *Sonderkommando*. I, along with other strong Jewish young men were picked for this wicked job and not for instant death, like my parents, brothers, and sisters. Our job was to open the doors of the gas chamber after the people were gassed and carry their bodies to the ovens. Then they forced us to crush their bones by pressing the bodies through a coarse sieve. After we were finished, the ashes were thrown into the river."

"So when I found out about this," Irv recalled, "I asked Jakob if he wanted to confront your father. At first he wasn't sure, especially because in 1957 no one was interested in outing former Nazis. But I had this friend, Moe Solomon, who was a New York City cop; he's living in Florida now. He was always very militant, loud, and impulsive. He said that while no one really cared about Nazis back then, we could scare Rudolf Schmidt, which is your father's real name."

Brian's face had turned white—drained of all color. He held on to the edge of the table as if to steady himself and turned to Jakob. "So, what did he say when you confronted him?"

"At first, he denied it, saying he was fighting the Russians during the war and didn't know what was going on. But when we told him we knew he was lying, he caved, admitted it all, and gave us his SS number."

The room fell silent.

"I thought maybe I'd have some closure or revenge, but I was wrong," Jakob said, breaking the silence.

"You know they say sometimes you should let sleeping dogs lie. Well, I didn't. And I ended up feeling worse. I guess I could ask the same question of you. Why are you doing it?"

"I have to know," said Brian. "You're basically saying that my whole life and the life of my family is a lie. Our family name isn't even Smith. My father was a Nazi, but I can't bear to think my mother knows."

"Your father told Jakob, Moe, and me that your mother did not know," Irv said. "For whatever it's worth, he said she was a devout Catholic and would leave him if she knew."

"And what else did my father say?" Brian asked, quickly skipping to the next worry. He had no time to be relieved.

"If it's any comfort, he was terrified of losing his family."

Irv took a black-and-white, eight-by-ten-inch photo out of a cardboard envelope and handed it to Brian whose eyes and mouth both opened wide as he registered the contents of the photo. It was one that Irv had snapped of Brian's father and Jakob Zilberman, sitting next to each other at Brodsky's Deli in 1957.

"We told him that since he told us the truth, we wouldn't do anything for the time being. Of course, as I mentioned, there really wasn't anything we could do. But Moe threatened him. And as far as I knew, he behaved himself for sixteen years. But it looks like I was mistaken."

CHAPTER THIRTY-SIX

JOJO WAS NOT SPEAKING TO Bruce. Since he had missed her audition, she had kicked him out of the bedroom to sleep on the plaid sofa in the downstairs den, which she knew was uncomfortable because it had a big bar down the middle. *Serves him right,* she found herself thinking each night as she got into bed.

During the past week, she cried and cried, ate chocolate and drank white wine, and stopped taking Charlie's phone calls. True, what she had was circumstantial evidence, but as Faye would have said, it was *gezuntah* circumstantial evidence—big and strong—that he had been unfaithful. She was too ashamed to tell her mother—what if she were just imagining things? She had tried to talk to Bronka on the phone, but her twin was busy chasing some big story. This was unusual, since Bronka was normally so accessible to her. So, finally Bronka was coming to Syosset so they could discuss the situation.

When Bronka asked what she could bring, JoJo answered, "I stopped eating except for chocolate."

The sisters sat side by side on the couch. JoJo wore no makeup and her eyes were red and puffy. Her long blonde curls were tied with a rubber band in an unkempt ponytail. She wore a large white t-shirt that was stained and ripped in the sleeve.

"Is he here?"

JoJo rolled her eyes. "Of course not, did you really expect him to be here?"

The kids were on the floor in a sea of toys.

"This looks like a nursery school classroom," said Bronka. "I hope they don't have what I brought them."

"You don't always have to bring them something. You're spoiling them."

"Hey kids," Bronka called out. "I brought dinner and I guess you don't need it, but if you want it, I have something else for you too. Or I can give them to some other children. But I need a hug first."

Ian, wide eyed, five years old and earnest, perked up when he heard there was something for him. He walked over to Bronka with little Tracy crawling behind.

"What do you have for me, Auntie Bronka?" Ian said. "A toy?"

"Don't be rude," said JoJo.

"He's not being rude. Well, I also brought hot dogs and French fries for dinner. You like that, right Ian?"

Ian nodded.

"And something else if you want it."

She handed Ian a package of Matchbox cars and for Tracy a stuffed honey-colored Winnie the Pooh with black button eyes and nose and a red shirt.

Ian jumped up and down, shouting: "I knew you'd bring a toy. You always bring us something!"

"And what do you say?" JoJo said.

"Thank you Auntie Bronka," Ian called out as he ran to hug her and Tracy raised her hands for Bronka to pick her up so she could get a hug too.

After dinner when the kids were fed, bathed, read to, and put to bed, there was finally quiet. The sisters sat on JoJo's unmade bed, finally alone.

"Your reading material is as eclectic as your night clothes," Bronka quipped as she spotted two books on JoJo's nightstand. One was a plain paperback with red print, *The Joy of Sex: A Gourmet Guide to Lovemaking* by Alex Comfort and an orange book: *Between Parent and Child* by Dr. Haim Ginott. The top of the book sported a gold sticker, which read, "The book that teaches you how to talk CHILDRENESE."

"And when did you switch from negligees to t-shirts?"

"Let's lie down on the bed like we used to do when we were little," JoJo said as her eyes filled with tears and she ignored Bronka's question.

"What's going on, JoJo? Seriously, you're not talking to Bruce and you're reading *The Joy of Sex*. Do you have a boyfriend on the side?"

JoJo began sobbing and Bronka's eyes filled with tears too.

"Of course, I don't have a boyfriend on the side. That's insulting, Bronka. I think Bruce is cheating on me."

Bronka's mouth opened wide, but no words came out.

"He was supposed to come home early from work and go with me to my audition at the Y," JoJo said. "And he didn't come home. He just said he had to work and he blew off the whole thing. I really wanted him to go with me; this was my big opportunity and he killed it. I was so upset by his behavior that I totally blew it. I didn't get the part of Polly or any part at all. He told me he had to meet with Charlie because she had a crisis and needed his help."

"So, from that you concluded that she and Bruce are having an affair. I think that's a bit of a stretch."

"It's not, Bronka. First he lied to me and said he had to work late. But it was only when I pressed him later that he admitted they went to dinner. Why couldn't he come home and do me this one favor? He's hardly ever home. I thought his father was working him to death, but now I don't think Leon's to blame at all. He's always been nice to me. Doris never had any use for me, but if he had told his father what was going on, he would have let him leave. Now I see he wasn't working late, but was out cavorting with my best friend . . ."

"I thought I was your best friend," Bronka interrupted, squeezing her sister's hand.

"I made a mistake. I never should have married him."

"Don't say that, JoJo. Look, Bruce has his faults, but I'm quite sure he loves you and he loves the kids."

"I'm not so sure. If he did, he wouldn't be doing this. He's completely lost interest in our family.

"And I'll tell you something else, Bronka. You're the only one I'm sharing this with. I keep having these terrible dreams. Bruce and I and the kids are in a bunker in the forest and it's freezing and we're starving. Bruce says he's going to find food for us and he disappears for a very long time. And the next thing I know, men in uniform remove the tarp and are aiming their rifles at me and the kids."

"Then what happens?"

"I don't know, that's when I wake up in a sweat, screaming. And I'm afraid to go to sleep now because every time I do, there I am facing Nazi soldiers in the bunker with the kids, and Bruce has abandoned us."

"Honestly, JoJo, I've always wondered how you managed to brush away this cloud that hangs over our family. I've been having recurrent nightmares for years. I suspect your doubts about Bruce probably triggered them; it shows you're human. But you really need to talk to him and let him explain. You have to confront him."

CHAPTER THIRTY- SEVEN

UNCHARACTERISTICALLY, BRONKA WAS A BIT late for work the next morning. She had left JoJo at eleven o'clock and then, once in her own bed, tossed and turned for hours thinking about their conversation.

Before last night, Bronka always thought that JoJo was not scarred in the same way as she was by their father's tragic past. But now, it was clear that it had just been buried. The trouble with Bruce had manifested itself in nightmares, like hers.

On her way into the office, Brian practically bumped into Bronka, almost knocking her down on the pavement. He ignored her and kept walking, his face grim. With his camera bag and backpack, he walked fast without looking back.

She ran down the street after him, calling: "Hey Brian! Stop! Talk to me. Please tell me what happened."

He sneered at her. "You and your helpful suggestions. I trusted you and your pal, Irv Rosen."

He shoved *The Daily News* in her face.

"Look at this and tell me you're not responsible for it."

The headline read: *Neo-Nazi Identified!*

The front page displayed two pictures—the original photo of

Brian's father at the Neo-Nazi rally and another taken yesterday while he worked behind the counter at Brodsky's Kosher Delicatessen in Floral Park.

"I had nothing to do with this," she blurted out.

She felt her face getting flushed as she turned to page three. The article reported that several readers had called the paper to report that the man in the Nazi uniform at the Fatherland Gardens name-changing event was Roy Smith who worked at the Jewish deli.

Bronka didn't know whether to cry or scream. Her heart broke for Brian, but she was furious.

"How is this my fault, Brian? I've been there supporting you every step of the way and you lash out at me. What do I have to do with this if people recognized your father from the deli?

"But the timing of it is suspicious. We just met with Rosen and Zilberman and the next day it's in the paper."

Bronka was not one to yell, but all of the emotion she usually kept bottled up, came forward.

"You're blaming me? Irv and Jakob had been sitting on this information for sixteen years. They have known who your father is since 1957. And as you heard, they know much more than his real name. Are you really so dumb that you think they ran to the paper the minute we left them yesterday? And that overnight, *The Daily News* sent a photographer to the deli and snapped a picture and now it's in this morning's paper? Brian, you're in the news business; you know things don't move that quickly. I can assure you that Irv and Jakob had absolutely nothing to do with this."

"Look," Brian said. "I can't think straight. Honestly, I don't know what to think. I gotta get out of here now. I'm going home."

Just like that, thought Bronka. No, "I'm sorry for attacking you." No, "I'll call you later." She realized that Brian still wasn't convinced that she and Irv and Jakob weren't to blame.

CHAPTER THIRTY-EIGHT

BRIAN GOT INTO HIS CAR and headed home down Union Turnpike. He opened the windows and blasted the radio as loud as it would go. They were playing John Denver's "Country Roads," and he imagined himself driving away from Queens and getting lost in some mountain range far away. That's what he wanted to do—escape from this nightmare. But first, he needed to confront his father—and yes, his mother too. No matter if she knew or not.

He drove up to his tidy Cape Cod where he had lived most of his life. Lawn well-manicured, bushes trimmed, annuals blooming.

At the kitchen table Brian found his mother, Margaret, with her head in her hands and sobbing, still in her flowered nightgown. She worked the four-to-twelve-o'clock shift at the hospital, but usually she was up and dressed by now. Doreen must have skipped class; her eyes were bloodshot and her face seemed swollen.

Brian was not crying; he was blazing angry. He kept thinking about the question the Watergate investigators constantly asked about President Nixon: "What did he know and when did he know it?"

"Where is he?" Brian barked.

"We don't know," Doreen answered.

With a snarl, he threw *The Daily News* on the table. It narrowly missed Doreen and landed with a thud.

"I suppose you've seen this, Mom," he said in an accusatory voice.

"Yes, of course we've seen it," answered Doreen. "And the phone hasn't stopped ringing this morning. Some from people we know and some anonymous hateful calls and a number of hang-ups."

"Well, what do you expect?" Brian said. "But I asked Mom, not you." He turned to his mother. "Where is your husband?"

"I told you I don't know. He was already gone when I got up. Doreen just called the deli and asked for him. Sid said he asked your father to leave and he stormed out. He has no idea where he is."

"Why are you attacking Mom, Brian? She's not guilty. Imagine how she feels."

"I'm trying to, but I can't even come close." The venom poured out of his mouth. "How does she feel being married to a Nazi for all these years? Don't tell me you didn't know, Mom. You must have had a clue."

Brian could see that his mother was sobbing and choking on her tears. Of course, she couldn't stop crying, he thought. It was a disgrace to have a husband exposed as a Nazi. And now, he, her beloved son—her sweet, complacent, loving child—was attacking her in this fashion. Even though he knew his berating hurt her to the core, he couldn't stop.

"Why are you blaming me?" She spoke in a shaky voice in between sobs.

"You know, I've been researching this since the rally in Fatherland Gardens," Brian continued. "Did you know about what's in Grandma Bernadette's cedar chest, Mom? A key to Dad's secret suitcase. Did you know your husband was a guard at Auschwitz? I just met someone who identified him from there. Did you know that your husband's own father—my grandfather, your father-in-law—was proud of his son for slaughtering Jews?"

"I was in the dark, Brian," said Margaret, "whether you believe me or not. I had my doubts when I first met your father after the war. But you know the story: he swore he spent the war on the Eastern Front. And when the war was over, he insisted he couldn't get out of Germany fast enough."

"And you believed him?"

"I did. I wanted to believe him," his mother said.

"And it never came up again?"

"No, not until now."

"You carried his babies, Mom. Now we have to pay for his sins."

"Whoa, Brian!" Doreen retorted. "That's just nuts. Guilt is not inherited. We had a good childhood. He gave us dinner every night when Mom was working. We watched TV with him. He didn't beat us. *We* didn't send Jews to their death. How we treat people now—all people—is what really counts."

"I feel responsible," said Brian.

"Brian, this is crazy," said Margaret. "I agree with Doreen; I don't believe in bloodlines. If you embrace Jesus, you're a Christian. It's what you believe and how you live your life. And Dad was a loving father to you.

"A Christian with a secret Nazi as a father? And Little League games wipe that out? Tell me, Mom, how could you have not known? I'm having trouble swallowing that."

"Look, Brian, I'm telling you the truth. Like I said, I had doubts at the beginning, but then he won me over. He helped raise the two of you. He was present; he didn't teach you Nazi propaganda or show any indication at all that he supported it. He was a good father. I had no idea." She crossed her heart and began crying again.

"I'm going to carry his guilt for the rest of my life," said Brian. "But what I really want to know is, does he have any remorse or shame? Or is it just a problem because he's now been exposed?"

CHAPTER THIRTY-NINE

BRONKA WAS BACK ON THE cooking column beat. And for the moment, it was fine with her. There was no drama. She needed a break from Nazi-hunting. Not to mention, the dilemma of how to help her sister. Mindless work was what she needed now. She still was amazed that people actually tried the recipes she wrote about. Along with the usual compliments, she occasionally got complaint letters, especially if an ingredient was omitted or there was a typo.

It was really a shame that I don't cook, she thought.

As she flipped through the cookbooks on her desk, Lillian buzzed her with a call.

"Hi Bronka," the familiar mellifluous male voice said, "it's Stan."

Bronka's face lit up and her anger at Brian faded.

"You promised to let me know how the meeting went with Brian and Irv. Just curious."

"It's such a long story," Bronka began. "I could give you a synopsis, but it's not pretty. In fact, the last thing that happened is that Brian just stormed out of here after he gave me a tongue lashing."

"You? Why? You've been so kind and generous to him."

"Brian has completely drawn the wrong conclusion and I'm sorry I ever got involved. He's making it seem like it's all my fault."

"That's crazy. Of course it's not your fault. I don't know what happened, but I'm sure he will come to his senses. He's probably just lashing out at you because you were in his line of vision and he's comfortable with you."

"Yeah, that's great," said Bronka.

"How about we discuss it all over a nice dinner? Tomorrow night after work?"

"Sounds good," Bronka responded as she felt a wave of exhilaration wash over her and her heart started pounding so loud she could hear it.

So, he was definitely not marriage material. Even if he were to leave the priesthood for her, she considered herself to be an observant Jew, so how would that work out? And her father expected her to deliver Jewish grandchildren to make up for the six million murdered. It was unlikely that a former Catholic priest would agree to that.

So, what exactly was she doing by meeting Father Stan for dinner? They needed to discuss the Brian situation, she told herself. Also, he said he was born in Poland and adopted. The reporter in her wanted to hear that story. But it was more complicated than that: she could not wait to see him again.

At home after work, she changed into a navy-blue bell-bottom pantsuit with a matching belt with silver studs, and took time to put on make-up, using eye shadow to highlight her eyes. She debated with herself whether she should wear jewelry. She decided on a small white gold Star of David that Faye had given her. Better to remind Father Stan—and herself—of who she was.

When she got to Annie's Tavern, Father Stan was standing outside in the parking lot waiting for her. She was surprised—but secretly delighted—that he was not wearing his clerical garb, but instead a blue sports shirt with the top button open, navy-blue sports jacket, and khaki pants. He looked like he was just a normal guy from Queens or Brooklyn, meeting a date. There was something strong and rugged about his looks—not at all the looks of a priest.

He walked to her car and extended his hand as she opened the door to get out, then took her arm and guided her to a long wooden staircase leading upstairs from the parking lot. They entered a reception area, where a waitress came and escorted them up another flight of wooden stairs.

The dining area was dimly lit with wooden booths, each separated from the other by a high wood partition. So much the better for privacy, Bronka thought to herself.

They sat across from each other and smiled. The waitress came and took drink orders. The priest ordered a scotch for himself and a white wine for Bronka.

"I know you're driving home so I won't ply you with alcohol," he quipped. "But the real reason I brought you here is because I know you only eat fish out and there are so many choices you might even have trouble deciding what to order!"

The menu was indeed expansive. Of course, there was lots of shellfish, but still there were more choices of kosher fish with fins and scales than Bronka even knew existed. In addition to flounder and salmon, there was tuna, and bluefish, Dover sole, and halibut.

"I'm going to have the halibut," he volunteered. "But the salmon is also very good here."

"I'll have what you're having." Bronka blushed as she spoke.

The priest started. "I guess we should begin with Brian."

"Yes," said Bronka. "Of course."

"I tried calling him a few times," said the priest, "but there's no answer at his home. The receptionist in your office said he was out sick this week."

Bronka explained what happened with Irv and Jakob, and the photo.

"That must have been incredibly difficult for Brian to take in."

"And then Irv showed him a photo of Jakob and his father. I have no idea what happened when he spoke to his mom and sister."

"I'll stop by the house tomorrow and see what's going on," the priest said. "That poor family, oh Jesus! And I wonder if Brian knows about the Braunsteiner–Ryan case—have you read about it or heard about it? The woman was a Nazi guard in a concentration camp and came to the U.S. illegally after the war. Somehow, Simon Wiesenthal got involved. Everyone just thought she was a regular Queens housewife and now she's going to be deported."

"Do you think that will happen to Brian's father?"

"There's no way of telling. If he came into this country illegally, it could be a problem, but there's really not a big apparatus here searching for Nazis. I think that will come in time. But, in the meantime, the U.S. government invited many former Nazis to come here after the war to work at Los Alamos or in the space program or to spy on Communists. So, you might say the government knows there are Nazis hiding in plain sight."

"By the way, the documents Brian gave me, which I translated, are sickening," the priest said over a dessert of apple pie a la mode.

"Did you share them with him?"

"No, I'm not sure there would be any purpose to that. Of course, if he asks me for them, I'll give them to him. But what's the point? The letter from his grandfather, which you heard, said it all. Everything else just reinforces it."

"I know," Bronka said, with tears in her eyes.

"I've spent the last two years studying Jewish history," said the priest, "and while the Jews have experienced countless catastrophes, this was simply the worst. What bothers me most is that the majority of Germans and those in the occupied countries just went along with it."

"You know," said Bronka, "my father wasn't in a camp, but he's also a victim not only of Hitler's Final Solution, but the aftermath of the war." She explained what happened to her father, how he lost his wife and unborn child who were killed in the Kielce Pogrom.

"How tragic," said the priest, as he put his hand over hers. "And, what of your mother?"

Without giving it a second thought, as simple as falling off a log, the truth rolled off Bronka's tongue. Her response was completely reflexive, telling this earnest man of the cloth to whom she was now profoundly attracted, her family's deeply held secret.

"How interesting—and unusual," Father Stan said when she finished her family's story. "One rarely hears about a Pole embracing Judaism, especially back then. Please tell me more."

"Well, it's a long story. But doesn't it offend you as a priest that my mother renounced Catholicism?"

"I don't think 'offend' is the right word. Perhaps it saddens me, but we must never forget that the roots of Christianity come from Judaism. The two religions are inextricably intertwined in my life too."

"What do you mean?"

"Do you really want to know?"

"I do, Father Stan. I want to know with all of my heart and soul."

"Bronka, you can call me Stan. I'm not your father."

"I'm not sure if I can do that," Bronka responded with a quiet giggle in her voice.

He gazed at her with his intense brown eyes and she imagined that the two of them were just any young man and woman out on a date hitting it off splendidly.

CHAPTER FORTY

WHEN BRONKA THOUGHT ABOUT THE evening afterwards, she honestly couldn't remember what the halibut had tasted like or even if she had actually eaten her dinner. All she could think about was her priest's revelation that he had been born a Jew.

They must have sat in the restaurant for hours until the waiter started dropping subtle hints. They then got into their separate cars and went to a diner for coffee.

There was so much to absorb. She had always been attracted to complicated men, but Stanley Kowalcyzk was an enigma within a puzzle. He was a cauldron of contradictions—more mysterious than anyone she had ever dated.

"I was born in 1943 to Jewish parents," he told her. "My biological mother, Ruchel Rabinowicz, delivered me in the barn of righteous Gentiles—and along with my father, Avram, stayed there for the first month of my life, where I was circumcised and given the Hebrew name, Shaul. But after a month, rumors reached them that the authorities were sweeping the area looking for Jews in hiding. They heard rumors that the Polish police were going from house to house to arrest the few remaining Jews.

"Avram knew that it was no longer safe to stay in the barn with the baby. He convinced Ruchel they must give me over to another righteous Gentile for safekeeping, one who would return me to them after the war. The righteous Gentiles, who allowed Avram and Ruchel and me to hide in their barn, had a cousin who was still nursing her one-year-old daughter. She agreed to take me and take care of me until I could be reunited with my parents. But I never saw my parents again; they were both murdered at Treblinka.

"A couple of years after the war was over, the Kowalcyzks, my adopted family, moved to the United States with their two children. I was six-years-old and their daughter, my sister, was seven.

"Although they raised me as Catholic, I did not look like them at all—with my dark hair and swarthy coloring. Neighbor children taunted me and called me names. My parents had become disenchanted with Poland. They had seen many of their friends and neighbors collaborating with the Nazis and there had been many concentration camps in Poland. They wanted a fresh start in America, both for themselves and their two children.

"I remember very little about my life in Poland. The family had animals on a farm and my parents were loving and indulgent. Both I and my sister, Magda, had great fun riding our pony, pulled by a cord held by our father. There was one memory that was especially clear, though: one day, when my father was taking me for a pony ride, some neighborhood teens started chanting, 'You little dark Jew boy, little Jew bastard. Why don't you look like your parents? You're a dirty Jew.'

"This was the first time I had heard this talk and back then, I didn't even know what a Jew was. But throughout my life, I wondered why I was dark and the rest of my family was fair, why my eyes were practically black and my mother, father, and sister had light blue eyes. Only on her deathbed a couple of years ago, my mother finally confessed the truth to me.

"Our family settled in Brooklyn. My most vivid memory from that time was my First Communion. In preparation for this holy occasion, I was required to go to my First Confession. I remember how it was to meet with my catechism teacher, Father O'Malley, a smiling, towheaded priest in a black cassock. When Father O'Malley asked me what sins I had to confess, I said: 'I fight with my sister sometimes.'"

"Do you hit her, my son?"

"Oh no, I would never do that. But sometimes I say bad words.

"I remember the priest giving me absolution, saying I could now go to communion if I recited two 'Our Fathers' and one 'Hail Mary.'

"Although I was young, I was deeply moved by my First Communion ceremony. Unlike some of my classmates who participated in the ceremony mindlessly, I embraced it with my whole being. The very scent of the church made me feel holy and feeling absolved of my 'sins' was freeing. Priests had the power to make me good again.

"I also loved the church itself: the fragrance of rich and heavy incense, combined with the oak and cedar wood of the benches. The burning candles in various sections of the church made me feel cozy, warm, and secure.

"I knew from the age of seven that I wanted to be a priest.

"The only problem is what I found out two years ago—that I had been born a Jew to two Jewish parents. My mother made her confession to me on her deathbed. Like Jesus, I was born in a barn.

"For the past two years, I have been studying and praying. What I have been trying to figure out is whether I can incorporate both religions into my life or if that is an impossible feat."

CHAPTER FORTY-ONE

BRIAN'S FATHER HAD DISAPPEARED AND still could not be located. Doreen was in school and Brian's mother was working, so all he did was think about his father all day long. He seethed with anger and resentment. He imagined a fistfight, where he bloodied his father's nose and knocked him to the floor and stomped on him.

After a week of trying to find him and moping around the house, Brian returned to work. At this point, he needed a distraction from his troubles.

"It's better that he's gone," his mother said.

While he was embarrassed to walk into the Jewish newspaper office, Brian knew he had to move on with his life. Perhaps he would look for another job, but first he had to keep the one he had. Everyone greeted him warmly and no one mentioned his Nazi father. But he could barely make eye contact with Bronka—he was so ashamed.

It was Bronka who had to approach him; she asked him to talk with her outside on the street in front of the office.

"I was only trying to help you," she told him. "Now I realize it was a mistake. I shouldn't have gotten involved. It wasn't my place. I never meant to hurt you. No one is blaming you for what your father did more than thirty years ago." Tears filled her eyes and she gulped.

Intellectually, Brian knew he was acting like a jerk. And he knew that Bronka—ultra-sensitive and kind person that she was—always thought everything was her fault. Rationally, he knew that she did not cause this, nor even expose it. She had just been there with him and had been a witness. Much like Father Stan, whom he feared he could also no longer look in the eye. Perhaps he needed to get away too. But how could he leave his mother and sister with his father on the run? He felt trapped.

Bronka extended her hand to him. "Still friends?"

He took her hand, but could hardly look at her.

"Sure," he responded with a far off look in his eyes

CHAPTER FORTY-TWO

BRONKA WAS LEAVING WORK EARLY to go to JoJo's with her mother. All the way home on the bus, she kept thinking that Brian hadn't really forgiven her. Her overzealousness had gotten her into trouble. She had only meant to be kind and helpful. But she had cared too much and gotten too enmeshed in something that was private. Or was it really? Herding innocent Jews into the gas chambers at Auschwitz—that needed to be exposed. If that wasn't public, what was? The United States was slow in holding Nazis accountable, but her mother always said, "The pendulum swings in all things." Maybe someday in America, attention would swing toward shining light on these heinous crimes. That day could not come soon enough, she thought.

At least Brian and I will be on speaking terms now, she hoped. She could not abide being in the office while he actively ignored her. But she was sad, not only for the lost friendship, but also for the excitement of following his father's narrative. On the other hand, she had great empathy for both Brian and his family. Their shameful secret had been exposed. What would happen to them?

This was definitely something she intended to discuss with Father

Stan. Ever since his revelation about his Jewish origins, they had been in constant phone communication. In reality, they had been in constant contact since that first interview, speaking frequently on the phone and going out for dinner regularly. They were meeting for dinner again the following night. And Bronka could hardly wait. But today, she was going home, picking up her mother and they were heading over to JoJo's to see if they could help her.

In the car on their way, Bronka decided to bring up the matter of the Nazi.

"Mama, any interesting gossip from the deli? I promise I won't tell anyone. Anyway, after we went to Fatherland Gardens, I promised Brian I'd never write anything about his father."

"OK, but you must not share this with anyone, including Brian."

"Brian's not exactly speaking to me."

"Well," said Judy, the story already on the tip of her tongue. "Sid told me that after he saw Roy identified in the paper, Roy had the nerve to show up to work. Sid said he had just had it with him anyway. He was a good worker, but over the years he'd made some snarky comments about people in the deli. So he just fired him on the spot—after working there for almost twenty years. Roy left in a huff."

"Where did he go?'

"I don't know. Sid said Roy's wife, Margaret, has been calling him every day to see if he's heard anything about his whereabouts. It seems like he's just disappeared off the face of the earth."

As Bronka drove along the Northern State Parkway in Izzy's old car, she put on the radio. She needed a few minutes to reflect on what her mother had just told her.

"You like this music, Mama? They're featuring two John Denver songs back to back."

"Yes, I love John Denver. Let's listen."

To the sounds of "Rocky Mountain High" and "Sunshine on my Shoulders," Bronka had a chance to think about what her mother had just told her.

So, the Nazi had disappeared. But where was he? Brian must be desperate trying to find out. Knowing him so well, she conjectured that he must want to confront his father.

Then she remembered: only she, Father Stan, Brian and his family, her family, Sid, and Irv and Jakob had any inkling that Rudolf Schmidt had been a guard at Auschwitz and entered the U.S. illegally. That was a well-kept secret. Irv and Jakob had sealed their lips for sixteen years. It was highly unlikely they would expose the Nazi now, especially after they had met Brian and seemed to feel compassion for him. Irv didn't need another award-winning photo; he was already past his prime. And Jakob Zilberman remained ambivalent. The rest of them would not spill the beans either.

So Brian's father fled. But what he did, leading that neo-Nazi march probably wasn't illegal. On the other hand, lying on his application to enter this country could very well be considered a crime. But first, there needed to be a critical mass in America more interested in hunting Nazis than Communists. Until then, Roy Smith/Rudolf Schmidt was probably safe.

Bronka pulled into the driveway and helped Judy carry the packages up the stairs to the front door of JoJo's house. The door was open and the kids ran to greet them. Bronka gave a lollipop to each as they gave big hugs to her and their grandmother. The children ran into the den where JoJo was sitting cross-legged in a large sweatshirt and shorts with her hair in a ponytail.

Judy was all smiles, but JoJo kept her scowl.

"They shouldn't have lollipops right before dinner. They won't eat anything."

"I've brought their favorites, they'll eat," Judy replied with a cheery smile. "A little dessert right before a meal helps stimulate the appetite."

JoJo rolled her eyes.

After they ate, trying to keep it light with the children all through dinner, and the kitchen was cleaned up and the kids put to bed, the women sat on the blue sectional sofas in the den—Bronka and JoJo next to each other and Judy facing them.

"So, tell me sweetheart," she said to JoJo, "Talk to me. What's going on?"

JoJo began to cry. "Bruce is staying at his parents' house. I kicked him out."

"I hope you had a conversation with him first," said Judy.

"I did. I confronted him."

"What did he say?"

"His answer was unacceptable. He said ever since Tracy was born, I had let myself go and was just moping around all the time. So he discussed it with Charlie, and she said it wasn't unusual to be blue after the birth of a baby. But he told me that he thought after a year it was enough already and I should just snap out of it. He claims she encouraged him to be more understanding, but he thought I didn't seem like the same person anymore. And Charlie was so perky and upbeat by comparison and gave him advice about how to handle me. Can you imagine? My best friend and my husband are talking about me behind my back as if I'm a nut case."

"I'm your best friend," Bronka reminded her.

"I know, Bronka. You don't have to keep telling me that. You're probably the only friend I have."

"He said those things about you, Johanna? What is he talking about?" Judy asked. "You've always been so vivacious and popular."

"Not like your serious and humorless twin," Bronka added.

"Girls, this is ridiculous, we're not getting anywhere."

"So what's the bottom line?" Bronka asked.

JoJo went through the story again—how she had wanted to be more than a mother; that the audition was her first step into getting back to her old self; how Bruce didn't even show up. Then, she told them how he had been with Charlie instead.

"He admitted it?" Bronka's eyes opened wide.

"He said he was planning on coming home early, but then Charlie called him at work and said she had something important to discuss with him that couldn't wait. So he met her for dinner—instead of coming home! They drove out east where they were sure they couldn't be seen and then, according to him if you believe it, they sat in the car for hours, talking. He doesn't have a word to say to me, but he can talk with her for hours."

"What was so important about what she had to say that he felt it necessary to disappoint you?"

"She said she wanted to tell him that she had decided to leave Steve. Then, according to Bruce, she came on to him, but I don't know what to believe anymore. There were lipstick smears on his white shirt and it reeked of her signature fragrance, *Charlie.* He claims it never went farther than that. But damn it, he's certainly attracted to her, so what difference does it make?"

"I think it does make a difference," said Judy. "Do you believe him?"

"No, I don't," JoJo started crying again. "I was so stupid. I always knew that Bruce had no backbone, but I never realized what a snake Charlie was. She pretended to be my best friend and all along, she was trying to steal my husband."

"So, he's staying at his parents' house now," Judy said. "It's getting late, do you want us to sleep over, honey?"

"No, Mama, that's okay. Papa will be too upset if you don't come home."

"Well, I do want to speak to your father about this and see what he thinks," Judy said. "He always says: "There is a solution for every problem."

"Even this one?" JoJo asked.

"Yes, even this one."

CHAPTER FORTY-THREE

THE NEXT MORNING AT TEN o'clock, Aron took off his white apron and baker's hat and told Judy to hold down the fort in the bakery. He walked the few blocks home and entered through the side door to the kitchen. He picked up the receiver of the white kitchen wall phone and dialed Doris Stern's home number.

"Hello," she answered, in her haughty, yet surprisingly flirty voice for a woman in her fifties.

"It's Aron," he said. "Ve got to talk."

"Yes, we do," she said.

"Vat's going on with your son? He cheats on my daughter, the mother of his two children, the mother of our grandchildren. And you let him stay by you? It's a *shanda*."

"Whoa!" said Doris. "There are two sides to every story. And I'm sure you are aware that *she* kicked *him* out. I can't very well have him sleeping in the gutter. What would the neighbors say?"

"She has a name. Her name is Johanna. And *she* had good reason to. And perhaps if you were more concerned with your son's behavior than what the neighbors would say, ve could solve this."

"Aron, I think we should continue this conversation in person. We need to talk about this face to face."

"Yes, let's talk *tachlis*," Aron said.

"Just you and me," Doris replied. "Can you come over today?"

"I don't drive," Aron said. "I'll have to find a ride."

"Look, I'll send a cab for you, Aron. Can you be ready in a half hour?"

A cab was a luxury that Aron Lubinski did not indulge in. It seemed so decadent to him—so frivolous and unnecessary. You could get around Queens and the other four boroughs of New York City very nicely on public transportation, but this was not the case once you crossed over Lakeville Road and into Nassau County. So what choice did he have? He had no idea what a taxi cost, but he grabbed a wad of cash from his dresser drawer and stuffed it in his wallet. He would do whatever it took to save his daughter's marriage.

When the taxi arrived at the brown-shingled ranch house in Rolling Hills, Aron took his wallet out of his pocket to pay the driver. "No, that's not necessary, sir. Mrs. Stern has already taken care of it. And the tip too."

Suprisingly, the Doris Stern that greeted him at the door was not the pompous *ungapatchked* prima donna from their previous encounters. Now, she wore a casual pair of black pants and a blue blouse and she extended her hand to Aron, then ushered him into the kitchen. She wore no makeup, save for some pink lipstick.

"It's cozier in here," she said. "Do you prefer coffee or tea? I didn't know what to serve a baker, so I thought perhaps you'd like some fruit."

"Thanks," said Aron. "I really don't care for cake; fruit is better. And tea is fine."

"I have some thoughts," Doris began. "But if you want to say something first, go ahead, Aron."

"Your son really hurt my daughter."

"Yes, Bruce was foolish. He can be very weak, but there is a logical explanation, which is important for you to hear. And Johanna needs to hear it too. But she won't listen."

"Stop right there, I don't vant to hear you criticize my daughter. Your son is the philanderer and you are right on the money—he is very weak."

"Aron, Aron, please listen to me and listen well. Bruce is not a philanderer. He made a mistake by trusting the wrong person. And he trusted her because he wanted to help Johanna, but she won't let him help her. She refuses to open up to him."

Aron was taken aback to hear Doris's version of their children's marriage. According to Doris, Bruce had been brought up with a mother who expressed her opinion on everything. So, he just expected that his wife would tell him what she wanted him to hear. But she didn't. And Doris attributed that to her upbringing. Doris insisted that Bruce had asked JoJo what was wrong and she just glared at him or started crying. Then she would scream and cry in her sleep, had neglected her appearance and the house, and was prone to mood swings. So, he had turned to her best friend, Charlie, in an attempt to reach JoJo. It wasn't Bruce's fault, according to Doris, that Charlie had some other ideas. But Doris insisted that there was no affair—just an understandable attraction that developed because Bruce was vulnerable.

"I have to admit Bruce is not the best conversationalist," Doris went on. "But even when your daughter presents a perky, pleasant face to the public, I'm afraid that she's really upset and just doesn't know how to express it."

"What's the need to express?" Aron retorted. "If you ask me, there's way too much talking about feelings nowadays. In my day, no one talked about feelings, just survival. I'm alive and the rest of my original family is dead. That's all you need to know. I only want my daughters should be happy, marry nice boys and give me Jewish grandchildren. And what do I get—one daughter who's going to be an old maid if she doesn't hurry up and another whose marriage is breaking up?"

"The marriage doesn't have to break up," Doris reassured him as she lowered her voice. "We're just very different. I don't mean to be rude, but I've never really met anyone like you before. Your family just isn't like the typical families I know in Rolling Hills. My friends, the people at the country club, share their feelings with each other. At lunch or dinner or mahjongg, they complain about their spouses or their daughters-in-law. Women show off the latest pieces of jewelry they've received as apology gifts from their husbands. It seems to me that even within the intimacy of your family, there's no acknowledgement of how people feel."

Aron frowned, taking in Doris's words. But he had to admit that although he was put off by what she said, she was remarkably candid.

"Then I guess you were disappointed that our children married?" he asked.

"No, of course not. We have two beautiful grandchildren. They wouldn't have been born if our kids hadn't married. Sure, there was a time when I thought Bruce was going to marry Amy Levinson, the cardiologist's daughter from Great Neck. But Bruce only wanted your daughter. And of course, once there was a pregnancy, there was no choice. There's no point in rehashing the past."

"I understand, Doris," Aron said. "Your son married the girl who was born in the DP Camp. It was fine as long as she seemed cute and happy, but now because she's going through a difficult time, you think she inherited my inability to express her feelings—even to her husband."

"Look Aron. I don't want to fight with you. I respect you enormously. I can't even imagine what you went through during the war. Then you came here, started a new life and raised a family. I give you credit for that, and for calling me and coming over here. Honestly, I can't think of a single person from the club having the *chutzpah* or the guts to do that."

"Do you want them to get divorced, Doris?"

"No, of course not."

"You know more about these things than I do," Aron said. "And you have your son's ear. I don't care how you do it, just make sure he does *teshuvah*—he repents—and apologizes to my daughter in a way that is sincere. Make this go away. We don't vant our grandchildren should grow up in a broken home. Do we Doris?"

"No, of course not," she said.

"As long as we are all alive and safe, this is a problem that can be solved," Aron added.

"They will move on. Oh, and by the way, I think they will have to move; they can't stay in that neighborhood with the hussy living across the street."

"I hear you, Aron. You're right. I'll take care of it."

On the cab ride home, Aron felt conflicted. He had accomplished his goal. Doris would fix it—of that he was certain. He wasn't exactly sure what she had in mind, but he remembered how she had gotten her way with every detail of the wedding. The truth was Aron was not worried about her method; he was counting on Doris to get good results.

He thought more about their conversation. What did Doris even want him to do? That he should have conversations about how he was cheated out of being a doctor by Hitler? Did she want him to wear his heart on his sleeve? Feelings? Doris didn't have a clue. Aron was convinced that nothing positive could ever come from talking about what he felt.

But what of his daughters? Had he deliberately taught them to hide their feelings? It seemed to him that Bronka's main activity was analyzing her feelings (which he feared was interfering with her finding a husband). She was picky, but she had also inherited his legacy of suffering. But JoJo didn't dwell on things the way Bronka did. So what was wrong?

Back at the bakery, Betty was at the counter waiting on a customer. She motioned to Aron that Judy was in the back.

"Let's go for a walk; I vant to ask you a question," Aron said, waving his wife away from the kitchen.

"I want a report," she said, following him. "So, what happened?" she asked as they walked past the stores on Union Turnpike.

"Doris will take care of it."

"What does that mean?"

"I'm not sure, but I assume she will speak to her son and set him straight. She claims it wasn't actually an affair with the neighbor woman."

"So, what was it then?"

"Don't worry about it! It's in her hands."

"But what do you mean, it wasn't actually an affair? What was it then?"

"More like an attraction, maybe a flirtation, definitely a misunderstanding, but not worth breaking up a marriage and a family."

"That's as clear as mud," Judy said. "But what's the point? You're satisfied that Doris will solve this, so there's no point in trying to press you for more information."

"But I do vant to ask you a question," Aron said.

"Go ahead."

"Doris seems to think that JoJo is unable to express her feelings because we don't do that at home the way she and Leon do."

"How does she know what goes on in our home?" Judy asked first, but then grasped the opportunity to approach her husband deeply. "But since you're asking, I think you do keep your feelings bottled up. Except when you're yelling at me. You never wanted to discuss with the girls what happened in the war until you had no choice. You're better at communicating with God than with human beings."

"And the girls?"

"In that way, they're different," Judy mused. "I think this whole situation with Bruce has triggered something in JoJo that she didn't even know was there. Not to mention, her postpartum hormones and she's now tied down with two kids. And don't forget, she had big dreams. She probably feels left out. And remember that in spite of outward appearances, both girls share not only our genes, but inherited our family legacy."

"Let's get back to work," Aron said. *Genes, family legacy, all this newfangled jargon,* Aron thought.

"The next generation, just like ours," he said to his wife, "will have to learn to live with the shadows we all carry."

CHAPTER FORTY-FOUR

AS JUDY BENT DOWN TO pick up the newspaper at the bottom of the front stoop, she breathed in the fresh spring air. She admired the yellow and pink tulips sprouting among the shrubbery, ever since she had lovingly pointed out these burgeoning signs of spring to the twins the first year they had arrived in Queens, the spring flowers had lifted Judy's spirits. But now, she noticed there were so many other reminders that a new season had arrived.

Supermarkets began showcasing palm fronds for Palm Sunday and stuffed bunny rabbits and Easter baskets. Yellow and pink marshmallow peeps—shaped like baby chickens and made of soft marshmallow rolled in colored sugar, made their yearly appearance—along with special sales on Easter hams. And the Passover food section seemed to get bigger each year. Gone were the days of mainly matzohs and macaroons and jars of gefilte fish. Now, there were selections of Passover candies and cookies, cake, kugel and pancake mixes, jars of tomato sauce, and cans of vegetables, olives and fruit. And if she failed to miss a new product, she had Bronka, her food writer, to tell her about it or even bring her a sample.

Many of Judy's neighbors had dispensed or streamlined their

Passover preparations. But as a Jew by choice with a husband who was a stickler, she was intent on following the letter of the law. In the early years, Faye had taught her everything she knew, but now, twenty-three years later, it was second nature to her. It was a huge amount of work, but the men (who let the women do the bulk of it) said it was redemptive. Judy was not a complainer, but this didn't seem exactly accurate to her. After cleaning the house, moving and lifting dishes and pots and pans, and relining shelves, covering counters and scouring and re-scouring the kitchen, it was time to prepare a sumptuous meal for both of the seder nights, and then serve it and clean up. She felt relieved—true—but she did not feel redeemed.

Now, there was more reason to be excited: Faye and Izzy would be coming back to Queens for several weeks. Izzy had some medical issues and Faye wanted him to see a specialist in New York. Becky, unfortunately, was back in a facility because she had stopped taking her medication again. Of course, Faye blamed herself because she had been distracted with Izzy's illness.

"So, it's good news/bad news," Faye had told her. "We'll come the last week in March and we'll stay through Passover as long as Izzy's medical condition warrants it. So I'm excited to be with you for Pesach—just like old times. And to be honest, I could use some company. And Izzy could too. This is very tough for him and it will be good to have the family around to distract him."

The girls were really too busy to help the way they once did, so she was happy to have Faye around once more. Of course, it would mean a bigger seder—Faye was such a party planner—but Judy was happy for the help and the company. Besides, Faye would run the show, which was just fine.

As soon as the plans to come to New York were made, Faye started calling Judy every day from Florida to discuss the seder guest list.

"I think we should have Jennie since Al and Lenore are in Israel visiting Mindy."

Mindy had disappeared before Al and Lenore's wedding. Then they found out she was in Berkeley and went out there and reconciled with her. Now she was in medical school in Tel Aviv.

"Well, obviously JoJo and Bruce and the kids. Ian can do The Four Questions. But just a suggestion, and I'm not sure you're going to like it, but I think you should invite Doris and Leon."

"I don't think they go for all the ritual," said Judy. "It's such a long night. And Aron thinks Doris looks down on us."

"Maybe so," said Faye. "Look, I thought I had Doris pegged from the wedding. But you know, I was wrong. Yeah, she's a Rolling Hills snob, but she's stepping up to the plate to save the kids' marriage. She's helping them buy a house in Dix Hills. She's helping them get a fresh start. We can always talk about real estate with her."

"Or the stock market—that's Leon's favorite topic," Judy groaned. "I don't know."

"Trust me Judy, it will be a nice gesture. And when was the last time you invited them over?"

"But we don't even have a dining room. Where will we fit all those people? Maybe we can squeeze eight into the dinette, but no more. And you don't want to put the kids at a separate table for the seder."

"Yes, of course," Faye said. "*L'dor v'dor*, from generation to generation, we pass on the story of the Exodus. That's what it's all about."

"I have it all figured out," Faye added. "We'll move all the furniture against the wall and we'll set up a long folding table, maybe two, in the middle of the living room. We'll sit on folding chairs."

"For a fancy lady like Doris? She'll just turn up her nose."

"Judy, you should know by now that you're not competing with them. You could have moved to Rolling Hills long ago. Aron can afford it. You have different values—that's all. They need to respect that. And, if their grandchildren are being taught those values, they should be familiar with them too."

Judy had made it a point from the beginning of their relationship not to argue with Faye. She knew that Faye loved to entertain and to be in the middle of things. She also suspected that this was a distraction for her from Izzy's medical issues.

"I'll check with Aron and JoJo first. Don't want to embarrass anyone," Judy said.

"And," Judy asked, "Anyone else you want me to invite?"

Faye smiled and dropped the bombshell. "You know that priest that Bronka's always talking about? I think we should invite him too."

"Really? The priest? Are you serious?"

"I am very serious. My rabbi in Miami Beach said there's nothing wrong with inviting a non-Jew to your seder for educational purposes. It helps foster understanding."

"Hmm, I see," said Judy. "So we're going to educate Bronka's priest?"

"That's the idea," said Faye.

CHAPTER FORTY-FIVE

PASSOVER WAS BRONKA'S FAVORITE HOLIDAY. As a child, it was the one time of the year that she actually felt sorry for the Rosen sisters, whom she particularly envied at Christmas time. They didn't get to go to a seder.

While she thought they were adorable, she was not jealous of the cuddly bunny rabbits and sweet little chicks scampering around their backyard right before Easter. The colorful Easter baskets overflowing with jellybeans and chocolate eggs and bunnies, and even the sisters' new pastel spring coats with rhinestones on the collar and matching straw Easter bonnets—Bronka was not envious of any of it.

Easter, in Bronka's mind, never had nor ever would, compete with Passover. As early as she could remember, it was the seder that captured her heart and soul. The tastes, symbols, songs, and smells of the seder made Bronka grateful that she was Jewish.

When she and JoJo were little, they would recite The Four Questions together—first in Yiddish, then in English. Bronka loved the song, "Dayenu," sung near the end of the first part of the seder, and the way Izzy and Papa put the emphasis on the "nu" with their booming voices. It was one of the rare times during the year when she saw her father joyful and totally present.

And, as children she and JoJo would always look for and find the afikomen, the middle matzah that Izzy had wrapped in a special cloth napkin and hid. After the dinner, Izzy would say, "We can't continue the seder without the afikomen. Who has the afikomen?"

The girls would giggle and take out the hidden matzah and be ready to hand it over, when suddenly Papa would remind them, "You deserve a gift for finding it!" They would squeal, Faye would return with a small age-appropriate gift for each girl, and they would hand over the afikomen and the second part of the seder would begin.

Part two featured more lively singing and also the opening of the door for Elijah, the prophet. The custom was to have a single woman open it and it was supposed to bring her luck to find a husband in the coming year. In the years when they were small, their neighbor Lenore, Mindy's mother, opened it; or if Aunt Becky was there, she got the honor. Now, Bronka was called on year after year to open it and this was the one part that she dreaded.

At any time of the year, Bronka could conjure up the familiar and comforting aroma of the seder plate, which was the centerpiece of the table—the egg symbolizing fertility and the circle of life; the bitter herbs, a reminder of slavery; the shank bone, a symbol of the pascal lamb; charoset, a finely chopped mixture of apples, walnuts, and sweet red wine, representing the mortar the Jewish slaves used to build the Pyramids; the salt water for tears; and the curly parsley, a green vegetable representing hope and springtime.

So too, the dinner that remained standard throughout the years—gefilte fish, chicken soup with matzoh balls, brisket, potato kugel, and tzimmes, a sweet dish of carrots, sweet potatoes and prunes.

But this year, she had a new question herself: How would Father Stan react to this observance?

CHAPTER FORTY-SIX

HOW PRISTINE THE TABLE LOOKED, Bronka thought as she admired Faye's handiwork. Two long tables with a card table at the end filled the entire room, covered with beige damask tablecloths and Faye's sterling silver from her first marriage displayed. This set of silverware was only used during Passover, as was the white china with the blue trim.

"Where should we put the highchair for Tracy?" Judy asked as she entered the room.

"Next to her parents, of course. So what do you think of the table?" Faye asked.

"It's breathtaking—you really outdid yourself. All we need to do now is put out the matzah."

When JoJo and Bruce arrived with Ian and Tracy, all the work was done.

"Did you give them anything to eat?" Faye asked JoJo.

"No, it's still early."

"Well, I suggest we feed them now. It's a long night for little ones and we don't want them to be starving during the seder," Faye said. "I'll fix them something. How about some nice soft-boiled eggs?"

"I'm not hungry," said Ian.

"You're not?" said Judy with a smile. "You're going to be up late tonight and we're not going to eat right away."

"I don't want eggs."

What do you want?"

"A treat," Ian said.

"Come with me," Judy said.

She handed each child a kosher for Passover chocolate lollipop.

Bronka noticed that the Sterns came to the seder outfitted for a cocktail party. Leon was dressed in a sharp pinstriped navy suit—sporting a wide tie with yellow sunflowers. Doris was all dolled up in a colorful Pucci dress, ornamented with her signature oversized jewelry—large gold and diamond hoop earrings, a gold and diamond heart on a thick gold chain, a diamond watch, and thick gold bracelets. On her right finger was the three-carat engagement ring Leon had given her on their twenty-fifth wedding anniversary. The original ring, which was less than a carat, was stashed away in one of her jewelry boxes. On her left hand, she sported her latest acquisition—a gold band with varying sizes of marquise cut diamonds.

Bronka noted that Doris stood in sharp contrast to the humble priest, dressed in black with his white collar. All the other guests, while dressed in proper seder attire, were unremarkable when compared to the power of Doris Stern's presence. But despite her physical command, it was clear to Bronka from the beginning that Doris and Leon were the most uncomfortable in this unfamiliar venue.

As everyone took a seat at the festive table, Leon said, "This is so nice. We usually just go to dinner at the club for Passover. There's matzah on the table, but no service, no Haggadah. This beautiful table reminds me of my childhood in Brooklyn."

Doris rolled her eyes and was quick to change the conversation.

Bronka suspected that was because she did not like to admit that she did not have the advantage. She had been raised by secular Jews, who didn't practice most of the customs. And Leon didn't do much to encourage her to engage in home rituals. But they were active in their synagogue and attended High Holiday services and occasionally went on Friday night. Doris had been raised as a proud cultural Jew, but she was unfamiliar with most of the practices that were second nature to the Lubinskis.

"Thank you for having us," Leon said. "We know Ian has been practicing The Four Questions. We're looking forward to hearing him, right Ian?"

Ian shrugged his shoulders.

"I got you a special *kipah*," Aron said right before Ian's big moment.

But Ian wasn't interested in donning the blue and white yarmulke his grandfather offered him. JoJo, who was sitting next to her son, took the skullcap Ian had resisted in putting on and placed it on his head. Ian immediately removed it.

"You're a big boy now," Izzy said. "You should wear it when you say the *Fir Kashas.*"

"I don't wanna wear it," Ian replied with a big frown.

Doris piped in, "Put on the party hat."

"It's not a party hat," Faye corrected Doris. "All the men are wearing yarmulkes."

"But I'm not a man yet," said Ian.

"You're right. You're a kid. OK, you don't have to put it on. Just say the Four Questions like you practiced," JoJo prodded him.

Ian looked around the room at his parents, his two sets of grandparents and his aunt. While Bronka adored him, she knew that he wasn't used to everyone telling him what to do and was likely suspicious of the two people he didn't know. Jennie was an old woman with red lipstick on her teeth. And there was a strange man who wore a black shirt and a black suit. Unlike the tie worn by his father and grandparents, he wore a narrow, stiff and upright white collar that was turned around. Bronka sensed there was going to be a scene, just what she didn't want Father Stan to see.

"I would rather prefer not to," he stammered and began to cry.

There was a cacophony of voices, all directed at the boy. "Don't cry, Ian. You're a big boy, Ian. Just do it. Do it like you practiced. We can't go on with the seder unless you say The Four Questions."

Ian began to sob uncontrollably.

"Do you want to recite The Four Questions now or wait till next year?" JoJo asked him.

At first, Bronka thought that the words coming out of her sister's mouth were peculiar. Next *year*? Then she remembered that JoJo had told her about Chaim Ginott's book and the advice she tried to follow: *Give the child two choices that are acceptable to* ***you.***

"Next year." Ian replied.

"Why don't we all chant it together?" Bronka was quick to suggest.

Only Doris didn't join in because she didn't know the words. Everyone was surprised that Father Stan seemed to know the words and the tune.

The guests wanted to know how Father Stan was so familiar with the seder. As they ate, he explained that he had been attending seders for years with his Jewish colleagues, but for the past several years he had also undertaken the study of Judaism in depth. He shared how he had discovered his Jewish roots and how he was now immersed in learning about the religion of his birth parents.

"So was The Last Supper actually a seder?" Leon asked.

"I think I've been asked that question at every seder I've attended." Father Stan chuckled. "On the surface, there's a resemblance. Jesus and his twelve disciples are reclining and they say prayers and drink wine.

"But I think it's safe to say that they were not eating gefilte fish or hiding the afikomen. The traditional foods that we're enjoying right now come from Eastern Europe. Jesus and his disciples probably ate a lamb they'd sacrificed.

"And, in fact, when Christians attend a seder during Holy Week it's a way of connecting to the roots of Christianity and to bond with Jews. Captivity, freedom, and covenant are essential themes in both religions."

After Father Stan summarized the discovery of his birth origins during the Holocaust, Doris asked, "So, I see you are wearing the collar, but you are a more knowledgeable Jew than I am. Can a person be both Christian and Jewish?"

"Ah, that is the very question I have been pondering and studying. What I am finding is that neither religion embraces the idea. My impression is," he smiled sheepishly, "that you have to pick a team."

Bronka didn't know which amazed her more. That Leon and Doris were still at the table and hadn't made an excuse to leave early, or that Father Stan's answers were so on point. It was as if there was nothing he did not know. She watched her father squirming in his seat, anxious to put an end to this talk about Jews and Catholics, and finish the seder, which already had dragged on way too long. JoJo and Bruce had already left with the kids; it was way past their bedtime and Tracy had had a tantrum—crying and holding her breath. The parents had to extract Ian from under the table where he was playing with a truck that Izzy had slipped to him, deciding not to wait for another tantrum to give him his afikomen gift.

Bronka also noted that her mother had listened with rapt attention, smiling and shaking her head up and down, agreeing with the priest. Bronka believed that in her heart her mother just accepted it all—the difficulties and the contradictions—and remained sweet and kind. She hoped she was her mother's daughter in that she was a caring person too, but she knew also that she had some of her father's traits.

Her thoughts quickly turned back to Father Stan. She wondered if he was glad to have been born Jewish. She was beginning to suspect that while it was a subject of curiosity for him, he had picked a side—and it wasn't the same one that she had chosen.

After Father Stan finished, at Leon's prodding, he gave a long-winded explanation of *Nostra aetate*, a document published by the Second Vatican Council in 1965. Listening to the enthusiasm in his voice, Bronka sadly concluded that his heart remained with the church.

"Ultimately, the document affirmed the validity of Judaism as a religious way of life with which Catholics must establish relations of 'mutual knowledge and respect,'" Father Stan concluded.

Bronka noted how proud the priest was to explain this document, and she watched as he grinned like a Cheshire cat when Leon said, "Thank you so much, Father Stan. We've learned so much from you tonight. Surely, the Vatican will think of a way to use your knowledge and unique perspective."

Bronka's heart sank as she recalled Faye's other expression: "Every pot has a lid." But Father Stan was never going to be her lid; she was beginning to see the truth.

Aron was off to the synagogue early, but Faye gave Judy and Bronka permission to sleep in the morning after the first seder.

"We have to make another seder tonight. Let the men go to shul. We deserve a break."

Judy had not gotten out of bed yet when Bronka, still in her pajamas, came downstairs to the kitchen to get a cup of coffee.

"Good morning, Glory," Faye greeted her cheerfully. "Let me get you coffee and if you like, I'll whip you up some matzoh brie."

"That would be great," said Bronka.

"Just let me get the matzoh brie going, then we'll sit and talk."

As the melted butter sizzled in the large frying pan, she fried the mixture, turning it over like a matzoh pancake.

"If I remember correctly Bronka, you like sour cream with your matzoh brie," said Faye.

"You really do have a great memory."

"Thanks, I like mine with strawberry preserves and that's how I gave it to you when you were little. But you liked it the way your father ate it—with sour cream. You are your father's daughter."

Bronka grimaced.

Faye placed the container of sour cream and a jar of strawberry preserves on the table. Then she poured coffee for both of them and brought out two plates of the Passover concoction.

"Some people eat this all year long, but I only like it on Passover," said Faye.

"I agree," said Bronka. "So tell me about Izzy." Bronka had been concerned since she first saw him: aged and different and old in a way he had never been before. She had been waiting to ask Faye and now was the perfect time.

Faye's mouth turned down and her brows furrowed as she revealed the truth to Bronka. The cancer had spread throughout Izzy's body. That's what the doctors in Florida had told them, but she thought that perhaps in Manhattan there would be some treatment. But there was nothing that could be done and now, he had only a few months to live.

Bronka got up from her seat and walked to the other side of the table and sobbing, embraced Faye, who was now crying too. "I'm so sorry, Faye. I love him so much; he's the only grandfather I've ever known. What will you do?"

"I'll go on," Faye said. "But I will miss him terribly."

"And Becky's not doing well now, either?"

"I don't really want to talk about Izzy or Becky now. Izzy's still in the bedroom, and I don't want him hearing us talking about him in case he comes in. He wants you to always think of him as your big, strong, Uncle Izzy. And he gets so upset whenever I mention Becky. So let's talk about the seder; what did you think?"

"The kids were awful, but it was too long a night for them. JoJo and Bruce looked cozy together, and Doris and Leon behaved themselves. But what the heck was Doris dressed for?"

"Yes, she did look like Astor's pet horse," said Faye. "But come on, *shayna maydela*, you know that's not what I mean. The priest, I want to hear about. He's tall, handsome, and brilliant. What's the deal with him?"

Bronka began to cry. What was the deal? On one hand, Bronka was embarrassed to discuss the priest with anyone. Especially after the seder, she felt so foolish daydreaming about him. She had to admit she was attracted to him. And she didn't think she was imagining it that he was drawn to her too. Do priests have the same feelings as other men do? Of course, she thought. The difference was that he had taken vows and unless he wanted to renounce his vows, he couldn't act on them. But she felt like such a tangled-up mess inside, she knew she needed to talk to someone about it. Not her mother, not JoJo. It might as well be Faye. She was still pretty sharp.

"I think there's definitely something wrong with me," Bronka said. "I actually was beginning to believe that I was in love with him, just as I thought I was in love with Ned. Stan is perfect, but I was hoping that when he told me he had found out about his Jewish origins, he might abandon the priesthood and choose to be Jewish, especially because he became so immersed in learning about it. But after his dissertation on the Catholic Church last night, I've realized it's just a stupid fantasy."

"You mean that the gezuntah Catholic would embrace Judaism?"

"But he's technically Jewish."

"And your mother—and you and your sister—are technically not. Who needs technical Jews? We need living, breathing, practicing Jews. Catholicism is what he knows and loves. I could have told you he's not giving it up."

Bronka began to sob, deep wrenching sobs, which took her breath away.

"Bronka, my dear. You're young and smart and beautiful and you're fortunate to be living in a country that's free in a time when things are changing for women. Think of what your parents had to overcome when they were your age."

Although she knew it was true, Bronka hated the comparison. She did not have to be reminded. It was part of her psyche every day of her life.

"I know this is painful to hear, but I've always been straight with you," Faye went on. "The priest is a waste of your time; he's not going to marry you any more than Ned is going to marry you. Find someone who is kind and who perhaps loves you more than you love him. And while we're all damaged, maybe find someone who doesn't depend on you to save him. I've had two husbands, Bronka, and I've loved each of them in different ways. You will love someone who returns your love.

"And stop letting your fantasies get in the way of pursuing your dreams. You want to be a journalist and not a food columnist, so try for another job somewhere else. You're not married to *The Dispatch*. And don't care what people think. I was considered a businesswoman because I worked side by side with both husbands in the bakeries. It was *our* business and that threatened some other people, but too bad.

"And Bronka, one more thing. Your father will kill me for saying this, but get out of this house."

CHAPTER FORTY-SEVEN

WHILE FAYE'S ADVICE REMAINED IN Bronka's head, she didn't act upon it until a couple of years later. The loss of Izzy a few months after Passover had been a huge blow for the entire family. Faye, although devastated from the loss of her husband of thirty years, had an uncanny ability to carry on with her life. And she did so in an admirable fashion, traveling on Eastern Airlines between Queens and Florida, while trying to manage Becky's ups and downs, and finding new friends and activities wherever she went.

Aron, however, did not handle the loss as well as Faye. While the first time Aron actually met Izzy was the day the family arrived in New York from a Displaced Persons Camp in Germany, Aron always felt grateful to his older cousin.

Although it was more than thirty years since the end of World War II, Aron's nightmares and night sweats—along with long buried memories—returned after Izzy's death. Bronka could hear him screaming while Judy tried to comfort him. His lack of sleep caused him to be morose and exhausted during the day, snapping at his workers and Judy. He became increasingly concerned about Bronka's safety and well-being. He worried when she drove at night, when she dated a new young man, or when she took the bus to work. After all, weren't buses being blown up in Israel? While he made it clear he wanted her married and producing grandchildren, he was determined to keep her under his thumb until that occurred. Faye's advice that she should leave the house always felt out of reach.

But for Bronka life was changing in other ways. Her tightly knit little work family at the Dispatch had disintegrated over time. What began as the departure of Brian Smith to Chicago after the exposure of his father as a neo-Nazi seemed to become the inspiration the others needed to leave. Steve Arlin got a job with *The Jerusalem Post* and along with his wife and two kids, moved to Israel; Manny Gottlieb went to a big PR firm, doubling his salary; the cerebral Jeremiah Krinsky took his talents to *Moment Magazine*. And Max took a job teaching journalism and supervising the student newspaper at C.W. Post College.

The members of the new regime were suspicious of Bronka and viewed her as part of the old guard. They were eager to make names for themselves, especially Lynette Gershowitz, who had been brought in by the new editor/publisher, to be a general assignment reporter. Lynette and the new boss made sure to keep Bronka in her place, relegated to the food lane, forever typing recipes.

On July 4, 1976, the twins' twenty-ninth birthday and America's bicentennial, Bronka joined her parents, Faye, her sister, Bruce and their children to view the tall ships in New York Harbor. Bruce found an observation area off the Henry Hudson Parkway from which the family could park the car and view the parade of ships across New York Harbor and up the Hudson River. Bronka was awed by the towering masts and graceful hulls against the New York City skyline. Even Aron seemed touched. "This is the land of opportunity and second chances," he mused, strangely upbeat.

Right then and there, Bronka resolved that she would give herself a second chance. She was also buoyed by the daring hostage-rescue mission carried out by commandos of the Israel Defense Forces in Entebbe on the same day. Certainly, she could be courageous enough to make a new start. She was not married to a job typing recipes at *The Jewish Dispatch*. And her social life could consist of more than waiting to be fixed up by someone in the synagogue. What could her father actually do if she left the house?

Her father couldn't stop her from spreading her wings now; she was an adult. She had lived her entire life tiptoeing around him and worrying about his feelings. On her next birthday, she would be thirty. Her biological clock was ticking and her career was going nowhere.

It was now 1977, the year Bronka would turn thirty. She had been looking for jobs for almost a year with no luck. She scoured the want ads and regularly contacted local newspapers. She couldn't even get a position at one of the New York dailies. She had a few interviews but was told that her experience and skill set didn't match the paper's needs. Manny Gottlieb said he could get her a job at his PR firm, but that's not what Bronka wanted and she wasn't ready to settle. She made up her mind that she was going to hold out at least until her thirtieth birthday.

Not only was her job search disappointing, but her love life was nonexistent. She had recently been on ten dates with Avi Liebling, the scion of the famed Yussel's Smoked Fish Company. Her family—especially Faye, who swore by their lox—had been particularly excited about him. At thirty-four, she had labeled him as "ripe and ready" (and, of course not to mention, rich). But when his former girlfriend of two years came back into his life, he dumped Bronka unceremoniously. This was followed by a disappointing date with Norman Nachman, a good-looking blond-haired fellow from the shul. Unfortunately, his personality did not measure up to his looks.

Bronka thought it strange that he chose a movie without even asking her first if she had seen it.

So even though it was May and the sun shone and the flowers bloomed and the birds sang, Bronka had hit rock bottom—in her personal and professional life. Yet there was a strange comfort in knowing that there was nowhere to go but up!

The family was eating dinner in the kitchen when the phone rang.

"Can't they wait till after dinner?" Aron said, as Bronka got up, walked over to the wall phone and answered it.

"Hi Bronka, it's Irv Rosen. I just heard about a job and I think it has your name on it." Irv Rosen always got right to the point.

"Wow, what is it? Where is it?" Bronka asked.

"Well, it's not local, but it's a great opportunity. My old army buddy, George Stein, is the managing editor at the *Philadelphia Press*. It's a daily, right in the heart of the city. George is a great guy and he's looking for a general assignment reporter. He told me off the record he'd like a bright young woman since he also needs someone to do weekly lifestyle features. The pay is decent and it would definitely be a step up for you. Look, nothing is ever certain, but if I recommended you to George, I think you have a great crack at getting the job. Of course, I'm not sure you want to relocate. So think it over and let me know."

"Thanks so much, Irv," Bronka said, taking a big breath. "I don't need to think it over. I'd love to apply for the job."

Bronka confided in her mother and begged her not to tell Aron that she would be interviewing in Philadelphia.

"All right," Judy said. "But, if you take the job, you will have to tell him and he won't be happy."

"I know Mama. But it's time for me to live my own life. JoJo's been out of the house for more than a decade. I need some space."

"I understand," Judy said. "I'm not saying you shouldn't do it. I'm just letting you know that we need to handle this delicately if you decide to go."

"If I get the job, I'm going."

As Bronka got out of the cab in front of the massive brick building that housed *The Philadelphia Press*, she was struck by how small the storefront offices of *The Jewish Dispatch* now seemed. She entered the sparkling lobby and a receptionist directed her to the fifth floor and the offices of George Stein, managing editor.

Faye always said that if something was right, it was like falling off a log. This certainly felt like it. The job would be a little bit of this and a little bit of that, including women's features, George explained. He trusted she could meet the demands of a daily newspaper. Irv Rosen had raved about her. George said she reminded him of his daughter. He gave her a tour of the editorial offices and she saw that she would have a desk among a myriad of other reporters in a very large, bustling newsroom. He introduced her to a few of the reporters, mostly male.

Then he took her out for lunch and asked if she would be able to start July the first. Would that give her enough time to relocate?

Yes, yes, and yes! She would just make her deadline—three days before her thirtieth birthday.

"Vat did I do wrong? You vant you should leave our family? Is it so terrible here? You don't pay rent, you get your meals, Mama does your laundry. You are a spoiled American girl. I don't understand. You've met plenty of boys, but none is good enough for you. There are more Jews in New York than anywhere in the world. Now you go to a strange city for a job with a *goyishe* newspaper. Are there even Jews in Philadelphia? Is there a shul? How will you find a husband there?" Aron was disappointingly himself.

While her father's words stung, there was no turning back for Bronka. Although her heart still ached for him, nothing he said or did would deter her desire to pursue her own path. But although Bronka physically left her family home, the guilt and the worry remained with her. Distance meant very little, she realized. She would forever be who she was.

PART THREE

1977-1983

CHAPTER FORTY-EIGHT

THE REALTOR SHOWED BRONKA A beautiful one-bedroom apartment in the Rittenhouse Claridge, right in Center City near shopping, restaurants and museums. But it was unfurnished and still felt pricey and her father's frugality convinced her that a second-floor furnished apartment in a row house on Spruce Street near the art museum was a better bet. The area looked a bit seedy to her, but the realtor assured her that it was safe. There was a separate bedroom with a double bed, dresser, and a desk as well as a furnished living room with a couch, coffee table, and chairs. The eat-in kitchen had a small table with three chairs. The landlord, who lived on the first floor, was a widow in her seventies. She immediately took a liking to Bronka and helped her navigate the new neighborhood.

Bronka's first few weeks at the paper were filled with stories about local government, crime, and human interest, as she attempted to learn the lay of the land in the new city. Her first Sunday there, she visited the brand-new Museum of American Jewish History. She called home after to tell her father.

"I spoke to one of the docents at the museum who gave me the names of some shuls near my apartment. I'm going to try one out on Shabbos."

The second Saturday she was in Philadelphia, Bronka decided to attend services at the synagogue on Eighteenth Street. As she embarked on the mile-and-a-half-long trek, she thought how the apartment at the Rittenhouse Claridge would have been so much more convenient not only to the shul, but to everything. *At least I'm getting some exercise*, she thought.

She arrived at 10:30, right when the Torah service was beginning, and noticed immediately that attendance was sparse. The rabbi was of medium height with dark brown hair, twinkling blue eyes and a perpetual smile. He looked to be in his forties. The cantor was an older gentleman and those on the bimah looked even older than the cantor.

There were a few couples, and a few individual men and women sprinkled throughout the sanctuary. Towards the back, there was a woman with a toddler on her lap. Three older children were shepherding a basket of candy around the aisles offering some to the congregants.

After the service, the congregants gathered for a kiddush of sponge cake, pickled herring, gefilte fish and challah. The rabbi made a beeline to Bronka.

"So, Shabbat Shalom, welcome to our shul." He extended his hand and shook Bronka's. "I'm Robert Abelov, but everyone calls me Rabbi Bob. And what's your name? What brings you here?"

Bronka introduced herself. "I really don't know too many people here."

"Well, you've come to the right place," Bob said, inviting her to lunch at his home.

A half hour later, Bronka was seated at the table in the long, narrow dining room of the rabbi's row house, which Bronka learned the synagogue owned. The rabbi was on his third contract, having been the spiritual leader of the congregation for the past ten years. The woman in the back of the sanctuary with the four children was actually his wife, Tammy.

Bronka had to admire the seamless way she welcomed her, obviously accustomed to unexpected guests on Shabbat. Also at the table was Cantor Rosenstein, who was a widower and apparently a regular at the rabbi's home.

The four children—ranging from two and a half to ten—were well-behaved and clearly used to having company. After kiddush and motzi, Tammy served a spread of cold salmon, turkey, potato salad, cole slaw, and chickpea salad.

"Too hot for cholent," Tammy commented. "I like to keep it cool and simple in the summer."

After the meal the cantor excused himself for his Shabbos nap, the children went off to play and Tammy cleared the table. When Bronka got up to help her, she said, "No, please, you're our guest and I'm sure Bob would like to chat with you. Please sit. You can help next time you're here."

Three hours later, Bronka, lulled with wine and good food and congenial company, felt more relaxed than she could remember. She had not only learned all about the synagogue and Philadelphia and its Jewish offerings, but had opened up to the rabbi about her complicated family history.

Although initially reluctant to mention the fact that her mother had never converted, when she saw how forthcoming and embracing the rabbi was, she decided it was now or never. Either he would kick her out of his house or he would have a solution. And her intuition told her that he was a man with solutions.

"I want to marry a Jewish guy, live an observant life, and raise a Jewish family," she concluded.

"You'll find someone, I'm sure. Maybe it's bashert that you've come to Philly. Hmm, let me think who I know."

CHAPTER FORTY-NINE

THE FOLLOWING SUNDAY RABBI BOB and Tammy accompanied Bronka to the mikveh. When they arrived there, they were met by the cantor and the synagogue's 80-year-old Torah reader. The rabbi explained that the conversion ceremony is a two-step process, beginning with a meeting of the *Beit Din*, a panel of three observant men. "We will meet with you in the room adjacent to the mikveh," he said. "Normally, the convert is asked questions about Judaism and why she wants to be Jewish. But your case is a special one. You have practiced and studied Judaism your entire life. You will not be quizzed. This is just a formality for you."

When the meeting ended, the rabbi and the two other men waited outside while Tammy escorted Bronka to a changing room where she undressed and showered. Bronka then walked down seven steps into the warm, room temperature water, where she immersed herself completely. After the first immersion, she recited the blessing that was on the wall. Under Tammy's direction, she then immersed herself twice more and recited the *Shehechiyanu* blessing, thanking God for having kept her in life and enabling her to reach this occasion.

Bronka felt a visceral sense of elation. She was at peace. She found this somewhat surprising because she had always feared the mikveh. She thought it would be dirty, but it was sparkling clean. She believed it was only for the ultra-Orthodox and she would feel out of place there. She had heard about a few of her peers going right before their weddings because their mothers or mothers-in-law insisted upon it, not because the girls wanted to. But she had always thought of it as an archaic custom.

How wrong she was! It was a beautiful, mystical experience that had freed her. She was now who she was and where she wanted to be. Her dunk in the mikveh had given her new life and an authentic identity. It had exorcized the ghosts of her mother's birth family, especially the Nazi-sympathizing Polish policeman, her genetic grandfather. It had laid to rest the queasiness she felt when she recalled Shmuely Ehrenberg's doubts about her roots.

After she dressed, she was greeted by hugs from the rabbi and his wife.

"You can now live your life as the observant Jew you are," said the rabbi.

"Thank you so much, Rabbi and Tammy. I can never thank you enough," she said, surprised how strangely simple yet complex her conversion was.

"It's you we should thank; we now have a wonderful new member of our synagogue family. Can we give you a ride home?"

"Thanks, but I think I want to walk and reflect on the experience. I do my best thinking when I'm walking."

"Sure enough," said the rabbi. "We'll see you in shul next Shabbos and for lunch following services."

As she walked, she felt like skipping down the street, singing Shehechiyanu, praising God for having kept her in life and enabling her to reach this joyous occasion.

Rabbi Bob and Tammy were true to their word and soon it seemed as if the entire congregation had a son or a nephew or a brother to introduce to Bronka. Most of these lasted no more than seven dates, but Bronka was busy and happy. So, too, at the office, where everyone wanted to fix up the newly confident and radiant young reporter who treated every assignment as if it were the most important story in the world, focusing intently on the article at hand. Most of all, she began to relax about finding a husband, putting herself in God's hands, convincing herself that when it was meant to be, she would meet the right person. When the time was right, she would give her father the grandchildren he so desperately wanted from her.

CHAPTER FIFTY

BRONKA HAD PLANS TO RETURN to Queens to be with her family for the seders, but two weeks before, George Stein called Bronka into his office, along with Marc Katz, a 36-year-old ace reporter who had an uncanny knack for getting his byline above the fold. George explained that NBC was launching a massive advertising campaign about its forthcoming miniseries, *Holocaust*. In addition to the ads, it included the publication of one million educational guides for teachers' organizations and Jewish and Christian religious groups, and special timing that coincided with events on the Jewish calendar. NBC also declared the first day of the broadcast, Sunday, April 16, to be Holocaust Sunday, ushering in a week of thought and reflection leading up to Passover. The final episode coincided with the thirty-fifth anniversary of the Warsaw Ghetto uprising.

"I want you to find refugees and their children," George said, "and follow them as they watch the four episodes. I want to know their reactions, not only to the series, but also to NBC's outreach. Do they think NBC is trivializing this sensitive topic? How do they feel about the story line, the acting, etc, etc? You guys know what to do. This will be a series, so I want you two to get started on it right away."

"We're on it," said Marc breathlessly, as Bronka answered, "Yes, of course."

Bronka and Marc walked out of George's office and into the coffee room.

"I can start with my shul; there are a couple of people who are refugees and the rabbi will know about the kids. But I'm ashamed to say, other than my childhood friend, Esther Zilberman, whose father identified a Nazi who was delivering cold cuts at our tenth birthday party, I don't know a lot of people who have similar experiences, especially here."

"Don't you worry; I'm on it. I have just the guy who will lead us to all the people we need."

"Who's that?"

"Well, he's a second cousin or something like that. He was born in a DP Camp . . . ."

"Just like me . . ."

"Right, and they stayed with us for a few weeks in Brooklyn when they first came over. He was, maybe two or three years old. I was about eight. He tagged after me and I tried to teach him a little English and I played blocks with him. I introduced him to the Howdy Doody Show."

"Sounds familiar," said Bronka.

"Anyway, when he came to Penn for law school and learned that I was in Philly too, he contacted me. I see him when I'm covering the courts and we've gone out for lunch a couple of times. You'd find him intriguing, Bronka. Right up your alley—brilliant guy and passionate about the Holocaust. He's working for a judge now, so his hours are basically nine to five. But believe it or not, in his spare time, he's tracking down Nazis. You should see his files!"

Although she was five minutes early when Bronka arrived at the restaurant, Marc and his cousin were already there. Marc waved to her from the table where they were seated, and Bronka immediately noticed the auburn-haired young man whose back was to her. When was the last time she had seen a man with that color hair? She tried to remember.

"Come sit next to me," Marc said. Bronka took her seat and looked at the young man at the opposite side of the table who stood to greet her. Along with his shock of reddish-brown hair, sideburns, and horn-rimmed glasses, he wore a yellow sport shirt without a tie and a brown plaid sports jacket with khaki pants. He extended his hand and Bronka, with her steel trap memory, suddenly remembered she had met him before, although now he looked more mature and professional.

"Haven't we met before?" Oren asked Bronka. "You look familiar to me."

"You went to Columbia, right?"

"Yup."

"We met at a party about ten years ago."

"That's right. Bronka. Of course—the girl with the unusual name. Do you remember that I called you, but you told me you were seeing someone?

"Sorry 'bout that. It didn't work out."

Marc had already briefed both Bronka and Oren on the basics of each other. Besides their common birth stories, he was thirty-two, had grown up first in Brooklyn and then in East Meadow on Long Island. He had a younger brother, who was a doctor. Both Bronka and Oren were currently unattached.

It would be no problem for Oren to hook the two reporters up with Holocaust survivors and their children in the Philadelphia area, he said. He was connected to a whole network.

"I told you Oren was a great resource for us," Marc said.

"Great," said Bronka. "How are you connected to all of these survivors and their families?"

"Well, I met a guy who is a Social Security investigator. He used to work for the INS and he quit because he discovered that the agency was dragging its feet on bringing these Nazis to justice. He told me that Congresswoman Liz Holtzman got wind of it and found out there was a list of more than fifty former Nazis hiding in plain sight in the United States. She sponsored legislation to correct this wrong, and in fact, she's hoping to move all of the Nazi-hunting efforts to the Department of Justice in the near future. I'm hoping to get a job there, but in the last few years, I've been doing a bit of detective work myself, researching this. And I've met lots of survivors and their children in my quest. Believe it or not, there's actually one guy on the list who lives right in this area.

"He was a guard at Auschwitz-Birkenau, and he's moved and changed his name several times. In fact, I think at one point, he actually lived in Queens."

"What name did he use in Queens?"

"Roy Smith."

"Roy Smith!" Bronka called out incredulously.

"Don't tell me you know him."

"Well, I wouldn't exactly say I know him personally, but his son was a friend and colleague of mine. We worked for the same Jewish newspaper and we covered a Nazi demonstration on Long Island. It turned out that his father was one of the leaders. To make a long story short, I found out later that his identity had been discovered earlier. He had been a Nazi SS Officer who used a whip at Auschwitz to herd naked Jews into the gas chamber. Meantime, Roy Smith worked in a kosher deli."

“You can’t make this stuff up,” said Oren. “Did you get a big scoop?”

“Not really because I had promised Brian I wouldn’t write about his father and then Brian left town. I think he’s in Chicago now. And the father just disappeared. Don’t know what happened to his wife either.”

“She’s with him, they’re living in a garden apartment in Wynnewood. She’s a nurse, working at Wynnewood General Hospital under the name of Margaret Dougherty, her maiden name. And he’s going by the name, Rory Dougherty.”

“You’re kidding; he’s trying to pass himself off as Irish now?”

“Looks that way. I think he’s just trying to blend in with his wife.”

“Is he working?”

“He’s the super at the garden apartment complex where they live. Neither he nor his wife leave Wynnewood, a suburb—interestingly—that has a big synagogue and many Jews. I’ve been after him for two years now.”

“Have you seen him?”

“I have. Taking out the garbage outside the apartment complex. And one day I was in the Wegmans in Wynnewood—by the way, they have a great selection of kosher food—and I saw him shopping there. The Social Security investigator dropped in on him, but he insists that he’s Rory Dougherty. He says his father was Irish and his mother, German.”

“So what are you going to do now?”

“Well, if you’d like me to take you on a field trip to either his apartment or Wegmans, I’d be happy to do it. But other than shaking him up a bit, there’ll be no result. He’ll just deny everything and insist it’s a big mistake. Think about it: he first came here in 1949—it’s almost thirty years. I think he figures he’s gotten away with it, and maybe he has.”

Bronka and Marc had more people to interview and more material for their series than they knew what to do with. Bronka was in daily—if not hourly—contact with Oren; in addition to being an invaluable resource for her story, she was mesmerized by all they had in common.

He didn't waste any time asking her out. Their first date was at a cozy Italian restaurant, where they both perused the menu looking for non-meat items.

"So, are you kosher?" He asked her.

"I'm trying," she said. "I'm not about to give up eating out, but I stick to dairy and fish—no meat. How about you?"

"Me too," he said. "I used to eat chicken out, but I gave that up about a year ago. Now, I'm strictly dairy and fish."

So easy peasy, thought Bronka. She didn't have to go into a whole explanation with him.

Neither did she have to make him understand what it meant to be the child of survivors. What it was to have spent your first years in a Displaced Persons Camp and then come to America as a child immigrant, not knowing the language or the culture.

"All of a sudden, we—the children of survivors—are a phenomenon," said Oren, as he took a forkful of eggplant parmesan.

"By any chance, are you familiar with the article Helen Epstein wrote in the New York Times?" he went on.

"Yes," she replied. "'The Heirs of the Holocaust.' For the first time in my life, I realized that what went on in my family wasn't unique to us. I found it so comforting to find out that we're part of a group with common feelings and behaviors."

Oren reached across the table and put his hand on Bronka's and she could feel the tenderness in his touch. She thought he looked at her as if she were the brightest and most knowledgeable girl he had ever met.

"I'm honored to be a member of any group you're in," he said.

"Ditto," she answered.

"How's the manicotti? Mind if I taste it?"

"It's delicious—go ahead, be my guest. This is such a huge portion."

Oren took his fork and ate from her plate.

Bronka felt as if she were watching an idealized version of herself in a movie. *Oh, I wish Faye and Mama and JoJo could see me now.* Bronka Lubinski—at last comfortable in her own skin, being appreciated for her own special qualities. The recipient of adoring looks, rapt attention, and respect. Who would believe it?

Faye had told her that when she found the right one it would be easy. She hadn't really understood what she meant at the time, but now it was clear. Oren made her feel comfortable and beautiful and smart and special. And she knew in her heart of hearts that this was no fantasy; everything about it was real. She could not stop smiling.

That first date, he took her home, right to the door of her rowhouse. Oren was a gentleman, she thought.

"I really enjoyed your company tonight, Bronka. Let's do this again soon."

"Yes, I'd love to."

"Would you mind if I kiss you good night?"

She smiled and nodded. They embraced and he kissed her sweetly, gently, as if she were precious. Bronka knew that she had finally come home.

Oren was as good as his word, a real mensch, Bronka thought. He would stop by her office at the end of the day and ask her if she wanted to go for a drink or dinner. He did not play coy. This man was genuine. She stopped wondering what happened with Ned and threw herself into her work and the new relationship, which overlapped in so many ways.

Those that Marc and Bronka interviewed expressed mixed reactions to the TV series. Several agreed with Elie Wiesel, who said it "trivialized" the Holocaust. But others were grateful that the series had portrayed both Jewish resistance and collaboration. They were also glad to see the way the program showed how average Germans began to believe and act upon the Nazi lies. The German Dorf family, whose father is a prominent SS member, and the German-Jewish Weiss family, whose mother believes the Nazis will not harm her upstanding, respectable family, were typical of the time. There were compliments on the scope of the series—from Kristallnacht, to euthanasia, to the Warsaw Ghetto, to Auschwitz. While some thought the commercialized show glamorized and colorized the Holocaust, others felt that it brought the grotesque story home in a way that black and white, grainy newsreels did not.

About 120 million people—half of the population of the United States—watched the series. And one thing was certain—the subject of the Shoah and Hitler's Final Solution was now out of the closet. It had a name—Holocaust—and after more than thirty years of pretending not to see what was in plain sight, the American public, Jew and non-Jew alike, acknowledged and embraced it. This would have tangible results in the years to come for the survivors, their children, and the general public. These were the conclusions of the final article in the series by Marc and Bronka.

Both George and Marc also asked Bronka to write an opinion piece about her perceptions as a member of the Second Generation of Holocaust Survivors. This piece would be the most personal thing she had ever written, and she worked hard, trying to get across her feelings and knowledge in an accessible but truthful way.

"Now I know who I am and that I am not alone, and I am proud and comforted to be a 2G (second generation)," her piece concluded.

"While it was a fictionalized version, NBC's Holocaust miniseries, gave my family's legacy—and millions of other families—a name and a voice. It is now up to all of us who care about decency and justice and human rights to learn more, to support the survivors, to punish the perpetrators and to speak out whenever we see prejudice and discrimination. If we learned anything from the Holocaust, it is that it took place in incremental steps while average people let it happen."

On the Friday morning of Passover eve, Bronka was finally heading home to the seders in Queens and Oren Lieberman had offered to give her a ride. He was going in the same direction to his family's home in East Meadow. He stopped in front of her rowhouse, honked, and she came out.

"I couldn't find a parking space," he said.

"Don't worry, it's a problem here; probably a good thing that I don't have a car." She climbed into the passenger seat of his car and they headed east towards New York.

While they had only known each other a few weeks, the chemistry was palpable. Bronka couldn't remember when she had felt so absolutely comfortable with a man. Their interests aligned and they finished each other's sentences.

"Your op-ed was magnificent. I'm so proud of you and I hope you're proud of yourself," Oren said.

"Thanks, that means a lot. But as soon as I've accomplished one thing, I just move on and try to find the next thing to succeed at."

"You know, you may have found your niche with this 2G stuff. Perhaps write a column or a book."

"Thanks for your confidence. I think it's a little soon, but it's certainly a niche in which I'm comfortable and feel like I belong. I think we may need to wait a bit to see how it all shakes out."

"Not necessarily. Don't you want to be on the cutting edge?"

"Well, we'll see. I'm concentrating on the visit home right now. I haven't seen my sister and the kids for a while. I'm looking forward to spending some time with them," Bronka continued, telling him about JoJo and her plight and ultimate happiness.

"She's my twin, but she's all set and I'm still figuring out what I want to be when I grow up."

"Well, we definitely have that in common." He chuckled.

"Anyway, I don't want to talk about all that now. Tell me what's doing with Roy Smith," Bronka said.

"Nothing much. The fellow who gave me the list—the Social Security investigator—went to see him on a supposed issue, but he came up with nothing. He told me that he just lied and denied—and smirked."

"Oy, that's the guy," said Bronka as she continued. Then, "So listen, I may have something for you."

Bronka went on to tell him about Brian and the Gardens and Father Stan's translation of Roy's letters. If he could get ahold of them, they would be incriminating, as well as an amazing story. She couldn't write about it, but perhaps Oren could put the information to good use. She still felt conflicted suggesting it, but knew it was the right thing to do.

"So how do I get in touch with Father Stan?" Oren asked.

Oren dropped Bronka off at her home and while she had not intended to invite him in, Faye came running out of the house to greet them when she spotted the car in the driveway. She and Judy were preparing for the seder and she insisted he come in for a minute to taste her charoset with the raisins.

"Wow," said Oren once inside, swallowing the spoonful of charoset with raisins, "I'll have to tell my mother about your secret ingredient, Faye. But I must be going, I have to help set up the tables and chairs for our guests."

"Well, don't be a stranger, Oren," said Faye. "*Ziesen Pesach* to you and your family."

"*Ziesen Pesach* to you and all of the Lubinskis," said Oren.

The minute they heard the car pull away, Faye, with a big smile on her face, ran over to Judy and hugged her tight. She appeared to be jumping up and down, which was quite a feat for someone pushing ninety.

"This is it! He has the right look. And he's such a lovely young man," Faye exclaimed.

Judy smiled approvingly, and Bronka blushed, knowing that Faye spoke the truth.

When Oren got home, he helped his mother bring the tables and chairs up from the basement. Then when he was finished, he put in a call to Father Stan, introduced himself and told him what he wanted.

"Any friend of Bronka's is a friend of mine," the priest said. "I haven't seen her for a long time. How she's doing?"

"She's doing great, living in Philadelphia and making a name for herself as a journalist."

"I'm glad to hear that," he said. "As far as your request goes, I'm going to have to make a phone call first. The information was given to me in confidence, and while it was not strictly a confession, I believe I must ask the person who brought them to me whether I am free to share them."

An hour later, Father Stan called Oren. "I have permission to give you the documents, and if you want to pursue him, they're a smoking gun. If you want copies, I'll make them for you. I can't believe that scoundrel is still free. But there's still not much of a taste for bringing those Nazis to justice."

"I'm hopeful that will change soon," Oren said.

"Please bring Bronka with you when you come to pick them up." The priest said. "I'd love to see her."

"Oren, I really don't want to go," Bronka said when Oren called her to ask if she would accompany him to meet Father Stan.

"I have to get back to work," she said. "I thought we were going to leave at six a.m. for Philly. Now, you're meeting him at ten."

"I'm sure it won't take long. I'm taking the day off, and you should too."

Bronka was embarrassed to tell Oren that she simply did not want to see Father Stan. While at least she hadn't told the priest how she felt about him, she figured he knew that she had had a crush on him; she didn't want to humiliate herself, especially in front of Oren.

"What are you going to do, take the train?" Oren asked. "Doesn't make sense when you have a door-to-door escort?"

Oren was right, she thought. And besides, she wanted to be with him every minute she could.

When they arrived at the diocese, the monsignor greeted them warmly, effusively shaking their hands.

"This is one special young woman," he said to Oren.

"Yes, she is."

The priest looked at her intensely with his dark brown eyes twinkling, and said, "You know I quote you all the time."

"No, you don't. You're the quote-worthy one," she said, worrying that he was playing with her, while hoping to hide her feelings from Oren.

"No, I do. I remember what you said about keeping kosher—that it's a discipline and it reminds you that you're part of the Jewish people. It elevates what would be an animal act."

"And how does that come up in conversation?"

"Parishioners ask me about the ban on eating meat on Friday that was lifted in 1966. I think you made such an eloquent case for those types of restrictions. I, myself, still observe the ban. I can't bring myself to eat meat on Friday."

So, the priest hadn't forgotten her, she thought. And she supposed she would never forget him either, but she was glad that she had come and that she was moving on. But first, she needed to ask about Brian.

"How is Brian?" Bronka asked the priest.

"Well, you know he's in Chicago, making a name for himself as a news photographer."

"Does he see his parents?"

"He said he speaks with his mother on the phone from time to time, but he will have absolutely nothing to do with his father. I would not be handing these documents over to Oren without his blessing. He hasn't gotten over his anger; he still wants his father brought to justice."

The priest handed Oren a manila envelope that had been sitting on his desk. "Here are the materials. And what will happen to Rudolf Schmidt?"

"It's hard to say—probably nothing immediately," said Oren. "I'm hoping that there will be a new unit, which will be part of the Department of Justice, which will handle these matters. But we can only hope and do our best."

As they said their goodbye's, Father Stan took her right hand and raised it to his lips and kissed it. She was surprised yet pleased: she felt nothing at all.

CHAPTER FIFTY-ONE

ONCE HE GOT HOME AND was alone, Oren opened the envelope the Monsignor had given him and began reading the documents.

CONFIDENTIAL LETTER OF ACCEPTANCE TO OBERFUHRER RUDOLF SCHMIDT

20 APRIL 1943

Dear Oberfuhrer Schmidt:

You will begin your work at The Auschwitz camp on Monday, 26 April, 1943.

You should know that your position as a guard is of the utmost importance. Your work is highly confidential. Auschwitz plays a special role in the resolution of the Jewish question. There you will help carry out the most advanced methods to permit the execution of the Fuhrer's order in the shortest possible time and without arousing much attention.

The so-called "resettlement action" is as follows: The Jews arrive in special trains toward evening and are driven on special tracks to areas of the camp specifically set aside for this purpose. There the Jews are unloaded and examined for their fitness to work by a team of doctors, in the presence of the camp commandant and several SS officers.

The unfit go to cellars in a large house which are entered from outside. Your responsibility is with them. You will tell them that they are to be cleansed and disinfected for their new assignments and direct them to a cellar area, which is lined with benches to the left and right. You will order them to completely undress to be bathed.

To avoid panic and to prevent disturbances of any kind, you will instruct them to arrange their clothing neatly under their respective numbers, so that they will be able to find their things again after their shower. It is your responsibility to ensure that everything proceeds in a perfectly ordered fashion.

In the shower room are three large pillars, into which certain materials can be lowered from outside the cellar room. When three- to four-hundred people have been herded into this room, the doors are shut, and containers are dropped down into the pillars. As soon as the containers touch the base of the pillars, they release the poison.

After a few minutes, the door will open on the other side, where the elevator is located. The hair of the corpses will be cut off, and gold-filled teeth will be extracted. Then the corpses are loaded into elevators and brought up to the first floor, where ten large crematoria are located. The job itself is performed by Jewish prisoners—Sonderkommandos—who will never leave this camp alive.

The results of this "resettlement action" to date: 500,000 Jews. Current capacity of the "resettlement action" ovens: 10,000 in 24 hours.

Yours Truly,
Obersturmbannfuhrer Rudolf Hess,
Auschwitz Commandant

After Oren finished reading it, he looked up and thought: *the smoking gun.*

CHAPTER FIFTY-TWO

IT WAS THE BEST SUMMER of Bronka's life, even though she spent it in Philadelphia, a city that struck her as a bit dreary. Her life had become bright and shining because she now spent virtually all of her time—when she was not working—with Oren.

Her opinion of Oren was glowing. Oren was smart. Oren was articulate. He was kind and considerate. He didn't play games. They shared common interests and values. He hunted Nazis. He wasn't a wise guy. He was steady and consistent. He had no guile. He was a mensch.

He was a tender lover. He took his time, he didn't rush Bronka. He was patient and tuned in to her anxiety and lack of experience.

In his presence, Bronka became less anxious, more confident. Gone were the extreme highs and lows she had experienced with Ned. She was certain that this relationship was meant to be—*bashert.* Even when they had an occasional argument, he was always ready to smooth things over. He didn't hold a grudge. She did not even worry about whether she would lose him. That's how certain she was of his love. And there was no desperation to hers. It was right, comfortable.

On Labor Day weekend, Bronka felt a bit sad that the summer was coming to an end. They had spent Sunday at a barbecue, hosted by George Stein and his wife for the *Philadelphia Press* staff.

Bronka spent the afternoon hand in hand with Oren, stealing an occasional kiss. Much to her chagrin, Bronka's male colleagues had a field day teasing them.

"So, when are the two of you going to tie the knot? The girl's not getting any younger."

"Look at the lovebirds; that's because they're not married yet!"

"Wait til you find out what she's really like, Oren. If you want to know, just ask us. She's a piranha when she's chasing a story."

Bronka wasn't concerned about Oren's reaction, but she was annoyed that her male coworkers would play with her that way. Sexism was still alive and kicking, she realized. She doubted they would do that to a guy—one of their own.

They were among the earliest guests to leave and when they went back to Bronka's apartment, Oren kicked his shoes off and sat down on the sofa close to Bronka. He put his arm around her.

"I'm sorry my colleagues got carried away," Bronka said. "They do think they have the right to tease me, but they're usually not that bad at work. Must have been drinking too much."

"They're obnoxious," he said. "Don't give it any thought."

"I'm not."

"Anyway, I have something I've been meaning to discuss with you. Just wait a second." He reached into his pocket and took out a little datebook.

"Honey," he said, "I need to make a date with you."

"When, for what?"

"I'm thinking sometime in December. Do you have any free Sundays then?"

"I don't think I have anything planned then. Why?"

Oren got off the couch, got down on his knees and reached into his other pocket.

"Will you marry me?"

"Oh yes, of course, yes."

He placed a diamond ring on her left ring finger.

"How did you know my size and that I always wanted a round stone with baguettes on either side?"

"I had a little help from your mom."

"You mean, she knew this was happening—and she didn't let on?"

"Yes, she promised me she'd keep the secret."

"Well, keeping secrets is one of her strengths."

A couple of weeks after the proposal, the newly engaged couple traveled to New York so the two families could meet in advance of the December wedding. They both agreed that the festivities would be held at the East Meadow Jewish Center, the congregation where the Liebermans belonged. It had a beautiful ballroom and a parking lot, which Aron's synagogue in Queens lacked. They also had the bulk of the guests; although both Marek and Chaya Lieberman were Holocaust survivors and had lost most of their family in the Holocaust. Unlike the reclusive Lubinskis, they had more than a hundred substitute relatives in the friends they had acquired. These included people from the DP Camp and other refugees they had met and bonded with throughout their years in America. Unlike the solitary Lubinskis, they observed holidays, attended picnics and other events, and celebrated simchas with them. Even though it was traditional for the bride's parents to foot the bill, the Liebermans offered to split the costs.

Whereas JoJo's wedding had been whipped up last minute, Judy and Faye and Chaya accompanied Bronka to Kleinfeld's to choose her wedding gown—an ivory satin A-line dress with lace applique and delicate beading. Even Aron rented a tuxedo, following the dress code Bronka and Oren had decided upon.

Standing under the chuppah, Aron beamed. His new son-in-law and his family had been worth waiting for. His heart soared as the final of the seven blessings were sung: *Kol sasson v'eKol simcha, kol chatan v'ekol kallah* . . . .

"Blessed are You Who causes the couple to rejoice, one with the other."

After Oren stomped on the wine glass and shattered it with his shoe, the couple kissed and led the bridal party in marching back down the aisle to the band playing 'Kol Sasson' . . . .

The reception that followed was exuberant and raucous with the guests engaging in a forty-minute hora. Not only were the bride and groom hoisted on chairs while the guests sang and danced around them, but so too, were their parents. As Aron clapped his hands and allowed himself to be swept away in the joy, he recited Shehechiyanu to himself.

CHAPTER FIFTY-THREE

IN 1979, OREN LIEBERMAN WAS among the first group of attorneys to be hired for the Office of Special Investigations (OSI), whose purpose was to investigate and prosecute cases against Nazi offenders. The group was tasked with conducting civil proceedings that could result in denaturalization and deportation, and for finding and prosecuting those who had participated in Axis-sponsored persecution on the basis of race, religion, national origin, or political views. Naturalization and visa fraud were also prosecuted since there was no statute of limitations on civil immigration and naturalization fraud claims.

Oren was thrilled to be where he wanted to be, but soon found that he spent more time in archives looking at microfilm and in meetings than he actually spent in courtrooms. Still, he loved it, and with the copies of the documents the Monsignor had given him, he continued to build a meticulous case against Rudolf Schmidt/Roy Smith/Rory Dougherty.

Oren's new position meant a move to Washington, DC, where Bronka quickly found a synagogue to join, and she began her job as a reporter and biweekly columnist at the *Washington Jewish Times*.

She also focused on getting pregnant, which was not happening as fast as she would have liked. She wanted children desperately, both for herself and Oren, and—secretly—for her father.

In October, her editor asked her to take a look at the National March on Washington for Lesbian and Gay Rights. It wasn't exactly an assignment.

"Just take a walk over to the Mall and see if you can find a Jewish angle. I know you're not going to see Chassidim marching, but if there's anything that strikes you as Jewish, write it up."

With her notebook in hand, she observed what seemed to be more than one hundred thousand gay men, lesbians, bisexuals, transgender people, and their straight supporters, demanding equal civil rights and the passage of legislation. The march started at Fourth Street and the National Mall, turned left onto Pennsylvania Avenue, proceeded towards the White House, and ended in a rally between the Washington Monument and the reflecting pool. She and Oren walked along as she scoured the marchers for Jews.

She spotted a few synagogue members and stopped to interview them. There was a couple supporting their twenty-five-year-old son. Also marching were two women who shared a household and were happy to be quoted in the paper.

As she finished writing in her reporter's notebook, she heard someone call her name.

"Hey Bronka Lubinski, is that you?"

She turned around and to her surprise saw that it was Bobby Bass, JoJo's costar in the high school production of *The Boyfriend*. She noted that he looked very buff and handsome in a tight tee shirt and jeans.

"So, Bronka, what are you doing here? You're not gay, are you?"

"No, I'm covering it for *The Washington Jewish Times*."

"Wow, do you want to quote me?"

"Only, if you want to."

"Sure, I'll go on the record. Just wait a minute 'til my boyfriend comes back. He went to find a porta-potty."

"Look who I found, Ned," said Bobby as he approached.

And there he was, the bon vivant, world traveler, erudite philosopher. She had spent a decade wondering about why he had rejected her. He looked shrunken; he was slight, compared to the robust Bobby. And who was he with? Bobby Bass, a mediocre singer, an average guy from Bellerose, Queens. He got by in high school with his affability and good looks. Bobby was never a heavyweight. Preston had seemed more like Ned's speed; he was sophisticated and smart and debonair. Bobby was just so ordinary. She had thought that Ned was a cut above all that.

Not my problem, she thought as she decided to be gracious and extended her hand to Ned, who looked very uncomfortable.

"So this is my husband, Oren. Oren, meet Ned and Bobby, my friends from high school."

The men shook hands.

"So, you want to talk to Bronka on the record about why we're here, Ned?"

Ned looked as if he had seen a ghost. He looked like if he could have willed the pavement to open up and suck him in, he would have done it.

"Bronka," he said, looking like he might cry. "I'm going to be honest with you. I just can't do it. My mother doesn't know."

Ned's response only confirmed in Bronka's mind how dense Bobby was. Clearly he must have known Ned was keeping his orientation a secret from his mother. Bobby was ordinary and insensitive to boot. It also made her realize that she never could have healed Ned's pain. But if he had been open and honest with her, perhaps she could have been a good friend to him. It had not been about her after all.

"Sure, no problem." Bronka said. "Thanks anyway, great to see you again, guys. Good luck."

She walked away arm in arm with Oren, exorcised of one more torment in her life.

CHAPTER FIFTY-THREE

IN DECEMBER 1980, BRONKA AND Oren had been married for a year and had been trying for a child for much of that time. They had hoped to announce a pregnancy by their first anniversary. Every time she saw her father or spoke to him on the phone, he would say, "*Nu* . . . so do you have any news for me?"

She wished she could tell him how much it hurt and distressed her when he asked her that. Every month when she got her period, she was despondent. Didn't her father know that she would tell him if she had news? Oren's younger brother, Josh, and his wife, already had two kids and JoJo's son, Ian, was approaching bar mitzvah age. Bronka went from specialist to specialist, who told her that there was nothing wrong with her and she just needed to relax and keep track of her ovulation schedule.

Finally, she became so frustrated and disappointed checking every month that she decided to take a break. She suggested to Oren that they consider adoption.

"We can look into it, honey, but I believe in my heart of hearts that we'll have a biological child of our own," he said, trying to comfort her. "And it's only been a year. Why don't we just forget about it for a while? Maybe you need a project to take your mind off this. There's that gathering of Holocaust Survivors planned for June in Jerusalem you told me about. Why don't we go and invite our parents and siblings to join us? You can write it up for the paper."

Bronka had never been to Israel and began to get excited about the idea. It made sense to go to Israel before she had a child. And maybe it would be therapeutic for her father to be with other survivors.

But by early 1981, even before Bronka and Oren could finalize plans to go to Israel, she found out she was pregnant.

She was surprised and thrilled, but also a little concerned about how this would affect the plans to go to Israel for the World Gathering. She had done such a great job of putting pregnancy thoughts on the backburner; she was consumed with the planned conference. Four months into the pregnancy, Bronka got a big shock.

"You're going to have twins, young lady," said the ob-gyn. "Are there twins in your family?"

"Well, I'm a fraternal twin. I have a sister."

"Yes, fraternal twins run in the family. Identical are a fluke. Let me see, you're due in October, but twins often come early, so figure it could be September or even earlier."

"So, will I be able to travel to Israel in June?"

"I don't see why not, unless, of course, complications develop. This is always a possibility, especially with twins."

After she told Oren, Bronka got on the phone to convey the exciting news to her parents. That was all Aron had to hear.

"The trip to Israel is off," he said. "We're not taking a chance."

"I think June will be all right. I won't be in the third trimester yet."

"And what if something happens there?" Aron asked.

"They have wonderful doctors and hospitals in Israel," Bronka countered. "Hadassah Hospital is in Jerusalem."

"We'll go another time," said her father.

"But Ernest Michel, the head of UJA-Federation, says this will never happen again. It's a once in a lifetime event."

"Never again, when have I heard that?" Aron said. "Trust me, if it's a success, there'll be another one. Your mother and I are not going and if I could I would lock you in the closet to make sure you don't go either. The most important thing is the health of the *kinder.*"

While Oren's parents still wanted to go, Chaya said she did not want to tangle with Aron. She had already recruited several of their survivor friends to go with them, so she wanted to make the trip anyway. Oren encouraged his parents to go to the Gathering with their friends and he and Bronka deferred to Aron and stayed home.

Bronka got bigger and bigger and was delighted to feel the babies moving in her womb. She bought a comfortable maternity wardrobe with a few nice pieces she could wear to the office. But as time went on, she began to feel like an elephant. They discussed names. She and Oren ordered nursery furniture for their spare bedroom, which would be delivered once the babies were born. Bronka would not hear about setting up in advance; she was much too superstitious.

Oren was still busy at work tracking down former Nazis. And, just about the time they would have been in Israel for the Gathering, his supervisor gave him the go-ahead to move in on Rudolf Schmidt/Roy Smith/Rory Dougherty. During his tenure at OSI, he had augmented the dossier, adding to the microfilm, priest's documents, the testimonies from Irv Rosen, Jakob Zilberman, Moe Solomon, and others as well as the newspaper clippings from the Fatherland Gardens affair. It was clear that he was guilty on two counts: he had lied to get into the United States in 1949, and he had been directly responsible for the persecution and murder of Jews, shepherding them into the gas chamber.

Oren, along with his supervisor Neal Scher and the OSI Director Allen Ryan, traveled to Philadelphia in the middle of July to meet with Schmidt in his Wynnewood apartment. It was a small one-bedroom with a narrow dining room and living room and a tiny kitchen. He met with them alone, sitting at the laminated wood kitchen table, with no lawyer present. Schmidt's appearance and demeanor had changed over time. He was now obese with a red face and breathed with a wheeze. He tried to assume a pleasant façade, attempting to convince them that he had tried to comfort and assist the prisoners instead of threatening them with a whip on their way into the gas chamber. He had just been doing his job. He had no choice. But his story was simply not believable in light of the overwhelming evidence Oren had amassed.

The OSI team returned to Washington and decided to meet with him once again to give him the opportunity to have a lawyer present. The meeting was scheduled for August 28. Oren told Bronka that he was concerned about leaving her alone since she was huge and it was getting dangerously close to September, the month the doctor said she was likely to deliver.

"I don't want to miss the birth of our babies," he said. "I'd feel terrible if I was off Nazi-hunting when you gave birth."

"You're not going to miss either," she said. "We've both devoted years and years to tracking down this demon. You go, and I'll just make sure the babies wait. Anyway, it's still August. The doctor is talking about September."

The OSI trio returned for a second meeting, and this time Schmidt's lawyer was present.

"Look, his wife is a respected nurse in the community, his son is a photographer with the *Chicago Times* and his daughter is in the Air Force. Can we cut a deal?" the lawyer for Schmidt asked.

"What kind of deal?" Oren asked.

"He'll give up his U.S. citizenship voluntarily and leave the country," his lawyer suggested. "You won't have to take him in or bother with court proceedings."

"I suppose we can do that," said Ryan. "We'll go back to Washington and prepare the paperwork. I don't think it will be a problem."

On the way home on the train, Oren asked his boss why he so readily agreed. "I'm not really convinced that this is such a great idea; why do you think it is?"

"It would take years to litigate. We're getting the result we wanted. It's a win."

Oren returned home and embraced his very pregnant wife, who looked like she was going to pop any minute. An hour later, the phone rang and Ryan was on the line with some shocking news. He told Oren that he had just received a call from Schmidt's attorney. The lawyer reported that after the OSI team left, Schmidt became agitated, began breathing heavily and sweating profusely. He said that when he asked what was wrong, Schmidt collapsed and fell to the floor.

"I called an ambulance, and he was rushed to Wynnewood Hospital," the attorney said. "He's unconscious and in critical condition in the ICU. It doesn't look good."

Four days later, at six o'clock in the morning, Bronka's water broke and she began to have contractions. At nine o'clock, before they headed for the hospital, Oren called the office to say he wouldn't be in.

"Rudolf Schmidt died this morning," said his supervisor, Neal Scher. "You know it's September first—forty-two years since Hitler started World War II."

At one seventeen that afternoon, twin boys were born to Bronka and Oren. They came into the world with lusty cries, both more than six pounds each—a substantial size for infants born more than a month early. Their parents named them Elijah and Samson.

Bronka was thirty-four years old, and she could not remember a time when she had not dreamed of having children. As she held her babies for the first time, she wept with joy. She had waited, hoped, and prayed for this moment. And now, these perfect infants were here—and they belonged to her and Oren. They had been doubly blessed. She uttered a silent prayer of thanksgiving.

CHAPTER FIFTY-FIVE

ARON HAD BEEN RIGHT. THERE was another Gathering. The American Gathering of Jewish Holocaust Survivors took place in Washington, DC, in April 1983. The entire Lubinski clan joined with fourteen thousand other survivors and their families. Some survivors set up tables or held signs—or even wore t-shirts with names of hometowns and long-lost relatives and friends they had been searching for since the end of World War II. Surprisingly, there were even a few reunions.

The formal ending of The Gathering was marked by the announcement that two federal buildings near the Mall would be set aside to house a permanent memorial to the six million Jews murdered as part of Hitler's Final Solution.

When the ceremonies were over, the Lubinskis gathered on the capitol steps for a group photograph. Bronka was covering the event for *The Washington Jewish Times* and she asked the photographer who was assigned to the story to take some pictures of the family.

"Say 'cheese,'" the photographer said as he ran forward to tickle the little ones to make them laugh in between shots. When he was satisfied that he had employed all the tricks of his trade and captured the entire group smiling, he told Bronka he'd have some photos in a few days.

Aron looked at his wife, Judy, his daughters, Bronka and JoJo, his sons-in-law, Oren and Bruce, and his four grandchildren, Ian, Tracy, Elijah, and Samson. He smiled as his heart soared and he asked the entire family to recite the Shehechiyanu with him, right there on the steps, all of them together.

"Blessed Art Thou, our Lord our God, King of the Universe, who has kept us in life and preserved us, and enabled us to reach this day."

It had been a long time in coming, but as Aron Lubinski surveyed his family, he felt pride and joy—and hope. He remembered the family he had lost in Europe, but now he and his wife had built a new one. In his mind, he had finally defeated Hitler.

GLOSSARY

Aliyah – The Hebrew word aliyah means "going up." It has a double meaning. It is the honor given to a worshiper of being called to say a blessing during the Torah reading. In addition, it means moving to Israel.

Balabosta – Efficient Jewish homemaker.

Bashert – Yiddish word meaning destiny, commonly used to refer to finding one's soulmate.

Beit Din – A Jewish court of law consisting of at least one rabbi and two other observant Jews.

Bubbie – Grandmother.

Bund – Pro-Nazi organization.

Charoset – A mixture of apples and nuts that is displayed on the Passover seder plate and eaten during the seder. It symbolizes the mortar the Israelites used to build the pyramids for the Egyptians.

Cholent – A slow cooking stew of beef and vegetables, traditionally served by Orthodox Jews on the Sabbath.

Chuppah – Marriage Canopy.

Chutzpah – Nerve, audacity gall.

Dayenu – Traditional Passover hymn, literally meaning "It would have been enough."

Farputzed – Over dressed, decked out in clothing and jewelry—over the top.

Fir Kashas – The Four Questions the youngest child asks at the Passover seder.

Gottenyu – "Oh, God!!"

Gezuntah – Big, large.

Goyische – Not Jewish.

Haggadah – The book containing the text recited at the seder on the first two nights of Passover, including a narrative of the Exodus.

Kashrus, Kashrut – The Jewish dietary laws and the rules of keeping kosher.

Kavannah – Intention.

Kiddush – Literally means sanctification. It is a blessing recited over wine or grape juice to sanctify the Shabbat and Jewish holidays. It also refers to refreshments served after Sabbath or festival services.

Kipah – Skullcap, yarmulke.

Kol Sasson v' Kol Simcha – The last of seven blessings sung in Hebrew under the canopy at a traditional Jewish wedding. "Let there speedily be heard in the cities of Judah and in the streets of Jerusalem the sound of joy and the sound of happiness, the sound of a groom and the sound of a bride . . ."

Kosher – The Jewish dietary laws.

L'dor v'dor – From one generation to another.

Matzoh – Unleavened bread eaten during Passover.

Mazal Tov – "Good luck!"

Mechitza – Partition in an Orthodox synagogue to separate men and women during prayer.

Mensch – Decent human being; a person of integrity and honor.

Meshuggene – Crazy, mad, insane person.

Mikveh – Ritual bath, representing spiritual cleansing.

Minyan – Quorum of a group of at least ten Jews required for a prayer service.

Mishpacha – Family.

Motzi – Blessing over bread.

Nostra Aetate – In Latin, meaning "In Our Time." The Second Vatican Council made historic changes to church theology in 1965, which repudiated the centuries old charge of deicide against all Jews. Nostra Aetate was the document which promulgated these changes.

Oberfuhrer – Senior leader, a paramilitary rank of the Nazi party.

Oy vey iz mir – "Woe is me!"

OSI – Office of Special Investigations established in 1979 under the jurisdiction of the U.S. Department of Justice. Its purpose was to bring Nazis to justice.

Rachmonos – Compassion, mercy, pity.

Seder -- The ritual meal and home service Jews observe on the first two nights of Passover. The word, "seder," comes from the Hebrew word for "order," referring to the instructions, readings, and songs detailed in the Haggadah.

Shayna Maydela – Pretty girl.

Shehechiyanu – Prayer of Thanksgiving.

Sheitel – A wig worn by strictly Orthodox women in accordance with covering their hair as a sign of modesty.

Shiva – Seven-day mourning period.

Shoin genug – "That's enough!"

Shul – Synagogue.

Siman Tov u Mazal Tov – Sung on happy occasions, the literal meaning is "Good Sign and Good Luck!"

Smicha – Rabbinical ordination.

Sonderkommando – Jewish prisoner forced by the Nazis to perform duties in the gas chambers and crematoria in Nazi concentration camps.

Tachlis – The heart of the matter.

Tallis – Prayer shawl.

Tefillin – Cubic black leather boxes containing Torah texts on parchment that observant Jews wear on their hand and their arm during weekday morning prayers.

Teshuvah – Repentance.

Torah – The Five Books of Moses.

Tzadik – A righteous person.

Ulpan – A school or program for the intensive study of Hebrew.

Ungapatchke – A Yiddish word that describes the overly ornate, busy, ridiculously over-decorated, and garnished to the point of distaste.

Yenemsvelt – A faraway place; off the beaten path.

Yenta – Busybody.

Yichus – Pedigree, ancestry, family background.

Yizkor – Prayer Service in Commemoration of the Dead.

Yom HaShoah – Holocaust Remembrance Day in Israel.

A NOTE FROM THE AUTHOR

THE CHARACTERS AND EVENTS OF *Shadows We Carry* are all figments of my imagination. But the settings of the story are real. The late Sixties were a time of political turmoil and unrest.

The war in Vietnam became increasingly unpopular, especially with young people who protested in a variety of ways, including marches, demonstrations, and sit-ins. Although President Lyndon Johnson won by a landslide in 1964 after he assumed the presidency following the assassination of John F. Kennedy in 1963, he became increasingly unpopular in the years after. While he was very successful in getting civil rights legislation passed, he became bogged down in the war in Vietnam. As it escalated, opposition to his policies mounted. This culminated in his dropping out of the presidential race in 1968 after Senator Eugene McCarthy came in a close second to him in the New Hampshire Presidential primary and Senator Robert Kennedy entered the race. During the 1968 Democratic National Convention in Chicago, there were riots in the streets outside the convention hall, during which police clubbed and tear-gassed protestors.

The story of the abortion doctor in Queens is based on news reports at the time. Abortion was illegal in the United States until the

U.S. Supreme Court decided Roe v. Wade in 1973. The court ruled that the U.S. Constitution protects a pregnant woman's right to have an abortion without excessive government restriction. The decision struck down many U.S. federal and state abortion laws. Prior to Roe, young women who were pregnant out of wedlock would generally get married or give a child up for adoption. Prior to 1973, those who wanted an abortion had to resort to illegal means or go to a legal venue outside of the United States.

But in June 2022, the U.S. Supreme Court officially reversed Roe v. Wade, declaring that after almost 50 years there is no longer the constitutional right to an abortion. Writing for the majority, Justice Samuel Alito said that Roe and subsequent high court rulings reaffirming it "were egregiously wrong" and "an abuse of judicial authority." The ruling left the issue of the legality of abortion up to individual states.

During the Sixties, there were quotas for women in professional schools. In addition, females were often discouraged from attending by their families or male professors. It was a societal expectation that women get married and raise a family. In addition, during interviews, young women were asked routinely whether they planned on getting married and having a family. In the late '60s, Columbia University Graduate School of Journalism had a quota of twenty percent women. Not only was there little emotional support in many traditional families for women who blazed their own path and pursued male-dominated professions, but reliable childcare was difficult to find and keep. It was mostly done privately; the extensive networks of daycare—public and private—available today were rare or non-existent.

All these sexist practices and beliefs were eventually toppled by feminist writers who launched a revolution. Women like Gloria Steinem and Germaine Greer attracted media attention through their popular writings and their media savvy. In 1966, a group of feminists including Betty Friedan, who had launched the first wave of the Women's Movement in 1962 with her book, *The Feminine Mystique*, founded the National Organization for Women (NOW). This organization fought gender discrimination through the courts and legislatures. It lobbied Congress for pro-equality laws and assisted women seeking legal aid as they battled sex discrimination in the courts.

During the time period of the book, it was not unusual for LGBTQ individuals to remain in the closet and even to seek out relationships with persons of the opposite sex in order to publicly conceal their true sexual identity. In fact, the struggle for gay rights only first began in 1969 when the police raided the Stonewall Inn, a bar located in New York City's Greenwich Village that served as a haven for the city's gay, lesbian, and transgender community. At the time, homosexual acts were illegal in every state except Illinois, and bars and restaurants could be shut down for having gay employees or serving gay customers. The police often raided gay bars, but on the night of the Stonewall Riot, members of the city's gay community decided to fight back. This sparked an uprising that would launch a new era of resistance and revolution. The National March on Washington for Lesbian and Gay Rights took place in Washington, DC, in October 1979. But it took until 2003 to overturn all remaining laws against same-sex sexual activity. Some states have not yet repealed their sodomy laws and local law enforcement officers have used these statutes to harass or arrest gay people. Same-sex marriage was legalized in 2015. In 2022, President Joe Biden signed into law legislation that all states must recognize same-sex marriages performed in other states.

The Catholic Church finally discredited the notion of Jewish deicide in 1965 in its "Declaration on the Relation of the Church to Non-Christian Religions" (*Nostra aetate*), published by the Second Vatican Council. In no uncertain terms, the Declaration states that the crucifixion of Jesus "cannot be charged against all Jews." Pope

John XXIII convened the historic Second Vatican Council in 1962, which led to the promulgation of this ecumenical document after his death.

Yaphank, a hamlet in Suffolk County, Long Island, became one of the American Nazi movement's main centers of activity prior to World War II. In 1935, the German American Settlement League bought a large tract of land in the hamlet, which was named German Gardens. Fatherland Gardens is modeled after this neighborhood. German Gardens soon became a Nazi community meant solely for those of pure Aryan extraction. The fliers that were distributed at the time inviting German Americans to move there read, "You will meet people who think like you."

The main street, which ran the entire length of the community, was named Adolf Hitler Strasse. This and other street names honoring Nazis have also since been renamed. The name changing ceremony in the book is a figment of my imagination.

About fifty acres of the property was dedicated to Camp Siegfried, which was established in 1935. It was dedicated to training teenagers as future leaders of the Nazi movement. The camp held German Day observances, where more than 40,000 people came to celebrate "German Day." In 1945, the FBI officially shut down Camp Siegfried, but the community still exists. In 2017, New York State eliminated restrictions that permitted only those of German heritage to live in the community.

Der Stürmer literally, "The Stormer / Attacker / Striker," was a weekly German tabloid newspaper published from 1923 to the end of World War II by Julius Streicher. It was known for its virulently anti-Semitic caricatures, which depicted Jews as ugly characters with exaggerated facial features and misshapen bodies. In his propaganda work, Streicher furthered medieval stereotypes accusing Jews of killing children, sacrificing their bodies, and drinking their blood.

Until 1979, the question of who was a Jew was determined by the mother's religion and conversion. If your mother was Jewish, you were Jewish. But that year, the Reconstructionist Rabbinical Association declared that a child would be considered Jewish if the father alone was Jewish and the child was raised as a Jew. In 1983, Reform rabbis adopted the same position. Conservative and Orthodox rabbis still insist that for a child to be Jewish, the mother must be Jewish. A rabbi must perform conversion, which requires immersion in a mikveh.

From the end of World War II until 1978, Nazis remained safely in the U.S. and were not pursued with a few notable exceptions, including Hermione Braunsteiner-Ryan. News reports began to suggest that agencies within the United States government, some of which had actively recruited Nazis into sensitive positions, were now deliberately shielding Nazis from prosecution. The INS (Immigration Nationalization Service) began to be a target of this criticism.

Representative Elizabeth Holtzman introduced and secured the passage of what has become known as the Holtzman Amendment. This law expanded deportation criteria to include anyone "in association with the Nazi government of Germany who ordered, incited, assisted, or otherwise participated in the persecution of any person because of race, religion, national origin, or political opinion."

Holtzman's efforts closed a loophole that previously prevented Nazi war criminals from being asked whether they'd engaged in illegal activities during the war. The amendment also made "ex-Nazis ineligible for visas and eliminated the attorney general's ability to admit them as temporary non-immigrants."

Holtzman was perspicacious in calling for action to replace the INS with a unit that was part of the Department of Justice. This action increased the unit's reach and prosecutorial strength. The new unit opened in 1979 and was housed in the DOJ. It was called the Office of Special Investigations (OSI) and would soon become known as the "Nazi-hunting unit."

Allen Ryan was the OSI Director and Neal Sher was a supervisor in the department in 1979 and later went on to head the unit. They are mentioned in the meeting that Oren attended with Rudolf Schmidt, but this is a fictional event and Rudolf Schmidt is a product of my imagination. Famed Nazi hunter Eli Rosenbaum first came to the OSI in 1980 and later became its director. His example inspired me as I researched and wrote this novel.

Holocaust Survivor Benjamin Meed and his wife Vladka helped to organize the first World Gathering of Jewish Holocaust Survivors in Israel in June 1981. As a result of that event, that year the Meeds and other survivors established a North American organization called The American Gathering of Jewish Holocaust Survivors and Their Descendants. The American Gathering organized a reunion event for survivors that was held in Washington, DC, in April 1983.

The initial focus of the organization was to hold national and local reunions of survivors and their families and to combat isolation that survivors sometimes experienced, even within the wider Jewish community. The 1983 reunion was led by honorary chair, Elie Wiesel, with a speech given by President Ronald Reagan.

ACKNOWLEDGMENTS

SHADOWS WE CARRY WAS PROPELLED and inspired by the many readers who reached out to me asking what happened to the characters after *The Takeaway Men* ended. Thank you also to the members of the more than eighty book clubs and other groups whom I virtually visited with during the pandemic and who asked the same question during our meetings. I hope this sequel answers those questions.

I am deeply grateful to Brooke Warner, Lauren Wise, Crystal Patriarche, Tabitha Bailey, Rylee Warner, Krissa Lagos, Julie Metz, and everyone at SparkPress and BookSparks for their encouragement and assistance.

I truly appreciate all those who supported me, including my cherished friends, family, and enthusiastic readers. My editor, Rachel Sherman, read my first draft with a keen eye and helped me craft a better book. Thank you especially to the individuals who helped me by making valuable suggestions to the manuscript in its early stages: Arthur Fischman, Valerie Taylor, Sarrae Crane, Phyllis Lader, Curt Lader, Rabbi Jonathan Waxman, Jennifer Feingold, and Audrey Atlas.

I am especially thankful for the support and encouragement of my 2G friends: Thane Rosenbaum, Ellen Bachner Greenberg, Lisa Pollack, Andrea Bolender, Meryl Menashe, Harry Wagner, and Charlie Goldgrub, among many others. Their insights and experiences have informed and supported my work.

Thank you to Pam Stack, the intrepid Executive Producer of Authors on the Air Global Radio Network, who enthusiastically embraced my podcast, People of the Book. To Grace Sammon, who introduced me to her, and to Kerry Schaefer for her ongoing assistance. Thank you also to Annie McDonnell, who first gave me a platform on World of the Write Review and has been an enthusiastic cheerleader for both of my novels. And many thanks to all the talented guests who have shared their insights and experience with our listeners.

I am grateful for the ongoing and enthusiastic support of book reviewers, book bloggers, readers, librarians, book clubs, book shops, podcasters and everyone who supports authors. I would be remiss if I didn't acknowledge the overwhelming support I've received from the Jewish community throughout the world – including rabbis, lay leaders, synagogues, Hadassah groups, Holocaust museums and organizations, sisterhoods, UJA-Federation, JCC's and the Jewish Book Council.

I am blessed to be part of a virtual community of author friends who have nurtured and encouraged me, especially through the pandemic. Zoom has been a lifeline and I have so enjoyed "meeting" both authors and readers. There are many outstanding virtual book groups, and I would be lost without them. Thank you to Eileen Sanchez and Valerie Taylor, my co-administrators at Books Live Forever! And I am so grateful for the enthusiastic support of the members of Jews Love To Read! We have created an amazing community of readers, writers, reviewers, authors, bloggers, and bookworms from throughout the world! I am filled with gratitude for those who have offered words of encouragement, support, and praise. Your outpouring of kindness and consideration has made all the difference.

Heartfelt gratitude to my precious family—my sons, daughters-in-law, and grandchildren. You were always in my mind as I crafted this narrative about what things were like back in the day. While the characters and story line are fiction, the history—with all the limitations and obstacles of the time—were very real. Throughout your lives, I hope you will make the most of the possibilities and choices available to you.

Through sickness and health, my husband supports me in all my endeavors. So, too, do I draw inspiration from the loving memory of my parents and grandparents; they were in my heart and my head as I wrote this book.

BOOK CLUB DISCUSSION QUESTIONS

1. *Shadows We Carry* explores the issues of gender identity, historical upheaval, and family relationships. Which is most important to you and how are these issues relevant today?

2. How did the times in which JoJo lived impact her decisions? Do you think she should have married Bruce? How might her decision be different today and why?

3. What would happen nowadays if the Dean had spoken to Bronka the way he did during her interview for Journalism School? How were Bronka's perceptions about her personal and professional choices shaped by the times in which she lived?

4. Describe the twins' relationship. How did it change over time? How were they alike and how were they different?

5. How were each of the twins a product both of their times and of the impact of the Holocaust? Explain.

6. What do you think motivated Ned in pursuing Bronka? Why do you believe Bronka allowed the relationship to continue for years?

Was she/should she have been suspicious? What would their connection look like today?

7. What is your opinion of Mindy? Was her reaction to the news about the identity of her father justified? What do you think about her mother's decision to hide this from her for so many years?

8. Bronka asks Father Stan, "Do you think the children and grandchildren of Nazis and their sympathizers bear any responsibility for what their relatives did during the war?" How would you answer this question?

9. Do you think it was necessary for the federal government to track down former Nazis who had slipped into the U.S. after having committed war crimes?

10. Do you feel it was important for Brian to learn about his father's Nazi past? Do you believe his mother was hiding the truth or was she really ignorant of her husband's actions at Auschwitz?

11. Bronka writes in her op-ed about her reactions to the NBC miniseries, *Holocaust*: "If we learned anything from the Holocaust, it is that it took place in incremental steps while average people let it happen." Do you agree that this is the most important lesson of the Holocaust? If so, why? If not, what is?

12. Why was Bronka so attracted to Father Stan? What do you think was his interest in her?

13. Is the religion into which a person is born or the one in which an individual is raised more important? Do you believe it's possible to practice two religions at once?

14. Do you think JoJo should have forgiven Bruce? Did your opinion of her mother-in-law, Doris, change after this incident?

15. Do you agree with Doris that JoJo grew up in a house where feelings were not discussed? If so, why do you think this was the case?

16. Do you think Faye was correct in telling Bronka to move out of the house? Why do you believe Aron was so opposed to the idea?

17. What did the conversion to Judaism do for Bronka? Do you think JoJo should have converted too?

18. Why was Oren the right person for Bronka?

19. Why was it so important for Aron to have grandchildren?

20. Many people today have their DNA tested. How important are family bloodlines in the life of an individual?

21. The characters in the book are products of their time. Give a few examples of this. How are the choices we make influenced by the time and place in which we live? Which do you think is/was a better time to come of age—the present or the '60s or '70s? Compare the societal opportunities, constraints, and pressures then and now.

22. Were you surprised to learn that Brian's mother was again living with his father?

ABOUT THE AUTHOR

Photo Credit: Diane Berrent Photography

MERYL AIN IS A WRITER, author, podcaster, and career educator. *The Takeaway Men*, her award-winning post-Holocaust debut novel, was published in 2020. Her articles and essays have appeared in numerous publications, and she is the author of two non-fiction books. A member of The International Advisory Board for Holocaust Survivor Day, she is the host of the podcast, *People of the Book,* and the founder of the Facebook group, *Jews Love To Read!*

She holds a BA from Queens College; an MA from Teachers College, Columbia University; and a doctorate in education from Hofstra University. She and her husband, Stewart, a journalist, live in New York.

SELECTED TITLES FROM SPARKPRESS

SparkPress is an independent boutique publisher delivering high-quality, entertaining, and engaging content that enhances readers' lives, with a special focus on female-driven work. www.gosparkpress.com

The Takeaway Men: A Novel, Meryl Ain. $16.95, 978-1-68463-047-9
Twin sisters Bronka and JoJo Lubinski are brought to America from Germany by their Polish refugee parents after World War II—but in "idyllic" America, political, cultural, and family turmoil awaits them. As the girls grow older, they eventually begin to ask questions of and demand the truth from their parents.

Echoes of War: A Novel, Cheryl Campbell. $16.95, 978-1-68463-006-6
When Dani—one of many civilians living on the fringes to evade a war that's been raging between a faction of aliens and the remnants of Earth's military for decades—discovers that she's not human, her life is upended . . . and she's drawn into the very battle she's spent her whole life avoiding.

Murmuration: A Novel, Sid Balman Jr, $16.95, 978-1-68463-091-2
One of the first Muslim women to graduate from West Point, a Jewish US Army captain, and a Somali migrant nicknamed Charlie Christmas risk everything for a refugee boy on a three-decade odyssey that takes them from Africa and Europe to Texas and Minnesota—and redefines what it means to be American in the twenty-first century.

Child Bride: A Novel, Jennifer Smith Turner, $16.95, 978-1-68463-038-7
The coming-of-age journey of a young girl from the South who joins the African American great migration to the North—and finds her way through challenges and unforeseen obstacles to womanhood.

That's Not a Thing: A Novel, Jacqueline Friedland
$16.95, 978-1-68463-030-1
When a recently engaged Manhattanite learns that her first great love has been diagnosed with ALS, she is faced with the impossible decision of whether a few final months with her ex might be worth risking her entire future. A fast-paced emotional journey that explores whether it's possible to be equally in love with two men at once.

CPSIA information can be obtained
at www.ICGtesting.com
Printed in the USA
JSHW080936090623
42979JS00001B/1